D0357121

WENDY J. FOX

f the Ice
Had Held

Library of Congress Cataloging-in-Publication Data
Names: Fox, Wendy J., author.
Title: If the ice had held / Wendy J. Fox.
Description: Santa Fe, NM : Santa Fe Writers Project, [2019]
Identifiers: LCCN 2018033010 (print) | LCCN 2018034201 (ebook) |
    ISBN 9781939650924 (epub) | ISBN 9781939650931 (mobi) |
    ISBN 9781939650948 (pdf) | ISBN 9781939650917 (paperback : alk. paper)
Classification: LCC PS3606.O97 (ebook) | LCC PS3606.O97 I36 2019 (print) |
    DDC 813/.6—dc23
LC record available at https://lccn.loc.gov/2018033010

Published by SFWP
369 Montezuma Ave. #350
Santa Fe, NM 87501
(505) 428-9045
www.sfwp.com

To my sisters.

Contents

Chapter One Kathleen *Winter, 1974* 1

Chapter Two Melanie *Spring, 2007* 3

Chapter Three Irene *Winter, 1974* 5

Chapter Four Melanie *Spring, 2007* 9

Chapter Five Kathleen *Winter, 1974* 19

Chapter Six Melanie *Spring, 2007* 23

Chapter Seven Brian *Summer, 2001* 29

Chapter Eight Irene *Winter, 1974* 39

Chapter Nine Melanie *Spring, 2007* 41

Chapter Ten Brian *Summer, 2001* 51

Chapter Eleven Kathleen *Winter, 1974* 55

Chapter Twelve Melanie *Fall, 1986* 63

Chapter Thirteen Irene *Summer, 1974* 73

Chapter Fourteen Melanie *Summer, 1987* 77

Chapter Fifteen Jenny *Fall, 2005* 83

Chapter Sixteen Irene *Summer, 2007* 89

Chapter Seventeen Melanie *Summer, 2007* 93

Chapter Eighteen Jenny *Winter, 2005* 97

Chapter Nineteen Kathleen *Winter, 1974* 101

Chapter Twenty Melanie *Summer, 2007* 107

Chapter Twenty-One Lucy Estelle *Summer, 1970* 115

Chapter Twenty-Two Melanie *Summer, 1988* 127

Chapter Twenty-Three Lucy Estelle *Fall, 1970* 137

Chapter Twenty-Four Melanie *Fall, 1988* 143

Chapter Twenty-Five Simon *Winter, 1974* 149

Chapter Twenty-Six Melanie *Spring, 2007* 163

Chapter Twenty-Seven Jenny *Winter, 2005* 167

Chapter Twenty-Eight Melanie *Winter, 2007* 177

Chapter Twenty-Nine Irene *Winter, 1974* 181

Chapter Thirty Melanie *Summer, 1988* 183

Chapter Thirty-One Brian *Spring, 2007* 185

Chapter Thirty-Two Melanie *Summer, 2007* 195

Chapter Thirty-Three Irene *Winter, 1974* 207

Chapter Thirty-Four Melanie *Summer, 2007* 219

Chapter Thirty-Five Jenny *Fall, 1988* 227

Chapter Thirty-Six Melanie *Summer, 2007* 237

Chapter Thirty-Seven Kathleen *Summer, 1975* 241

Chapter One
Kathleen

Winter, 1974

Kathleen wondered why, if half the human body was really made of water, how water could be so dangerous. Her brother Sammy had split the ice of the river trying to cross, and he floated to the shore—found by a townie cop before he was even missed.

She didn't understand, if he wasn't sunk, why the river couldn't lift him, glide him to the banks until his toes touched gravel and he put his legs down and walked back into the night. Glistening with cold, yes, lips blue, yes, skin brittle to the touch, clothes sopping and the hem of his jeans just starting to freeze, but still with breath, heat from his lungs condensing the air around him.

Instead, the officer heaved him from the water in the dark of the winter evening, Sammy's teenaged body sharp with ice.

Chapter Two
Melanie
Spring, 2007

The software company in Denver where Melanie worked was in the majority of how start-ups ran—less glamorous than the swanky dot-coms of Silicon Valley, with their organic catering menus, on-site yoga, and complimentary Rolfing massage coupons; and more high-acid paper files sweltering under the heat of a hundred laptops, payroll cobbled out of questionable revenue recognition processes, and strings of code written under the damp pressure of a hangover. Their space was not sky-high and bathed in clean, filtered light, but rather it occupied the ground-floor wing of a crumbling office park where the air-conditioning was troubling and unreliable.

All through her twenties Melanie had bounced back and forth between jobs, and then finally, on the eve of her third decade, she landed this one. Through the issue of a company phone and a five-page document explaining how the 401(k) vested, she transformed into her idea of an adult and had stayed tethered to the company since then. The job gave her enough money to secure and pay a mortgage on a small condo close to downtown, to help her mother, Kathleen, out once in a while, and it gave her enough order to dampen the feeling of spinning she'd always had, even if only for moments.

Since she worked in tech, the model was acquisition, and she was not naïve to this. The model meant that the founders and a few of the earliest employees would cash out, and the rest of them would stay in the office, typing toward a different destiny—same keyboards, same products, just new letterhead that sat in the same place as the old letterhead, in a crumpled box under the printer. Still, when it actually happened, she had no idea the company had been for sale until she was asked to proofread the press release. Like an iffy check, it was postdated by several weeks and gave her a queasy feeling.

"Are there going to be layoffs?" she had asked her boss. She was in a small department where she did marketing and market analysis. She was hired without any training back when the company was not profitable; they'd taken a chance on her, so she felt a kind of loyalty. Still, she had read enough to know how acquisitions went. A team from corporate would make people redundant, and then the rest of the employees would plow through, taking on more and more work and living in terror of their cable bill.

Her boss told her not to talk about it. Her boss told her not to make any stock purchases of the publicly traded parent.

"You could be considered an insider," her boss had said and raised her eyebrow to a dangerous slope, like they were talking about a real tip, a life-changer.

Melanie did not think their little company being absorbed into a conglomerate would make even a blip in the markets, but she swore to secrecy anyway.

Later, when she was not let go and she told her new co-workers at headquarters in Chicago that she had to look them up, they were shocked. *We are on the Fortune 500*, they had said. *Right*, she had said, *there are five hundred of those?* She wondered if people who had gone to business school memorized this list, like the state capitals or the names of the saints.

Chapter Three

Irene

Winter, 1974

Irene wasn't sure if she should go to the funeral, but she also couldn't stay away—she thought that was just like Sammy, pulling at her even after he was gone. It was hard to remain contained. The flowers, the handful of people sweating in their formal clothes that were too warm for the church with the heat cranking, the way there was so much silence because the pastor, or the minister, or whoever he was, didn't know Sammy, so he just did the usual passages, the ashes and such, and no one from the family got up to speak.

The only other funeral she had been to was her aunt's and uncle's, when they were in a car accident with a tractor-trailer carrying crates of chickens. They hadn't even been the vehicle directly involved, they'd only swerved to avoid the wreckage on the highway. She had been very young, but she remembered that after that, she didn't see her older cousin, Lucy Estelle, as much anymore. At the service, her father, her rigid and snapping father, was like a boy. She had been only ten, but she knew what it meant to see him cry for the first time. It wasn't even really a funeral, just a memorial at the VFW, but she saw her father bare then, raw from sobbing and from having drunk whiskey all day, and then from sobbing some more. In front of the people who had come to pay their respects to the man and the woman who had taken their last breaths in a crumple of iron while the down from the spilt chickens clung to them like frost, her father had opened. Her father had told the story of him and his brother as young enlisted men, briefly, and then he moved backward—two boys on a farm at the end of a dirt road and how they were so lucky. *Your closest sibling is your first friend,* he had said, and her father and his brother had stayed that way, the first person to notify of trouble and of joy.

She was fourteen now and so Irene had planned something to say if there were words at Sammy's funeral. *I know you do not know me,* she would say to the small group of people who had gathered, *mostly family, but I loved your brother, your son. I know you do not know me, but I know how Sammy spoke of every person here, though I am sorry if I might not get your faces. Mikey and Kathleen, your brother loved you. Jeannette and Rose and Darlene and Thomas. Mom and Dad. All he ever wanted was to be with you. I never had jealousy toward other girls, only you all.*

If she was very, very brave, she might tell the rest of it—that she was pregnant, that they had planned to marry—but since no space was offered for anyone to speak, she only hitched a ride to the gravesite with someone she didn't know, keeping her silence through the drive to the cemetery, where she watched Sammy's casket get lowered into the ground. After, she turned and walked back toward home, the weight of the baby like a penance, like a gift.

* * *

When Kathleen came walking up the hill behind the school towards Irene, it was easy to see how Sammy's sister was like him. He had been the same—direct about what he wanted.

Kathleen introduced herself and she offered some thanks for coming to the service. Irene was not sure if she was supposed to shake the sister's hand or cry. Irene took a drag from her cigarette, even though every time she smoked, her stomach turned over. She had tried to stop, but it had been hard with her father puffing in the house, and so she gave up, and she told herself she had bigger things to worry about than cigarettes. There was a knot in her shoulder that ached when she turned her head, and a dull pain in her lower back all of the time. There was her messy room, and the way her body was changing—if she had thought the beginning of adolescence was bad, she felt a fool now, not even on the other side of puberty.

The way she'd prayed for her breasts to bud and her cycle to begin, because she thought these changes would make her a woman—what she didn't know then was the change that comes when the cycle is interrupted: the blooming of the breasts, the tension at the belly, the smell of everything, and the hunger.

Irene was a freshman and the fact that her body was starting to form a child before she could drive or vote or legally live on her own was not lost on her; she understood she was young, even if she was the oldest that she'd ever been.

The other girl, the sister, Kathleen, was tall, like Sammy, and also resembled him in the face, though Irene was not sure how much she could trust this girl who came to her in the snow, who came to her seeking the part of her brother that Irene carried. She was sure the sister knew, even though they had not yet gotten very far past introductions. Irene put out her hand.

"He mentioned you," Irene said as the school's bell rang. She wanted to give something else like, *It seemed like he loved you best,* or *He mentioned what an amazing auntie you would be.* Both were true but it was hard to feel like anything was worth telling with him gone.

"We should talk," Kathleen said, but Irene turned to go back to class.

The sister followed like a dog would, half a length back and a few paces to the side, determined.

The words Irene had inside of her at the funeral had seemed so whole, a little orb, and though she'd been able to imagine saying her piece—*I know you do not know me, but I loved your brother, your son*—like the child inside her, getting something into the air of the world was harder than thinking about it.

It was stupid of them to get pregnant, and it seemed stupid, now that he was gone, that they'd not just talked to Sammy's folks, even to the sister, Kathleen, whom he was the closest with. His people wouldn't have cared, but he was trying to do right first: get a ring on her finger, get a better job than working at the stockyard. She and Sammy were trying to smooth it out, trying to show they could be responsible by making a plan and keeping it before they told their secret.

Now Kathleen was tracking her through the snow, and Irene was sure Sammy's sister would not give up in trying to know her.

Irene did not want to be known. She'd let Sammy get close to her, and see—just look at what had happened.

Chapter Four

Melanie

Spring, 2007

It was spring in Colorado, and the April temperatures swung in wide, dramatic swaths. Melanie's potted petunias were wiped out one chilly morning, but by the time she came home, the gerbera daisies were sizzling in the afternoon sun, and she poured an entire can of water across the wilted leaves, hoping.

At work the day after the acquisition announcement, the air-conditioning would not come on. The administrative assistant called building maintenance, and one of the developers opened up the door to the server room—a frazzled, wheezing center of physical technology linked by frayed cables and tethered to overworked outlets. The door was propped open with old manuals, like *C++ for Dummies* and *Mastering the AS400.* There was a fan, ordered specifically for the purpose of cooling the server room, and it was switched on.

Melanie went back to her office, which shared a wall with the parking garage, making it extremely noisy. She followed the business journals, and she knew that the trend was to move everyone into pods or low-walled cubicles. This depressed her because she understood that *collaboration* was code for *you will never take a personal call on the clock again, ever!,* and she clung to her private space—sneaking in during a three-day weekend to paint her office walls the same yellow as her childhood bedroom, bringing in an enormous palm that she cultivated in a red ceramic pot, and changing out the overhead fluorescent lights for Repti Glo terrarium bulbs. From the packaging she learned that there were only three elements of light that were required for reptile husbandry: ultraviolet, visible, and infrared. The package read that a combination of different light sources was necessary in most cases.

With the yellow paint and the faintly pink glow of the repti-lights, Melanie felt that she was creating a productive environment. Her palm had healthy green leaves, and her office had a more rarified ambience than those around her. Some of the other spaces attracted miller moths when they migrated from the Kansas plains to the Colorado foothills, but even with the lights blazing, her work area was clear of the dusty wings and cocoon debris, and while she had no intention of actually breeding reptiles, the fact that she could sustain creatures outside of *Arthropoda* was sometimes a comfort for her when a long night had turned the glow of her champagne walls to the pissy shade of decaying newspaper.

The office was heating up as Melanie worked on an analysis of the industrial marketplace. She was disturbed by how many times the word *penetration* was used in the report request, alongside the more benign words *fastener* and *HVAC*. The report had been assigned to her a few months ago, and now she understood that it was related to the acquisition. There were growth targets to maintain. Markets to *penetrate*.

She started to sweat. While she thought, she read *The New York Times* online. She created a chart (she was very good at charts). What Melanie liked even more than the *Times* were advice columns; the whole genre was enthralling. In a different life she would like to have this job, offering wisdom on a variety of topics from etiquette to sex. As teenager, she had pored over her horoscopes.

* * *

On Wednesday Melanie flew to San Antonio.

On Thursday she woke up in San Antonio with a headache, her return ticket safely duplicated in her email, and a snoring man in her bed. This wasn't unusual for her, really, and in software, in technology in general, there was the industry advantage (or disadvantage, depending on how it was sliced) of men outnumbering women by four to one.

Usually they were easy—either introverts or married so long that they had temporarily forgotten how their bodies worked. She spent days on the road with the ones who were her co-workers, hawking a product she did not always understand. They called the software a *suite*, like in a building; they talked about *enablement* and velocity and *time-to-value*.

They all knew many acronyms, and the man lying next to her was no different, even if her skin touched his.

This San Antonio Man had sideswiped her some, a bright spot at an otherwise dull tradeshow. She had broken one of her own rules—never co-workers, never customers. While she felt she had a flexible relationship with consequences, accepting them mostly, she still groaned as she collected her clothes and put them on in the bathroom. She focused on how amazing a cup of coffee and a shower would be.

A month ago, Melanie had been in Chicago, with a man named Brian, who seemed to solidly hate his life. She wasn't sure if this was worse than the San Antonio Man, who was just starting to hate his.

What some women liked about the kind of job that she had, when they could get them, was that it was a profession similar to being a wife, except it paid. When traveling, she reminded her colleagues to catch every loop on the waist of their trousers with their belts, and she sent them back to their rooms if there was powdered sugar from breakfast donuts sprinkled on their shirts, and she liked, even, doing it cheerfully. She made sure everything ran smoothly. *Just saying*, sometimes she said, *that's not a good look*, and flashed a wide, toothy smile. She offered wet wipes for grubby hands and antacids for rumbling bellies. She sched-uled their lunch breaks and made dinner reservations. Her real job was market research and keeping the teams on track with corporate message points, but she had found this was much easier when no one was hungry or had diarrhea.

The night before, the San Antonio Man—who, when Melanie came out of the bathroom, she could see was still asleep but had flopped onto the middle of the bed—had said to her something about unhappiness, about the pressure of family, of economics, about the way he thought he was doing everything right but still felt horrible.

Fucking me is not going to change anything, she had thought to say to him, but instead she offered her bulletproof smile.

"I get it," she had said instead. "It's tough out there."

"It *is* tough," he had said. "I'm trying so hard."

It was this kind of conversation that would perpetually lead her, and others like her, to spend their company's money on too many beers, resulting in shacking up in Austin or Anaheim, with one of their rooms—usually hers—left sitting empty: $179 a night to hold a discarded lip gloss. The men she met on the road liked her because she fucked, and they liked her because she asked questions. When the wheels came down in their towns, they would go home to their wives, energized by the reminder that a sex life was still possible, and she would go home to her townhouse in Denver and take a long shower, shave every place on her body they could have possibly been, and move on.

* * *

Usually it was in early spring that the moths fluttered through the office. Melanie had read that moths were a rich food for predators like brown bears, because 72% of the moth's body weight was made up of fat, making it more calorie-dense than elk or deer.

Also she wondered about her colleagues' home lives. Did they like spending their days in a cramped office among the hum of machines, and did they like fighting traffic back to their wide, open-floor-plan homes in the immediate suburbs and beyond? Did they like wrangling a car seat into the rear of their Honda and going home to the production of dinnertime, or would they rather be with her, tangled in hotel sheets with their cell phones on mute, pretending to have a different life where no one ever had to make the bed or run out of beer? It seemed obvious to her what the right answer was. The right answer included room and laundry service, but she also did not blame them for returning to their families.

At work on Friday, she was composing an email when one of the sales staff—the one she had spent the night with in San Antonio—came into her office and closed the door. Her indoor windows looked into the hallway, carpeted in blue-gray, and she looked past him, past the articles and cartoons she had taped up in reverse so that the text faced the outside. One of her clippings was in anticipation of Easter, with two chocolate bunnies, the first, missing his hind-side, who said, *My butt hurts*, and the second, missing his ears, who said, *What?!*, and she focused on this as he was speaking.

He said that he had been thinking of her, and Melanie thought the force of his breathing was making her potted palm rustle, but she listened. She knew she deserved this, since she had broken the rule. Customers were about propriety. Co-workers, proximity.

He said that he had told his wife and that his wife was not happy, but that she understood, or she said she understood, except that he was not really sure she understood.

"Understands what?" Melanie said. The bunnies were a classic, she thought, relevant beyond the crucifixion at Calvary, beyond Peeps.

His eyes opened a little wider and then closed all the way. "I can't stop thinking about you," he said.

Melanie turned her head. The palm leaves were definitely rustling. "You should," she said. "You have to. You have children. I haven't been thinking of you," she said.

She flashed again on Chicago, a month ago, Brian—another married man with kids. She wondered about their problems.

The San Antonio Man, Alex, looked at his hands.

Her email was beeping and the room was growing warm.

"Okay, I did think of you once," she said to him. "I thought of you when I was thinking how creepy San Antonio SeaWorld was. Because remember that? Remember the beluga whales?"

He remembered. He said that he remembered she was upset that the dolphins and all of the sea creatures were so far from the ocean, and Melanie affirmed that yes, she had been very upset. She had eaten meat her entire life, but there was something about an inland-Texas shark tank that made her want to swear off the flesh of animals forever, and she had even checked her GPS, appalled to confirm that San Antonio was indeed landlocked.

"So I was thinking that you made that easier, and I was appreciative for that," she said. "Thank you," she said.

The night after the driest SeaWorld in existence, Melanie had drunk too much cheap tradeshow Chardonnay, and she took Alex to a bar near their hotel that she had been to once before, on some other trip, with some other San Antonio Man. The bar served nothing but off-brand spirits and peanuts; peanut shells covered the floor. When she complained that she had husks between her toes, wedged in her open shoes and demolishing her pedicure, he had done something that she thought was ridiculous and charming, which was to throw down his jacket over the discarded hulls to allow her to crunch unmolested to the bar, where she ordered a Crystal Palace vodka tonic, because it was all they had. He was sweet then. She wondered what his dry cleaner would think, and also, he was in a junior role, so it was probably his only good coat. After that, they had gone to his room, where he had been kind and polite and tentative, like an inexperienced young lover, but she liked this. In the morning they were at a breakfast seminar that reeked of pork. She had oatmeal.

They were silent in her office; her laptop hummed. She had it plugged in to a larger screen to prevent eyestrain, but the screen was flickering and making a concerning electronic sound.

"But, I told my wife," he said.

Her palm tree, lush from the repti-lights and her diligent watering, swished in a way that meant she needed to end the conversation. "I have to make call now," she said, and she picked up her desk phone to punctuate. It was 11:17 a.m., and she started to dial her own mobile, which she hoped he would not notice vibrating next to her.

* * *

Melanie lived in a townhouse that had a tiny yard and nice trim. It took her seven minutes to mow the lawn, but four of that was getting the lawnmower started. The lawnmower sounded like a train coming off the rails, and the dull blades seemed to push the grass over more than cut it, but she didn't mind. She had planted irises and sunflowers, a cascade of purple and yellow. She had also planted lilies, which stubbornly came up in the same shades, even though she was sure she had picked orange and red.

That night, she sat in her yard and ate a reduced-calorie microwave meal and thought about Alex, the San Antonio Man. He thought he was different, but he wasn't different. She felt bad that he had told his wife—she didn't like that he had felt guilty, but mostly she didn't like that he had then passed his guilt on to his spouse. One of the things about married guys, she had found, was that it was hard to get them to use condoms. Either they were just enough older than her that they didn't quite believe the reality of modern sex, or, like Alex, because they were partnered, they believed they were clean. Melanie did not say to any of them that if they were considering sleeping with her, their wives might be sleeping with the nanny; and if Melanie was considering sleeping with them, then probably she had slept with someone else like them.

The grass was cool and her entrée warm. She had her BlackBerry with her, and her email was beeping; she wanted to think her email was beeping again, but it was always beeping, and she opened an all-staff message from central HR.

We have just received news that Kyle Walker passed away this evening. Kyle faced his battle with cancer bravely, and we will always remember his service to the company. Many of you knew Kyle well, and we suggest that you keep his wife, Amanda, in your thoughts. Some of you have already inquired if there is a memorial fund for Kyle: management asks that you please refrain from soliciting or collecting donations on behalf of the Walker family on company property as this could have tax implications. The Company Foundation has provided a fruit basket and as a courtesy, your name is signed on the card as it appears in Human Resource records; please expect to see a $2.18 automatic deduction on your next statement from payroll.

Melanie read the message again, then tossed her phone into the yard, irritated. She ate some more of her noodles. The magnolia tree she had painstakingly weaned off of a big-box home-improvement store fertilizer addiction was drooping in the corner against the cedar fence planks. Sometimes she sprinkled a little Miracle-Gro around the base of it, just to give it a taste of its old life, and she wondered if now would be a good time. What she liked about the magnolia was that it could reproduce with the help of beetles. The leaves and flowers were tough and ancient, having evolved before there were bees. She hadn't ever seen a beetle in her yard, but she imagined their hard bodies doing the delicate work of pollination, and this seemed practical and calming to her.

After discarding the cardboard tray and the plastic fork from her meal into the trash, she looked for the red LED light of her phone. When she picked it up, there were more emails beeping about Kyle. She had worked with him since before the acquisition.

She remembered talking to him just before he went on leave, only a few months ago. She had told him how good he looked, because he had lost so much weight. She didn't know it was because he was sick—he didn't know then, either. He was wearing a purple shirt, and the fabric had a nice sheen against his dark hair and eyes. Kyle said that he was happy he was reducing, but he felt like shit.

"Maybe you're hungry," she had said.

"I'm not hungry," he had said. "And I'm usually always hungry."

"Me too," Melanie had said.

They talked about work after that, and the next time she saw him, he asked her to keep an eye on the orchid in his office.

The food turned over in her stomach. She only ate the reduced-calorie microwave meals because traveling was making her gain weight.

She was thirty-three years old. Kyle had been thirty-two. The orchid had bloomed, twice.

The next workday, the office was not so much somber as disorganized. Kyle had been on sick leave for some time, but he was the Adam Smith of the technical staff, the invisible hand who governed, who corrected, who offered perspective, who had taken the role of making the distinction between foreign (parent conglomerate!) and domestic (them!) interests. The air-conditioning went out again, and it was a very warm day, and the wind was blowing west. When they propped the door, warm air whooshed into the office like an oven being opened. The server room was becoming dangerously hot, and Melanie overheard one of the engineers say that he was sure Kyle would know what to do, and that set the rest of them off nodding and blinking back tears.

Melanie ducked into the server room and switched the portable fans, since the engineers were in shambles. In the kitchen she found disposable bowls left over from a picnic and filled them with ice, hoping to get a few degrees of coolness.

"Hi," said Alex, her man from San Antonio.

"Hi," she said.

The machines were whirring. There was a smell of melting plastic. The bowls were already soggy from condensation.

"I don't think the ice will really help," he said.

"What if we just shut it all down and went home?" she said.

"Let's wait," said Alex. "I'd rather see it blow."

The room got hotter as they waited for something to happen, and by the time they were back in the hallway, Melanie was sweating through her blouse, and the faces of Alex and the engineers were damp. She stayed, listening to them talk, working out their carpools to Kyle's memorial at the Masonic Lodge on Saturday. She arranged for a ride with Alex. *What's the harm*, she thought, *it's a funeral?* She traveled with people she knew and didn't know and people she had fucked and hadn't fucked all the time.

When the air-conditioning resumed, they all filed back to their offices and cubes, the mechanically cooled air cold against their moist clothes. In her office, she shopped online in an idle way for a portable AC or even a swamp cooler, and then she shopped for shoes. She thought about San Antonio and the way the river snaked through the city, flanked with a low boardwalk dotted with margarita joints and platters of TexMex aching under the weight of American cheese. What had she wanted when she let Alex court her when they had no business courting—she had already known what would happen.

The palm rustled, lush and vibrant under the shine of her multi-spectrum bulbs.

Chapter Five

Kathleen

Winter, 1974

At first, all Kathleen could see was the girl who was carrying someone made from her brother Sammy. It seemed one of the women in her family was always pregnant and there was something about the girl's look that made her feel sure, though her mother would be able to be positive.

Two more people he had left behind. There was her and her brothers and sisters and parents, but it was this girl, Irene, who Sammy had chosen.

Kathleen weaved through the cloud of tobacco and fogging breath, stepping carefully though a ring of ice and stamped-out butts. The girl saw her coming, and her eyes narrowed.

"You knew my brother," Kathleen said as a greeting, and put out her hand.

"Sure," the girl said, turning a little.

They heard the bell ring, and the few other kids around flicked their cigarettes, popped gum, and headed back toward the building. She turned and looked at the sky, a clear blue with clouds slung low over Pikes and Longs Peaks, streaks of gray at the top, more snow.

"He mentioned you," the girl said. She had on purple fingerless gloves, an oversized pea coat, and tall black boots. She lit another cigarette, and the smoke curled from the tip.

Kathleen tried to remember if she had seen her somewhere else, but she could only see Sammy alone, in the casket her father had grumbled about paying for, staring at the sum on the sales receipt, incredulous this was the last thing he would give to his boy. Then this girl, graveside, crying into a bandanna. When the bandanna was so soaked it was useless, she took off her stocking cap to cry into, her mascara streaming. When everyone eased back into their cars, she set out walking.

She finally extended her hand, and Kathleen reached immediately. Her name was Irene, and she shivered.

"Thanks for coming to the service," Kathleen said, and wished she had more to offer. They heard the bell sound again, marking the start of class, and they both turned toward school, walking together, but not close, as if Sammy were between them, ready to link both of their arms.

She wondered where the girl Irene had been when Sammy had drowned, when crashed through the slick plane of river ice to pure cold. It had been city police who had found him, less than fifty feet from where the river cracked. From the vantage of where he touched ground, it was obvious no one should have tried to cross—the water was marked, in the slower eddies, by patches of a crystalline patina that broke apart when the current shifted even slightly. Haste, bad judgment, or just misperception at a dark angle, she didn't know.

As they neared the school, the girl sped up, and Kathleen let her go. The next day she packed two lunches, and she brought one to Irene, saying, *Eat, you need to eat, you're too tiny*, and Irene looked at her in the hallway, mortified. Still, she took the crumpled paper bag, soft on one side where jelly had leaked through.

She could not pay attention in any of her classes. She wrote Irene's name on the margin of her notebook and then crossed it out so firmly that the paper shredded. In the hallways of her small school, she was constantly searching for Irene's black hair, but she knew after the first day she'd tracked the girl down, Irene would be avoiding her. She kept bringing extra lunches to school, but only one other time had she been able to press the brown bag on Irene.

In each of Kathleen's class periods, she asked for a hall pass to use the bathroom and peeked under every stall—dirty pink on the floor, beige stall dividers—to see if perhaps Irene was hiding there. Then she washed her hands and went back to class. She had already decided that if any of her teachers noticed the frequent bathroom breaks, she'll claim lady problems or diarrhea, two bodily functions that were hard to argue against.

Sammy probably didn't drown so much as freeze, she figured, trying to take a short-cut across the river that looked frozen but was not. Kathleen knew the way ice could look solid at the river's edge, thick as a floe, really, but be brittle towards the center. He was typically cautious.

He must have been in a hurry to come home, and she realized that while he may have been cautious with her, or with the younger siblings, she didn't know how he was on his own, in a rush, and heady from sex— was that it? Was it sex that had made him reckless?

Her parents hadn't asked, or as far as she knew, hadn't even speculated where he was coming from, why he was on the other side of the river, but Kathleen was sure it was the girl.

The winter was average, cold, but not unseasonable. Still, after Sammy's service, Kathleen stopped wearing her coat, stopped wearing long johns, stopped wearing her double-socks.

How cold do you have to be before you die? she wondered.

Her mother would not let her leave the house without the coat, but once Kathleen was out of sight, she peeled it off. Once, she had rolled the waistband of her skirts so they barely skimmed her thighs, now she shoved her gloves and her hat and scarf into her book bag. The air was bitter, and it made her feel alert and tired at the same time, but she was surprised how accustomed she became to it. Her skin was red and chapped, and sometimes it burned when she came inside, but she felt close to Sammy in the cold.

She took cold showers, she brewed her tea and then poured it over ice when her mother was not looking. She ate her food cold, she kicked off her blankets in the night and lay in the cold air with the window open. Even if she shivered, she found she could sleep, and she could survive. At school, her classmates complained of the chill in the drafty rooms, but she welcomed it, working off her socks and slipping back into her thin, cool shoes.

Always, she kept an eye out for Irene—if they passed in the hallway, Kathleen made eye contact, but Irene looked down. If Kathleen followed Irene up to the smoker's hill, Irene could see her approaching and she would cut back towards the school, leaving ash where her boots had been. They'd only spoken briefly, and then she had pulled away.

Kathleen wasn't sure what else she wanted to say, but she needed Irene. The closest she could ever have to Sammy again, especially if she was right the girl was pregnant.

Just two weeks had gone by and Kathleen's clothes were already becoming loose. She welcomed the gaps. After school, she walked to the river and ventured out on the ice, carefully—she didn't want to follow Sammy, only understand. Where the ice seemed stable, but where if she reached out some, she could start to see through, she kneeled and stretched to plunge her fist through the crust.

The ice was strong this close to the shore, so she had to punch, and she felt the skin at her knuckles tear, but when she broke through, the chill of the water numbed the ragged skin. Kathleen managed to break enough of the crust to sink her arm sunk up to her elbow, and the shock of it made her want to pull back immediately, but she didn't—she let the arm hang in the water, so cold there was almost a heat to it, and for one flash, she hoped this was what Sammy felt with his entire body submerged, pain at first, yes, but then something like dissolving.

She pulled her arm out, backed away from the puncture she'd made.

Irene, she thought. She wanted to go to her.

Is that what Sammy wanted? Only Irene? Sticking half a limb in the icy water didn't help her understand how he must have felt at all, she thought. She didn't understand anything.

Chapter Six

Melanie

Spring, 2007

They were two among many strangers killing time in a hotel bar in suburban Chicago, both mid-thirties, both in the jeans and branded polo shirts of a corporate travel day. After they had finished discussing the weather and the rocky approach by air, they had discovered they both lived in Denver—another place where the wind blew fierce and urgent.

Melanie had been trying to describe to Brian how Chicago had looked as her plane descended, the high-rises piercing through a low fog and the afternoon light gloss against the building windows and the mist, but she could tell Brian wasn't really listening. She was saying that she loved the approach, and she described again how the Windy City looked like a myth, mists of gray around the skyscrapers and the jag of Lake Michigan cutting at the shoreline. He ordered another beer and checked his phone.

They were both in Chicago for a conference, though not the same one.

Brian, she learned, was a seasoned business traveler, and he had a wallet full of foreign money, which he displayed on the table. She wondered what kind of person kept bills as a souvenir and carried them everywhere. Melanie's mother had worked as a teller in a bank, so she was aware that when it came down to physical tender, there were two types: currency and coin. He had both. Euros, which he was inflating the value of as he talked about the food in Bratislava, then some Indian rupees that he spun across the bar, and a few pounds from Britain—*these*, he said, *are really worth something.*

But they were not, she knew, worth anything because, like love, money was regional. One lover changes geography and forgets the other; a wad of lira departs its country and becomes nothing but confetti. She did not say this because she thought he would contradict her, she thought he would say something about it all being easy to exchange, but she knew people rarely did this. Instead they packed the change and the paper into an envelope or a plastic bag and forgot about it or thought they were saving it for the next time.

She said that she had been to Athens, backpacking just after college with some girlfriends, and he told her about a tiny café he had found while trying to exchange some drachmas—*before the European Union*, he said. *Of course*, she said—and she could picture perfectly the waiter and the rickety tables, the sheen of olive oil across the silverware, the lamb, the man's lips, because she knew there were a thousand spots like this across the Mediterranean, tucked under crumbling tile work and bougainvillea.

She leaned into Brian because she was bored, and March in Chicago was cold, and what she was trying to say about the fog was the soft shimmer of it and the condensation on her skin and how she always loved this, how it made her feel light.

He continued to excavate his wallet, finding travel cards and receipts with the heat ink fading from the thermal paper and bits of lint, until it all fanned around them like a reef.

When Brian produced a one-thousand-yen note to Melanie, the lamp glinted off the mustache of the crumpled face on the bill. He was talking about Japan's vending machine sake, and she noticed he didn't even try to hide his wedding ring. Some people took theirs off when they were scooting up next to other people in bars, and she would look for the marks where a band had worn the skin smooth or made a crease.

She could do math in her head, and she watched the markets, so she wasn't impressed by the zeros on the yen, even if she acted otherwise.

Melanie had spent a decade never going home alone unless she decided to. *That is a lot*, she tried to tell herself. *That is more than I deserve.* She was never stunning—a little thick around the thighs, hair always stringy or too short, and she was about an inch taller than most men liked. She knew more beautiful women, and women who worked harder at being beautiful, but she also knew, at least for those years, she had the other part, some charge that made men like her. Even if it wasn't always about looks, now that the reliability of the appeal of her physical body was starting to go, it became harder.

She figured she must be around the same age as Brian's wife, give or take.

Typically, Melanie wore low heels and chose her jeans carefully. In public, she watched her alcohol. Sometimes she felt creased, like paper folded and unfolded too many times, though there were moments when she felt smooth, flat. A dress that fell just right in a low-lit room. The smell of gardenia at a summer party that reminded everyone of a different place. The attraction that comes from perseverance, when she would be one of two standing after a long night.

Brian was on his last stop before going home for a week, a little hurrah for him. He had noticed how much of his wallet was spread around them, and he started to reassemble it. There were a few slips of paper that he crumpled up and brushed to the side. He was talking about his children, but she didn't find this attractive. She thought if he gave two shits about his kids, he would spend more time with them— he could do it, during summers at least, and his wife didn't work, probably, so he would have some room to maneuver. Instead of complaining about the cost of private preschool and first grade, he could have a snapshot of the daughter, front teeth missing, at the Taj Mahal, and a snapshot of the boy, cowlicked, posing as if he was holding up the tower at Pisa.

"So stop," she said. "If you're unhappy."

"Excuse me?" he said.

"Nothing," she said. Then, for a few minutes she kept her eyes down and her tongue tight.

If she thought he was interested, she would have told him his children probably didn't care about schools that have uniforms and college-bound standards. They cared about slow nights of homework and eating dinner on a blanket on the lawn. They cared about the things that a parent can do, like drawing a firm line against an F to make it an A, and they cared about how funny he might look going after the escaped science-project mice with a broom and a newspaper. They wouldn't have heard of a safety school yet.

"Do you want another?" he asked, and traced the rim of her beer mug. The top was charred with lipstick, the bottom with foam.

She wasn't sure she did, but she nodded at him and the bartender brought her a full glass of beer. The bubbles stung her tongue. The bartender was wiping down the counter and loading the dishwasher. The glasses made a pinging sound against the rack.

She had been traveling for a seminar that would take place the next day, and Brian had something, he had something that she could not remember, and suddenly her beer was already half gone. She saw that he was wobbly on his chair, and with his wallet all packed up his hands were idle. He had a tumbler of whiskey, and the ice was pretty in the liquid.

She finished her drink as the bill arrived. Brian flicked down enough twenties to cover it and asked if he might walk her to the elevator.

"Sure," she said. She hadn't fully decided whether she liked him or not, but she did like the line of his face, in particular the way his evening stubble was peeking through his skin, suggesting more gray than the hair on his head.

When Brian pushed the button for the elevator, the polished doors slid open with a *thunk*. When they stepped inside, the elevator jerked, and the car lurched the rest of the way to his floor while they groped some. When he exited, she followed, not even pretending she wasn't going with him.

When she was underneath him, she thought of what it must be like to be his wife, caring for the children. She thought of the passion they might have had, distilled now to a quarterly fuck and a conversation about the price of tuition.

She was clear with herself, when she woke up next to Brian that she wasn't angry.

She had nothing to be angry about. She hadn't been that drunk, and she wasn't married, so that wasn't *her* husband under the over-bleached sheets.

The shades were drawn, the room was dark, and her clothes were folded on a chair. *That's how hot it was*, she thought—there was time to fold. She used her phone as a flashlight.

Gathering her things in the dim hotel room light, she wanted to wake him. *Congratulations*, she would say. *You're another person who doesn't want to go home.* She supposed that if they had anything in common, this was it.

She dressed and smoothed her hair for her walk back to her own room. She wrote *Call me!* on the hotel stationery and stuffed it into his trouser pocket to be found by his wife, his dry cleaner, or him. She penned the telephone number of her most recent ex instead of her own on her note, because she thought this was mean but hilarious.

So maybe she was a little angry.

As she walked to the elevator, she wanted him to call.

Is Melanie there?

I haven't seen Melanie in a while.

And then silence—not *wrong number*, not a simple *click*, but an indication that she had been there once and now she wasn't. She hoped she would feel it when they both remembered her simultaneously; she hoped she would feel it when one disconnected the line and severed the only connection either of them had left of her, two strangers trying to think of what to say next.

Chapter Seven
Brian
Summer, 2001

When Brian's wife Jenny was first pregnant they went house hunting—leaving their efficiency condo in the city and venturing into the spiderweb of suburban living, looking for space and yards and wide, gleaming appliances. He had been surprised by her readiness to trade in her patent leather boots for plush carpeting, surprised by how mesmerized she was by the size of the developments and their pastoral names: Foxglove Run, Sage Hill, The Horizons at Rock Creek.

As their child transformed from pea to lima bean to lemon, Brian ran his fingers across slabs of granite countertop that were bigger than the entire bathroom of their condo. It takes only a drop of water cycling into ice to crack rock, but the finishes were glossy and smooth. The flecks of quartz sparkled. He wandered through the houses and tried to see Jenny brushing her brown hair in the master bath, or himself shaving at the sink. He thought of the little specks of razored-off whiskers that sometimes dotted the white-cream porcelain, and how he was always very careful to get it all down the drain. He thought of how they had their toiletries organized in miniature tubs under the sink, and of how in their early days, when sometimes he had woken up and she was gone, he would stare at himself in the mirror and wonder if he had done something wrong, if she was angry.

Now married, they fought, just as he had feared. They had even fought when Jenny found out she was pregnant. He was drinking a beer and she had tossed the home test casually onto the coffee table.

"Two lines," she said. "Bingo."

He was not sure what it meant. "How many lines are there supposed to be?" he asked.

"Depends on what you're after," Jenny said.

"Okay," Brian said. He thought he was being even, measured. "What are we after?"

Jenny looked at him, frowning. He heard each bubble of carbonation in his beer fizzing.

When their friends asked them if they had been trying, Jenny said they were not *trying* but they were not doing anything to prevent it, either.

We aren't? Brian wanted to know.

"Well, I'm not," Jenny said, when he asked. "Have you been doing something? *I* was doing something, but *I* stopped."

He considered this. He had never asked about Jenny's birth control—not when they were dating, not now that they were spouses—it had seemed secret and narcotic, something that was not his business. He could not tell if Jenny did not care what he thought, or if she had done what he had done and not inquired. He felt very stupid when he thought of it like this.

Their life had mostly gone forward, in an ordinary way: one day, after they had been dating for a few months, Jenny had moved into the condo, and after this had gone on for a while, she had become his fiancée.

They had married in a small ceremony. His family had not met Jenny's mother before, though his grandfather thought he recognized her, but he had been a small-town cop—people called him Officer Frank, his first name, and he was eighty-three then—and he had seen a thousand faces in a thousand different stages of expression, and he always thought he knew people. Jenny's mother, Lucy Estelle, had gotten very drunk. It had been a nice night.

By the time of the news of the pregnancy, Jenny and Brian had only just celebrated their second wedding anniversary, and the kitchen was already a tangle of prenatal vitamins.

"I guess we need to move then," Brian said.

"I think we do," Jenny said. "Hopefully soon."

When they looked at houses, he imagined himself slogging through miles of commuter traffic with only the company of drive-time radio, and he felt a rift forming in their marriage. He also thought he and Jenny were arguing more lately—was it because she was hormonal and he was terrified? He found this explanation to be extremely likely. Before the pregnancy, if they had heated words, one of them would take a walk to a local bar and meet a friend, or read the paper, or have a slow cocktail at the counter. He liked how just a little separation, just the tiniest bit of distance, cooled them both. He liked how it was accomplished very easily. With every foot added to their prospective patio, he would be farther and farther from a place where he could just step out for a few minutes, and then he would see himself, fuming, surrounded by the wide hallways and entryway arches of beige-y new construction, trapped by rows of fake wrought-iron fencing and hedgework.

In the middle of house hunting, he called his father. He was scared, and he wanted his dad, who was also a small-town cop like his grandpa, Officer Frank—everybody called him that, even Brian's father Simon—to tell him what he was doing was right.

"I don't understand why you were renting anyway," his father, had said. "Just throwing away money."

Brian considered this. Perhaps it was not a rift, just a little fissure.

* * *

When it came to real estate, Brian's boss told him it was impossible to negotiate with a woman with child, and to skip negotiations all together and set some boundaries, like not moving north of Park or south of Evans, and that even if they found the perfect home just a few blocks off, he should hold his ground and refuse to offer. Better yet, he should refuse to even look at it. Brian took a softer approach, and he went to every showing Jenny was interested in. As their lowball offers were consistently declined, the clacking of their real estate agent's heels against concrete driveways faded to the smoosh of tennis shoes; pencil skirts and blazers were traded for jeans and hoodies; she stopped trying to impress them.

Jenny was not ill much, but she was changing. Her belly was growing rapidly. She was more contemplative and more interested in cooking. For years, she had not done much in the kitchen besides heat water for coffee, and now she left work early and Brian came home to full meals spilling off their tiny kitchen table and mounds of dishes like debris from a war zone. She took off her wedding ring, the ring she had chosen, and placed it on her jewelry tree where Brian figured it would hang indefinitely with all of the other things she might never wear again, like heavy necklaces of bright glass beads, chandelier earrings, and silver bracelets. When he asked her about the ring, Jenny said her hands were swollen, but Brian thought her fingers looked as slim as ever, perfect, in fact, as she plucked leaves off cilantro stems or cubed potatoes.

When their real estate agent told them she did not want to work with them anymore, they both panicked and put an acceptable offer on an acceptable three-bedroom ranch that was farther from the city than Brian liked and smaller and more used than Jenny had hoped for. They moved in over one weekend, packing up everything from their old life, and watched the hired labor fill a truck.

Brian was surprised, almost, when all the boxes were unloaded into the new house, that their contents were unchanged. As if by not breaking or spilling or getting lost or just vaporizing, his socks and records and thermal mugs were complicit. Everything would be unpacked into a mortgaged space where neither he nor Jenny really wanted to live. It seemed so final. It seemed like they had so little.

"I think this will be fine," Jenny said, after their first night in their new bedroom. "It feels okay. I forgot how nice the tile is in the shower."

"I'm glad you like it," Brian said.

"I didn't say I liked it," Jenny said. "I said I thought it would be fine."

* * *

On the Monday after the move, Jenny got out of bed but didn't seem to be getting ready for work, and it was not until then that she told Brian she had put in her notice. She said she had known she would be tired from moving, and that she was already six months pregnant, and once the baby was born she did not plan on going back anyhow, so she'd given her office a quit letter.

Brian suggested she call and try to pull the resignation back.

"They'll understand," he said.

"Understand what?" Jenny asked.

He said he had thought they would be carpooling for the last weeks until she took her leave, and that he got that six months was, of course, very pregnant, but he also noted that there was another full business quarter left before the child came.

"It's done," she said. "There's no rescinding now."

He said he thought she might miss her job at the law office. She had worked in accounting, and he thought she liked it. When she had announced the pregnancy, the women had thrown her a shower, and the partners had given her a check inside a card signed by their admins.

He thought she should have consulted him. She had worked her way to a mid-level position, and before she was pregnant, she had gone to all of the office parties, to which she usually wore a wide smile and a flowery, cleavage-baring shirt.

He said they would miss her. She shrugged and said she would not really miss them.

"I think it makes more sense, anyway, that we are closer together during the day. What if the baby comes and I'm stuck in traffic?" Brian said. They only had one car, his.

"I can call the ambulance," Jenny said.

Brian thought an ambulance seemed unnecessary, but he did not say anything. At work—he was in sales—his boss had continued to remind him not to attempt negotiations. His boss had four children by three different wives. Brian did not aspire to be like him, but he could not deny that the man had more experience.

In the weeks that followed, it was difficult, and also ill-advised, for Jenny to lift very much, so as they unpacked and organized, Brian brought her boxes, opened them carefully, and then set them on a stool for easy reach. He was surprised at the quantity of packages that were initially piled in the baby's room, because he could not understand where these things had been hiding in the condo.

Jenny had decided they should wait to find out the gender, and while Brian found this infuriating, he painted the nursery a smooth, wasabi green. Every day when he was finally delivered from his commute, there were more parcels on the doorstep: a crib, which needed assembly, and a stroller, which looked suitable for off-road terrain.

In addition to unpacking, they had to go shopping in preparation. They purchased a bedroom set for the area Brian had hoped would be his home office, but one Saturday under Jenny's direction, it became a guest room. He shrugged and swiped his Amex through the slot in the terminal. He accepted the receipt, folded it into smaller and smaller squares, and shoved it into his wallet. He arranged for delivery, and he followed his wife across the store's parking lot and into the next store, her belly a compass leading them through shop after shop, where he pushed the cart, and she calculated. His feet hurt and he hated the plastic smell of the merchandise and he badly wanted a beer. She was frustrated with what she saw as the relative lack of gender-neutral clothing and wondered out loud why it was so impossible to make a few things in green or yellow.

"You wear blue," Brian said. "It's not only for men. I have a purple shirt you always say looks nice on me." The cart had one wobbly wheel and it squeaked on the waxed floor.

"It's not the same when they're little," she said. "I think I would feel weird."

"How many clothes does a baby need for one day, though?" Brian asked.

The wheel protested.

Jenny looked at him.

He heard his boss in his head. *Do not negotiate!* "I mean, by day one," Brian said, "we'll know if it's a boy or a girl. I'm saying how much green stuff do we really need, because pink or blue will be fine after that. Or any color."

"I don't think it will be fine, Brian." Jenny said.

"I think it will be fine," Brian said, and he wished they were not having this conversation in public.

"What if it's not fine?" Jenny said.

Brian pushed the cart around the corner. They were standing in a tall aisle of diapers shrink-wrapped into large bricks, and he questioned how these could be realistically maneuvered into the trunk of his car.

"It will be fine." He tried to say this with some authority, but the skin around his lips felt dry.

He was not really sure if they were talking about onesie colors or something else, but he wanted to be right. He wanted her to believe him, because the baby coming was very alarming. They chose one of the diaper parcels, and he pushed the cart onward, but the knot he had felt for months in his belly would not dissipate. He had speculated that maybe it was sympathy pains or indigestion, but he knew it was fear. He wondered if he should have prepared more, if he should not have fought Jenny so much on the house, because now he did not have an office. Now they had five times as much space as the condo, but they were running out of space anyway. He could admit there were some things that were nice about living out of the city center. Parking was nice. If they were going to have to do all this shopping, the proximity was nice. His commute was not nice, but it was also not unbearable. Recently, on his drive home, he had started to listen to a call-in radio show that offered advice to mostly women. Once he thought he heard Jenny's voice on the line—the program used a voice disguiser, but he recognized the cadence.

My husband is not excited for our baby, the caller had said, her voice graveled through the machine. *I asked him if he wanted a boy or a girl, and he said it didn't matter.*

Does it matter? the host asked.

No, said the caller. *Not to me. But I'm surprised it doesn't matter to him.*

* * *

As it turned out, Brian was not in traffic when the baby came. He and Jenny were sitting on their sofa—a new sofa—on a Saturday morning when she gave a little grunt.

"Are you okay?" he asked, but she was already up, jumping away from the upholstery as her water broke, beautifully, he thought, just a trickle on her jammy pants and house slippers.

And then it was happening. He drove carefully to their hospital. There was valet so he used that. The attendants brought a wheelchair for Jenny, and she accepted it gracefully. There was some waiting, some paperwork. Mostly, from his perspective, just waiting. When he went to Jenny in the room, she was reclined, and sweating. He had a hard time understanding it. Women had been having babies for thousands of years, but somehow the process had not sped up, unlike, say, intercontinental travel or building a fire. He wondered if there were drugs the doctor should be using or if there was something Jenny should be doing differently—or something he should have done, like driven her to yoga classes. She had talked about yoga, but after he got out of the car at the end of the day, he was incapable of getting back in. He had told her to drive herself and she had given him a sad smile.

"It's *couples* yoga," she had said, and the idea scared him enough that he went straightaway to take a shower.

After some more time passed, he was hungry and the hospital vending machine offered only questionable granola bars and candy. He chose a Twix that was stale enough to further affect his morale.

He tried to focus, but all he could focus on was that for weeks he had been thinking of getting a new car. For as long as he had known Jenny, she had never owned a vehicle. He was not sure she should be at home all day with the baby and no car. Also, he was tired of running errands. As he waited, he thought about the car situation extensively. Jenny in the car, driving with their baby. The child in the car, strapped in securely. The shine on the wheels, the new paneling. The gauges, glowing brightly against Jenny's cheeks and carefully illuminating the temperatures and pressures of the vehicle, in constant, quiet confirmation that everything was functioning normally.

It was hours later when their daughter came. He was in the room with her, and Jenny gripped his hand—still, her fingers did not seem swollen—and Brian's thoughts went blank for a moment, as if he had gotten an electric shock or the wind knocked out of him. When his head started firing again, he had a feeling not unlike successfully plunging out a garbage disposal, the pipes freeing with a satisfying gurgle.

They had a girl, tiny and new, with crumpled ears and gooey hair.

Finally, the knot in his stomach moved.

He had never seen anything like Jenny's face when she met their daughter. He had to sanitize his hands again, and put on a fresh gown over his rumpled clothes, but he held her while she screamed a perfect, whole sound, and he brushed his lips across her wrinkled forehead and whispered to her that her mother had done so well, that he was so happy to be there with both of them.

Her body was warm in his arms.

He thought maybe things were changing.

Chapter Eight

Irene

Winter, 1974

That girl Kathleen would not stop following her, and it was starting to piss Irene off, and it was also starting to make her scared. She didn't know what Kathleen knew, but she had to assume she suspected about the baby.

Twice Kathleen had brought her brown-bag lunches, and twice Irene had accepted them. She shouldn't have, but she was hungry. Pregnant and hungry.

Did Sammy tell? He had promised he wouldn't. The baby was supposed to be their secret, until they could sort it, and then Sammy had broken through the ice, and then Sammy could not be revived, and then Sammy's blue face was in the casket. She knew the funeral parlor put makeup on his face to make him look more alive, but it didn't work. He looked pinched and stoic, not like Sammy at all. And she could see the blue from the cold, even beneath the pancaked rogue.

What could Kathleen know of her guilt—Sammy had been sneaking out of her window, off to his sister's basketball game, but also away from Irene's father. She snorted at how stupid it was, and kept replaying the night. How much would her father have cared, that she had a boyfriend. Maybe she hadn't had to hide him. The sex, yes, but not the person himself, not Sammy.

Sammy might have charmed her father, and if he didn't at first, he would have kept after it with that same Henderson doggedness that this Kathleen had.

Leave me alone, she wanted to say to the sister, and at the same time *Come here*.

Could the sister understand?

I was going to be his bride—the word so formal, so weighted. She turned the word over on her tongue.

That's right, she thought, *bride*.

Chapter Nine

Melanie

Spring, 2007

One thing about Alex, her man from San Antonio, was that he was persistent. He stopped by her office; he emailed her links to articles about the parent company, or about the psychology of marketing, or analytics that he thought she would find interesting. Sometimes he instant messaged her and asked if she wanted a coffee; usually she did not answer, even though she did read the articles and did think about the coffee. On the morning of their co-worker's funeral, she thought she would come to regret giving him her cell number, even though it was in the company directory. He was adamant in ensuring she would not cancel, texting her a reminder and verifying where he was supposed to pick her up. An experienced dater, Melanie had given him just the intersection, not wanting him to know exactly which townhouse was hers.

That morning, she had the strange feeling of waiting, when the space between everything was too long. She clutched her cellphone and looked at her shoes and wished for something to do. When he pulled up—*finally*, she thought, though he was five minutes early, and she had only been waiting for five—she did not recognize him at first because he was in a sedan, and she had expected a minivan, as he had two children.

She had no idea about their ages, other than youngish. Maybe a girl and a boy or maybe two boys. She could not recall ever asking.

They said their hellos, she belted herself in, and he asked if she would navigate and handed her a sheet of directions. Even in the age of GPS, she also preferred to print her route. For the next thirty minutes, all they said to one another was, *It looks like you should turn right here on Evans*, and *Thank you*, and *You'll want to get into the left lane at 124th*, and *Okay*.

It was a relief to Melanie when they—*finally*—parked. Inside, the Mason's lodge had the same linoleum tiles and cinderblock walls and the same sagging paint as the average church basement, and she was struck by how sad it was: the toilet in the lady's room running, and the inkjetted meeting handbills curling at the edges on bulletin boards that were pinned so many times the cork was like a minefield. Their office had paid for the food, subs and chips. She would have thought the sandwiches, wrapped and sliced into halves so that their contents could be displayed in a cardboard catering box, were unbecoming for the occasion if she had not known it was Kyle's favorite lunch. Desperately, she wished she had a Bloody Mary with a beer back but made do with a warm diet soda and three bottles of water.

There were a few other people from the office, and Melanie thought she recognized one man in a very plain suit from corporate, but she was not sure. She felt strange sitting with Alex, but no one seemed to notice. They chatted with the other people at their table, who she understood to be Kyle's friends from high school, about nothing, mostly. When topics regarding the weather and the quality of the sub sandwiches were exhausted, they sat quietly, and Melanie tried to think of something else to say that was not about why they were all actually there.

She counted herself lucky that she had not been to a lot of funerals, and so she was not that good at them. Like any other event, she supposed, there was a skill to doing it right. Tradeshows required the stamina to smile and be extremely diligent about fresh breath. Weddings required the ability to pace trips to the bar and to wear shoes stylish enough to look good and comfortable enough to dance in. Work socials meant a willingness to talk to anyone and to ask them a balance of questions so as to seem interested and not so many as to appear prying. Funerals, she was not sure. Conservative dress, yes, but she thought most everyone would just like to close their eyes and cry. That is what she wanted, to close her eyes and cry, all of them silent except for some sniffling.

When people had finished eating, Kyle's wife, Amanda, stood at the front of the room, and the low chatter halted. She had brought a little portable stereo, and she asked for folks to come to the front and offer a remembrance of her husband. Melanie stared at the green plastic tablecloth and fingered a pepperoncini that had fallen from her sub; the first mourners approached the mic and others began to queue. The family told old stories of diapering Kyle, of how he had been as a child. Other co-workers talked about late nights at the office when the company had just been starting, long before the acquisition.

We solved a lot of problems, one said. *A few of these were related to work.*

A woman from her table told a story of sneaking out to meet him, when they were freshmen at school, and how she had fallen into the river and screamed for him because she thought she was drowning. Melanie could have told her that drowning is silent. As competent as the body is, the lungs, the mouth, the throat, cannot simultaneously vocalize and gasp for air, but she listened to the woman. It was a warm summer night, and it was only when Kyle came into the water fully clothed after her that she realized if she'd just put her feet down, she could touch the bottom. *That was the thing about him*, she said, *he helped first and asked questions later.*

Alex looked sobered, the heat of San Antonio knocked straight out of him, and Melanie dug into the pocket of her sweater for a tissue.

She hoped it helped Amanda to hear how her husband had been loved and that the words would dissolve the grubby walls and the paper plates, silence the leaky plumbing. When the eulogies were finished and people were making the motions to leave, she thought she should say something. She had sent Amanda flowers the day she had heard, and now the gesture seemed awkward and trite—she had only met her once before, in the parking lot of the office. Kyle and his wife carpooled, even though her office was not particularly close by, probably holding hands through the worst bits of traffic, or at least Melanie hoped they did. She hoped they felt safe and matrimonial in their Honda, cruising evenly through the urban dust and the potholes and past the single-occupant drivers who had nothing to do but be enraged at the taillights in front of them or stay absorbed on their phones.

As Melanie approached, Amanda turned and thanked her for coming. She said the flowers were nice. She said she loved lilies because the smell reminded her of being a girl in Kansas.

"We're all so sorry," Melanie said.

Amanda nodded. Melanie squeezed her arm—why did people do this, she wondered as she was doing it. To check to make sure a survivor was still alive? She wanted to fold this woman, this young widow, into her, but they embraced only lightly, and one of the aunties implored that Melanie take some of the sandwiches. She wanted to decline, but she thought about the family scraping food into a bin, so she agreed and bagged a couple of subs and a few more cans of diet soda. There was also a little basket of pine starts in plastic tubes that were meant to be planted in memorial to Kyle, and Melanie shoved three of the seedlings into her purse.

When they walked to the car, the sky was gray with rain, and she and Alex belted up again and drove quietly from the service. They had both liked Kyle, but had not known him so well. There were many things Melanie thought of saying, but she did not say any of them. The way the low afternoon light shone through the pewter clouds onto the recently blacktopped highway made her feel like she should be doing a better job with everything, being more industrious, being tough and productive, like her magnolia's beetles.

At the funeral, besides just wanting to close her eyes, she had wanted to hold Alex's hand. If she had his age right, he could not have been married long enough where an affair might be forgiven, she thought. While it had not been the case with her parents, she had seen this happen with some couples—a single transgression after many years, and the one night paling against so very many days. Alex was probably not in a place to test his marriage, and he'd only get staying together for the kids, until they started to hate each other, and then they would divorce anyway.

She remembered when sex still felt full of promise and potential, and going home with someone from a bar could be just an ordinary screw, or it could be the rest of a life. There was something magical in how hard it was to know who strangers might end up being, and she wondered what Alex thought about her, really.

As they made their way back to Denver, she wanted him to say something that would endear him to her, and she wanted to stop feeling choked and weepy every time she thought of Kyle. She was queasy even though the car was being driven well. What was it like for Amanda to be left behind with the wilting flowers and the soggy remains of the subs? What was it like for Alex's wife, at home, putting the children down for a nap, waiting?

When she reached across the seats of the sedan and laced her fingers through his, for just a moment, the accelerator jerked.

"Sorry," he said, steadying his foot on the pedal. "I didn't expect that."

They were picking through some of the more distant suburbs, and the afternoon rain was ready to break, the clouds low and dark. She reached for the printout of the directions.

"What happens if you stay out for a few hours?" she asked, and flipped the stapled papers to find the return route. He said he was not sure. She put the papers down, wishing she could ask him what he was thinking about, but it seemed far too familiar. The housing developments had thinned into a brief rangeland before the edge of the next batch of cul-de-sac communities, and they kept on towards Denver.

In any case, she believed they would not have a happy ending. There was so much she did not know. Perhaps he was deeply, and truly dissatisfied. Perhaps there were factors she did not understand. Perhaps he was confused. Perhaps she was.

She could not stop thinking that he was good looking, from an angle, and further, when people start to fall in love, it is the only angle they can see.

* * *

They went for a drink, ducking under an awning just as the clouds split and the smell of the rainwater came up, spores and lightning-cracked ozone. Melanie ordered a plate of chicken wings, and they ate these. They had very tall glasses of very cold beer. They talked about Kyle, and they talked about work. Casually, he put his hand on her knee. Casually, she put her hand on top of his. He had very dark hair cut close to his head. She assumed it was curly, because it seemed to her that this was what most men with curly hair did, crop it. She ordered another round.

It was different being with him in their town; she felt nervous. She found herself looking around the bar for people she might know. It might be network theory or it might just be the ease of picking out a friend's walk from a crowd, but it happened frequently, she thought, bumping into people. She worried there was a person who might recognize him, some friend of his wife's—the wife who he was now texting—or a friend of a friend, on their way back from the bathroom.

"Hey," she said. "I'm starting to feel uncomfortable being out in public like this."

"Okay," he said, "But how much does it really matter for you? I'm the one taking a risk."

He told her to relax, and while she understood that she was not the person with the most to lose, she pulled her fingers from where they were looped with his, because she did not want to get him into even more trouble, and because it did matter to her, being so close to home.

There was something sour coming from the kitchen, cold dishwater and bar rags, and she thought of the office and the way she, and all of them, spent so much of life with people picked by a hiring committee.

The waiter finally showed up with fresh beers for them both, and Melanie told Alex she did not think he should drive home. She was not entirely sure she was extending an invitation, but also not sure that she was not.

When he asked if he seemed too tipsy, she thought he might be accepting her offer.

"Buzzed driving is drunk driving, I heard," she said.

"Do I seem buzzed?" He sounded genuine.

The foam was pretty around the rim of her beer, and a song that was both angsty and popular rattled from a speaker. The room felt small. She remembered when they were in San Antonio how he had tossed his jacket over the peanut shells for her, and how she had crunched her way to the bar and giggled, and how his teeth had seemed to gleam, like polished stone. It made her very sad that he was with her now, in the afternoon, at a bar, after the memorial service for their colleague.

She was starting to feel the yeasty slosh of too much beer. Her choice of venue was poor, she decided. Everyone seemed so young, and this made her feel like she had cracks around her eyes, and dull skin. The San Antonio Man was texting again. She hoped he was making arrangements, but she did not ask. She got the bill and settled it. When he put down his phone, she suggested he buy her dinner, and he said he would.

She told him she was upset about Kyle, and she told him she was feeling alarmed.

"Me too," he said, and he reached his hand across the table.

They walked to a restaurant the way she remembered walking with her parents when she was still an adolescent, apart from each other, and she thought it was probably just as obvious that they were together now as it had been then. The rain had almost stopped, but the sidewalks were drenched.

At dinner, they were in a booth, though she would have rather been at the bar, where it was easier to talk. It was a cozy place with low seats and candlelight. Whenever he reached for his phone, the touch screen glowed like a beacon.

When the appetizer came, she asked him if he was still texting his wife, and he was irritated.

"Who else would I be texting?" he said.

They ate mussels and bread and ordered wine by the glass. Like a date, where an entire bottle seemed too presumptuous and picking the shells off the shellfish seemed tender and sophisticated.

"I'm not sure if this was a good idea," she said. She said she thought they should both go home, but he suggested they finish dinner and then decide, and she agreed.

She had ordered chicken, he beef. The plates were meant to be artfully prepared, but the tiers of garnish and painted-on sauce seemed fussy, and their server was letting her wine get dangerously low.

They ate politely, using both utensils, one in each hand. This was a skill she had had to teach herself; a mark of class was cutting food with the fork turned sideways. Someone had pointed it out to her once.

Melanie tried to make conversation, not knowing if he was scared of being with her, or scared of not having gone home yet. Now was not the time to ask about his children, but she still wondered.

Coffee came, dessert was declined. She ordered a whiskey and sipped it. Not sure what do next, she asked if he was going home.

"I'm supposed to," he said. "I don't really want to, but I think I will."

They decided to split the bill, and he waited patiently while she finished her cocktail. When they walked out, he gently put his arm in hers, and he left it there until they reached his car and he opened the door for her.

He drove slowly to where he had picked her up. At the corner, she told him to keep going.

"I'm down at the end, on the left," she said.

"That's cute," he said, as her townhouse came into view. "That's a cute little place." The booze had softened his voice.

She had worked very hard creating what her real estate agent called "curb appeal," so she could be ready to sell in case she ever needed to—a mortgage on a single income could get tight quickly. She had reproduced planters of flowers from a photo snipped from a magazine and replaced the concrete flagstone on the walk with brick. Her arms had hurt for days afterward. She thanked him for noticing and invited him up for a drink.

"If I do I'll be buzzed driving which is drunk driving," he said, and he reached across her, opening the passenger side door for her.

"You can stay, Alex," she said, and then she surprised herself by asking. "Please?"

After she unlocked the door, she slipped past him and flipped the light on in the small mudroom that was a jumble of shoes and scarves and her oversized laptop bag, empty and deflated in the corner. He followed her up the stairs. She opened a bottle of wine, pouring two generous glasses and immediately taking a gulp of hers. He set his phone on the counter and asked for some water, and she asked him if he wanted ice. In the time he drank the water, she had almost finished her wine.

His phone was buzzing madly, vibrating against the hard tile of her countertop, and she was starting to feel more than a little wobbly.

"You could turn it off," she suggested, nodding. The room spun a little, so she took a deep breath. "Or leave it on. Just leave it on. I'll put on music."

She padded into her living room. "Or, we could go outside," she called. "It's not raining anymore. Do you want to go outside?" She was tired of still wearing her funeral clothes, and she thought maybe they could keep it a little innocent. Curl up in pajamas on the couch. Watch a movie. She was not sure what kind of music to pick, so she decided to just go with whatever was already on the stereo. When she switched it on, there was a low guitar and drums being played with a brush, the Americana she listened to when she was sad and possibly drunk.

When she came back into the kitchen, he was scrolling through his messages again. "I think I really should go home," he said.

"Okay," she said. She tipped the goblet and drained the last drop. "Thanks for the ride and for dinner. I'll walk you out." The music from the living room was faint, and as she went with him to the door, she thought for a moment he might lean in and change his mind, but he did not. "Text me when you get home," she said.

He looked at her. "Mel, I get what you are saying, and it's nice. But I probably won't," he said.

"Then why did you even come in?" she said.

He didn't answer.

"Okay," she said, smiling her best smile. "See you Monday."

After she closed the door, she kicked her shoes onto the floor with the rest, refilled her wine glass, and went into the yard with the pine starts from Kyle's service. The grass and the earth were damp, perfect for planting. She made a space with her spade and filled in the dirt with Miracle-Gro. She knew the magnolia would be lapping up little tastes while she watered, but she wanted to make sure Kyle's trees rooted.

Digging, she was glad she was here alone, behind the protection of her high fence and the smell of the just-turned earth.

When she got the pine starts out of their protective plastic and snug into their little holes, the fresh green of the new shoots were bright against the dark.

Chapter Ten
Brian
Summer, 2001

The day after Stella was born, when they'd been home for only about an hour, Jenny's mother Lucy Estelle arrived, angry at the traffic coming into Denver and also at everything. Brian thought she had a ridiculous amount of luggage, but later recanted when he saw her packing included snacks and a large bottle of whiskey, which he would have picked up for her, and he told her so, but she said she was not sure if the store would have her brand.

They called their daughter Stella, which Brian had argued was a southern-sounding name or a kind of beer, after Jenny's mother, Lucy Estelle. Jenny told him Stella was Latin for *star*.

He was surprised at baby Stella's lull. He had taken time off work—his boss told him not to worry if he wanted to come back early, he said he would not judge—and Brian expected total chaos, but Jenny and her mother chatted in low voices, and Lucy Estelle bleached the bathtub so Jenny could soak, and, on day three, his mother-in-law cooked two huge pots of soup and two massive casseroles and divided everything up into labeled containers in the freezer. Stella mostly slept.

"Just in case," Lucy said, "you have a couple nights when all you can do is reheat. This snoozin' won't last." She winked and sipped from her whiskey. Brian went for a beer and clinked the neck of the bottle to the glass of rattling ice and liquor.

Brian had always thought his mother-in-law, in addition to being a drunk, was pushy, but he was grateful for her then, when Jenny was napping and Stella was fussing. She shoved his daughter into his arms and demanded that he change her or take her to Jenny to be fed or walk in a circle and bounce her.

On night five, Brian woke to Lucy Estelle leaning over him— Jenny had been up every other time and was dozing deeply. Stella was screaming.

"Get up," something about the dark always urging a whisper, "and go to your daughter!"

"I'm up, I'm up," Brian said.

"She needs you," Lucy said.

Brian padded through the unlit house toward Stella, Lucy trailing with a blanket. He knew she was training him for Jenny's sake; Brian did not have younger siblings or young cousins, and his father had not been the hands-on type.

He liked that: needs.

He cradled his daughter's head with his hands.

* * *

When he had first met Jenny, they had been at the show of a local band and he had spilled beer all over her shoes. She had been nice about it, though her friends were not, sneering at him and telling him he would have to buy her another pair. He hadn't argued, because he had been excited to see her again. Leaving Jenny with his number, he had said it was up to her, and the next day she had called and asked if he was ready to take her to Nordstrom. He picked her up in front of her building, and they had driven to the mall, like teenagers might have.

She had chosen a pair of suede platforms, but, when they were checking out, confessed her pumps from the other night had been from Payless.

"That's okay," he said, and signed his receipt. "Should we go somewhere else?"

They spent the afternoon on a coffee shop patio, until finally Jenny said that she really wanted to get going. When Brian said he would drop her home, she said no. *Your place.*

* * *

While Lucy Estelle was still in town, Brian got a new car. He chose a cherry-red sedan, and he fully admitted that his salesman training had dissolved when he thought of his daughter. He had been completely upsold on safety features. The interior was gray, and he felt it was extremely sharp. He asked for one of those large bows that he had seen on television, but the dealership told him they only had those in winter, and they were extra anyway.

Brian told the man who was helping him that the car was for his wife, who was at home with their daughter. The man told Brian that if it were him, he would give the old car to his wife and keep the new one.

"Kids, you know," he said. "They make a lot of messes." He was about the same age as Brian, but he did not say if he had children of his own.

"I'd rather have her in the newer one," Brian said. "More reliable."

"But that upholstery will show everything, man. Just wait."

"Okay," Brian said. He was becoming fine with waiting.

After the financing was sorted and the signatures collected, Brian realized he had no way of getting the cars back without Lucy Estelle or Jenny, so he gave the man another $50 from his wallet to follow in the old sedan, and one of the maintenance staff followed them both.

He liked his life, he had decided. He liked the women: Lucy Estelle, Jenny, Stella. He kept his radio silent and he repeated their names as he drove. The car was smooth against the pavement, and the wheel responded to even the slightest touch. Brian thought they were a little like the pioneers then, the three women and his two cars, caravanning across an unfamiliar landscape, headed toward a new idea of home.

Chapter Eleven
Kathleen
Winter, 1974

Seventeen now, Kathleen had grown up in a tiny house where she was the middle child by chronology, the youngest of the three girls, and the eldest of the three smaller boys. Her brother Sammy was the closest to her, just eleven months apart. As children, they were always together, grubby hands clasped. When Kathleen's sisters were rouging their cheeks and stealing cigarettes, she was in the trees, in a pair of hand-me-down jeans, hair tangled, hands scraped and scabby. One by one the sisters left, into the early marriages and cashier jobs of their small town, only Darlene, the oldest, had gone far, moving to Oregon. The summer before, Kathleen had taken the bus to see her, because she was the only one of the women from home who had time to go. Her parents took her to the station, and she rode for two days as the plains dissolved into mountains and then to plains and then mountains again.

Even without her sisters in the house, it seemed just as cramped. As the boys grew taller, their massive feet spread into the space vacated by the sisters, and the drains still clogged with hair as they passed puberty and proceeded directly to balding, like their father.

Kathleen was not sure what she wanted. Sometimes she passed her sister Rose, clerking at the grocery store, and sometimes she saw her sister Jeannette in line. Rose had graduated, just barely passing her final classes, but Jeannette had dropped out to get married, then her belly ballooned. Kathleen hadn't heard much from Darlene since the visit. Even though she traced their steps in the house, wearing their old clothes, it did not feel sad to her that her sisters had moved out. She had Sammy, her brother, her first friend, and like her, he was doted on by their mother. They all had the orbit of their parents, save Darlene, states away. They swirled around them, and Kathleen admired the static of her mother and father, she admired their pull. Even when she saw old pictures of them, they seemed the same. Her mother was tired, always tired, and years later Kath would wonder what her mother would have been like if she had not had so many children, if she had not spent so many nights without sleep and a baby at her breast, sometimes two, like with her and Sammy when Kathleen refused to wean. When Rose or Jeanette came to visit, they scolded her for not helping their mother more, but her mother defended her.

Kathleen was tall like her brothers, and she played basketball in the school's gymnasium, her hair reaching down her back, dangling from a ponytail. The team was new, but their uniforms were castoffs from the boy's C-squad. She guessed they were supposed to be grateful; some of the neighboring schools did not even give the girls uniforms, if they had teams at all. Wearing polyester with a sagging crotch was their toll for daring to train their bodies to be strong, a penance, like picking lentils from the fireplace.

And even if Rose and Jeannette rolled their eyes at her, all the sisters except for Darlene, as she was the oldest, were used to other people's clothes. Before their first match, Kath collected her team's uniforms, and her sisters happened to be visiting, so they helped her drag out the old dressmaker's tape and together with their mother they marked the uniforms in chalk, and cut down the shorts with pinking shears, cropped the tops to a slim tank. On her own bottoms, Kathleen made an extra slice on the edge of the side-seam.

She liked the effect, even if a little bohemian, of the zigzagged edges. In their first game of the season, when she was fouled and took the line, to the dismay of her coach, even the slow bend to bounce the ball before her shot revealed her leg. Sore from the scissor's handles, she wished she had had her fingers taped, but she heard her sisters and Sammy cheer as she swished each basket. They lost the game, but she played well, and Sammy walked home with her, giving her his jacket. He told her he knew she was doing a hard thing.

"It's just sports," she said.

"It's more," he said. "And you know it. I don't even care about basketball, but I like watching you play. Mom probably would have been good, I'll bet. Rose would be awful, though."

"Rose would be okay, she's tougher than she looks," Kathleen said. "Mom, though, I could see Mom being good on defense."

"She would be," Sammy said. "I think she'd foul a lot though. Slappy."

Kathleen smiled at him, and she wanted to hold his hand, even though she knew they were too old for it, so she walked the rest of the blocks, shivering even in his coat. He put his arm around her and she leaned into him, her brother.

For the second game, it wasn't her idea to go shorter with the uniforms, but after practice one night, her team had sat in the park under the crunch of the drying autumn leaves, clipping and tearing until their uniforms were mostly thread. They used scissors and a hole punch and stitched on rhinestones someone had filched from her grandmother. Kathleen liked the circle of young women, giggling and punchy from the thrill of defiance and making the uniforms theirs.

When they played again, their teenage bodies flashed on the court, like fish jumping in water, thighs exposed, the fabric just skimming the back of their butts. The away crowd rooted hard against them, and the referees had to stop to sweep bits of glitter and ribbon from the court. This time, they won, but they were all suspended for inappropriate dress.

They couldn't play in their modified uniforms, and the school said it had no budget to get them replacements.

At home, when she told Sammy and her folks, she saw the anger rise in her mother's face. Her mother understood.

"There's that law," she said. "The nine law—what was it called? You have the right now. You go talk to the teachers."

Sammy agreed. "You're right, tough on D," he said to her later, when she went outside with him while he smoked one of their father's cigarettes. "Mom's right. Go to the teachers. The ladies."

The school librarian helped Kathleen with the text, and the art teacher gave her some heavy paper like stationery. She typed carefully:

Dear Mr. Spencer,

It has come to our attention your school may be out of compliance with the provisions of Title IX, which as you know can have significant impact on your school's funding.

Kathleen thought the letter looked homemade, like the dresses her mother sewed, but she made up a name to sign it, and the librarian's sister posted it from the state capitol in Denver. Let Principal Spencer try to figure out if the funding threat was real or not. It had been two summers since the law passed, but no one had pushed him yet.

While there was still some time left in the season, new uniforms, women's uniforms, arrived. The colors were wrong, green and gold instead of blue and yellow, which made Kathleen think they were remainders or samples, but she didn't care, because when they stood in the locker room mirrors, they looked like a team.

It was in her crisp shorts and matching tall socks at a late season game that the whistle blew for no reason, and the coach and one of the referees approached Kathleen on the floor. For a minute she thought it was a late reaction to a push she had given a forward, she dreaded having to apologize to avoid a technical foul, but the whistle wasn't for the game. The ref was just one of the parents, and she saw his face above the faded stripes.

"It's Sammy," he said, guiding her by her elbow. "Go change."

* * *

Winter had come quickly—she had felt it walking home with him—and the nights fell into a fast freeze, turning the river to a bridge of glossy ice. This early in the season even a light boy's foot could crack it, the river still gushing underneath.

* * *

She would always remember how at Sammy's funeral there was nothing to say; he was young, and he was gone before he could do much. She would remember that she wished she had reached for his hand that night they were walking home, even if she thought it was silly. She would remember the way that he was special was for small things, like gripping two strings of fence wire between the barbs and pulling one hand up and the other down to make a door for her to pass through so she would not snag her clothes when they cut through a field. The way his blue eyes were almost navy. The way when it was his turn to do the dishes, he almost always dropped something, and whenever they pulled out a newly chipped mug from the cabinet, they would examine it, shaking their heads at him. Even years later, when Kathleen would feel the smooth edge of a cup with a fleck of the finish missing its ceramic glaze, she would think of her brother, his rough hands deep in the suds.

When she cleaned out the side of the room he had shared with Mikey, there was nothing but dirty clothes and magazine scraps. Her mother sat on the corner of his mattress so it sunk to the floor, her face ash, the same color as Sammy's had been in the open casket, washed clean and cold. The carpet in the room was old and worn. Mikey had been sleeping on the sofa since the night they found Sammy. Kathleen's father sat at the kitchen table chain-smoking cigarettes and putting ice in his whiskey to make it last longer.

After the funeral, except for a few T-shirts Kathleen stashed in her drawers, they burned his clothes—too sad to save. Her father splashed used oil and tractor gasoline on the pyre of ripped jeans, a motorcycle helmet Sammy never had a bike to match with, and the shards of his own chipped mug he used to drink coffee from, even though their mother thought he was too young to drink coffee, until the fire grew so high and so bright they all thought it might take them and the house. Kathleen held her mother's hand, and Rose and Darlene and Jeannette's babies cried, and she understood that even if Sammy had not been perfect, or promising, or even nice all of the time, he belonged to them.

He also belonged to the girl, with dark hair and hollowed eyes, who had cried into a soiled bandana, and who she recognized from school, wearing a black skirt and blouse at the service. There had been a handful of other kids, but this girl stood apart from them. Was Kathleen imagining the bump at her belly, the shine on her hair? She had never been in love, and thought if her brother had been, he would have told her.

* * *

She went over it again and again, how she had found Irene in between classes, just off school property, where the kids who smoked would congregate on breaks. There was a light and dirty snow on the ground. The girl had been easy to spot, a freshman, and glowing.

Kathleen sat on the steps of the school, peeling her jacket off to feel the cold.

"You're going to get sick if you keep undressing outside," she heard.

"I'll live," she said, and turned. Irene.

Irene sat next to her. Kathleen didn't know what had changed, why the girl had come to her now, and she didn't ask. She dug into her backpack for the extra lunch and handed it to Irene.

They sat on the steps of the school, and they talked about Sammy and about Irene's life. She lived with her father, and it sounded like he was not around much, working the night shift or sleeping, and Kathleen recognized her street as a place that had a reputation, fair or not, for being the bad part of town, but she could not say she had ever actually walked down it.

She saw what her brother could have loved about Irene, her earnest face, the way she looked to the side when she was talking, her dark eyebrows. She wondered if her brother had seen this girl and wanted to pull her in. He would have known, like Kathleen did, that there was always room for one more; this was the imperfect blessing of a large family. Kathleen asked if they could meet the next day, and Irene looked away but said, *All right*, and Kathleen could not tell if the girl was distracted or if she was embarrassed to have been given the lunches and to have eaten everything but the crusts of the sandwich. Next time, Kathleen would remember to trim them off.

That night she worried about how to get the girl to confess. She understood the consequences. If the school found out, they would make her leave, and her father might kick her out, so Kathleen started planning. It was just like the uniforms and the letter. She thought she could live at home for another year after high school, in a house with closets stuffed full of old infant clothes and the garage filled with boxes of toys, in a house that was impervious to children. Her father would still drink whiskey at the kitchen table, and her mother would still be tired, but they would have part of Sammy back. The other boys, Mikey, fourteen, and Thomas, thirteen (who they still thought of as the baby) would not be as used to a scream in the night or the low stink of the diaper pail, but they would survive.

She wanted to hear that her brother Sammy had wanted the baby. She wanted to hear that he planned to take the GED and get a job, that he would support Irene staying in school.

The next day, she tracked down Irene, and all she could do was grab the sleeve of her coat and hold on to it for a moment, saying, *I know, okay, I know.* She could not tell if Irene's face was fear or relief, but the girl accepted another lumpy lunch bag, and they chewed through their food quietly, while the other students spun around them.

In the following days when Kathleen couldn't find her, she wasn't sure if Irene was ditching school, or just hiding out again. Even with her own brothers and sisters, she had never felt such an urge to protect someone, had never known someone who seemed to need so much protection. Even Sammy, Sammy was gone, but it was from his own recklessness. She didn't blame him, only accepted that there was nothing to do, no fingers to point, no *if only*—if only he wouldn't have crossed the ice, but he did, and she couldn't have stopped him. He'd likely done it before.

Protection was for those left behind.

Chapter Twelve
Melanie
Fall, 1986

When she had been in fifth grade, they did their lessons in portable classrooms with squeaky walls and floorboards full of soft spots. She disliked, intensely, the school. In the spring and summer, her desk was always dusty because the classroom windows were left open, and the wind blew off of the Front Range in pressurized, howling bursts, carrying specks of grit, which Melanie was sure were made up of mostly dead moths and rotten leaves. Out of the windows they had a view of the Rockies, but she could live without it. She would rather have the glass tucked into the casements and the blinds down, to keep out the glare and the gusts. At school they told her she was lucky to live in a place like Colorado, where the sun shone often and the mountains kept watch over them, but all she had to do was look in any direction but west to see nothing but grass and flatland sprawl, and the Platte snaking pathetically along, with the same effect as when the boys peed into a dirt clod at recess and then jumped back so they would not get their own piss on their shoes.

At school they said that if you asked a kid in a big city where meat came from that they would say, *The Store*, and so children in the west should feel proud they possessed more survival skills, more expertise in the natural. Melanie did not feel proud, and as far as she was concerned, meat did come from the store. They took a field trip to a ranch once, but it was not like her parents kept a beef cow in the backyard. Usually they got everything at a club grocery.

Melanie thought it was boring, school, but she could not see what else she could do. She wanted to get on with it, but she understood she was a child and that part of being a child was years of waiting. At lunch, she ate in the cafeteria alone or with a friend and was depressed by the plastic trays and the plastic sandwich bags and the plastic smell of the food that had been either in the coat closet all day or recently scooped from a vat. It was hard not to feel like she was wasting her time. Every other Friday, hot lunch was pizza and maple bars, and these days were the worst because the entire school reeked of industrial pepperoni and fake syrup.

The school was in a suburban spot outside of Denver with a tiny historic main street surrounded by low-slung suburbs. Her parents lived in a one-story ranch house with pretty shutters and clean eaves. They bought the house when they were newlyweds, and even as the years went by and they could afford more, they stayed, because they loved the rooms and did not want to move. Some of her best memories were of the improvements they made, months of sawdust that poofed around her and softened every edge—like her mother's powder, or like glitter shaken from a jar. One year they put in another window in the kitchen to catch the early light, and her mother grew philodendrons in a line of clay pots on each windowsill. Her mother staked the vines until they were beyond the height of the walls, and then her father screwed hooks into the ceiling at tidy, six-inch intervals, each curve of tin cradling a rope of green. Kathleen watered faithfully and new leaves unfurled, the vines constantly reaching. It seemed important when it was time to mount a new hook. Her father would use his measuring tape for accurate distance, and little bits of the popcorn finish would scatter onto the kitchen tiles. Melanie remembered being lifted so she could pull the vine into its new support. It was like they had accomplished something. Another six inches, some proof that life was moving forward, even if it was only to the other side of the room.

Sometimes, she was surprised when she visited her friends' homes and the kitchens were dark and wallpapered or decorated with roosters. She loved the lush of her family's kitchen, and in the library at school, she learned that her mother's houseplants were poisonous to cats. Melanie kept this as one of the many secrets an only child has. When she walked through the kitchen, rummaging for dry cereal or a glass of juice, she thought of the chemical danger and imagined herself feline, padding safely out of reach on a linoleum jungle floor while her mother cooked whole chickens in a Dutch oven, stewed eggplants.

There were two small bedrooms, and a half bath off the master. The carpets had been replaced and the old wallpaper steamed off. Her parents helped her paint her room whenever she felt like it, and she went through coats of green, purple, cream, and finally yellow, taping the trim carefully and putting down a drop cloth to catch any errant blobs on the floor. She liked living there, the big backyard and her mother's irises. There were fresh flowers all summer in a vase on the kitchen table, and in the winter, cuts from the philodendrons rooting in murky water.

Her father traveled for work sometimes, enough that they missed him but not so much that they did not know him. He sold medical devices and this, to Melanie, seemed like a very important job, because what if your heart stopped and no one had the paddles to get it going again? Her father solved this problem. On nights he was gone, her mother would put on records, and they would sing along to Stevie Nicks or Carole King, waiting for their pork chops to finish.

In the living room they had a comfortable sofa and a few chairs. Sometimes the three of them would sit on the sofa and watch television, Melanie nestled in the middle. Sometimes they would work on the house, small chores like replacing the peephole or reworking the hinges of a sticky door. She liked these jobs, sitting on a low work stool in the garage with her father, polishing a cabinet pull or greasing an old drawer slider with paraffin until the glide was perfect. She had her own screwdriver with a pink handle and a small hammer that her father taught her to hold correctly, with her palm in the wide part of the grip, low to the base, to get the most leverage.

After school, her friends did cheerleading or basketball, but she would sit in the library, or on nice days take her books to the park and read. When Melanie's father was traveling, she liked to meet her mother at the bank where she worked as a teller, her fingers greased in glycerin from the tubs of pink Sortkwik, slips of deposit waiting for tally. Melanie would walk through the empty drive-up window and press the call button so someone would unlock the doors.

To her, the bank was order. Drawers of currency, counted. Bags of coin, rolled. Her mother was head teller, so she was always there late with the cash drawers. It was quiet after hours, and there was something calming about her mother's expert handling of money—the way she could, after years of practice, spot old dimes made of real silver or wheat cents, measure fifty-bill bundles by weight or by running her thumb along the edge of a stack. Her mother asked her if she knew why all of the presidents faced right on coin except for Abraham Lincoln's mug on the penny. Melanie did not know.

She came to love the incongruousness of it: someone who made just over clerk's wages working through thousands of dollars with more expertise than the richest gangster. Her mother did not actually care that much for money, but had the lingo anyway: a hundred bills was a *strap*, a thousand a *brick*. Melanie learned the treasury colors; she liked the wrappers for the twenties and hundreds the best, violet and mustard. At school, they had taken a field trip to the Denver mint, and she had felt superior because she already knew about money in large quantities, moving quickly.

At the end of a day, if her mother was in a good mood, they would walk home, arms linked, chatting. She would tell her about what she hated about school: her teachers, who were as interesting as a bar of soap, and how she had gotten in trouble for saying out loud that she thought studying American colonialism was boring.

"They boiled shoe leather in the winter at Jamestown," Melanie said. "I'd rather eat a dog."

"They had probably already eaten the dogs," her mother said.

"The map I drew of the settlement was mostly brown," Melanie said. "I left some blank spots because there was also a lot of snow."

Her mother told her stories of trying to educate her elderly customers when policies changed and explained why she alone could not open the safe (because half of the employees knew the beginning of the combination, and the other half knew the end).

When her mother was in a bad mood, they made their way down the sidewalk side by side, both staring at the pavement Melanie knew by heart—here was the square that looked like something heavy had been dropped on it; here was the one with the concrete cracked in the shape of a star.

It was not too far, she learned, the space between happy and sad.

At night her mother would peel off her stockings and rummage in the kitchen. The thing Melanie did not like about her father traveling was that it made her mother agitated.

She wondered what the house had been like before her and what had been in her room, but she did not ask. Emptiness was the idea she liked most—the floors glossed and the walls a shell pink, the air kept fresh by a slow-moving ceiling fan.

Once when her father was gone, they spent a week in school on Ponce de León arriving in Hispaniola and continuing on to Florida, searching. Pierced by an arrow anointed in poisonous sap from a manchineel tree, he took his last breath in Havana. *Who cares*, Melanie thought, but she colored the hand drawn map of the Caribbean anyway, making a hashed line to mark de Leon's travels. In school they always drew maps, and Melanie's mother saved them all in a poster tube in the hall closet.

"It looks like a heart," her mother said, putting beef roast with a crown of perfect onions on the table. Her father had not called, Melanie knew, because her mother slammed the pan.

"It's not," said Melanie. "It's just a circle and then he dies."

"He was the one who was looking for the Fountain of Youth, right?"

"He didn't find it," Melanie said, rolling up the paper.

"Thank God," her mother said. "Who'd want to do this crap forever."

But on the next night, he did come home. The weather was nice, and so they had leftover roast sandwiches with horseradish on the patio. The earlies were in bloom, and the daffodils rimmed the yard like a corona.

Melanie liked the way the food looked, spread on the glass table, and she liked it when her father was there with them. When he traveled, it was not only his body gone. There was less sureness in the house.

* * *

When she was in sixth grade, her parents sat her down on the center spot on the sofa and turned two chairs to face her. They would separate, they had decided, and the house would have to be sold. Her mother's face was caved in, like bread punched down after it has risen. Her father looked like nothing, almost, a tiny fleck of flaked-off veneer. The house felt loose to her then, the years spent oiling creaks and tightening joists unraveled in a moment, the tiers of birthday cake and fluffy soufflés collapsed to wobbly floorboards.

What is this place, Melanie wondered then, *without us?*

* * *

It was the first days after that were the hardest. The wind would blow and Melanie would feel it in every real and imagined crack in the house;

she would feel it in her body. Her mother came home with banker boxes and rolls of tape; her father hit the road, off to Omaha, Topeka, St. Louis. A Realtor came and drove a sign into the front lawn. It was fall, and Melanie came home from school one day to the white post and the red letters of *For Sale* with the leaves swirling around the place where the stake had pierced the grass.

She packed her things very carefully, wrapping even the softest items in a cushion of newspaper and a protective layer of cellophane tape. She filled the boxes slowly, labeling them with a permanent marker, and her mother did not rush her. It did not seem like there was much in her room, but it was surprising how much a small space could hold. When she was finally finished, her mother asked her to help with the rest of the house. Some things Melanie was instructed to pack, some she bagged for the Salvation Army. They also had a pile near the entryway that belonged to her father, mostly a heap of clothes and tools with a half-used tin of mineral oil on the top, leaking onto his old trousers.

While Melanie was sorting knickknacks and wiping windowsills, it was hard for her not to catalog improvements that needed to be made: a loose screen, an almost imperceptible ding in the drywall. She wanted spackle and her screwdriver. She wanted her father to return from traveling with a sheaf of orders, her mother to core apples for a pie, and the three of them to set out repairing a bit of scratched hardwood, all on their hands and knees with putty knives and sandpaper, her parents stooped to a height close to her own.

In the kitchen her mother was on a stool, loosing the philodendrons from their hooks, the vines in a coil in one hand like a lasso. It was terrifying to see the plants come down, the ceiling pitted and stained. As she stepped down to push the stool closer to the wall and then climbed it again to start on another section, Melanie heard her mother, under her breath, *Goddamn you, goddamn you*. It was rare for her to be angry like this, but even then Melanie knew. She was old enough to have already been stung—the kind of boys who talked her into showing her panties one day, her best friend the next, all while the meaner girls looked on, laughing.

The tangle of ties and hex wrenches by the door was growing, and still they had not touched the garage. Melanie had trouble with the pile, half of which was just household junk her mother had decided belonged to her father. The pile was not like him. It was disorganized. She kept working. It was the first time she had moved and the first time her mother had moved in many years, so they were slow.

She had a girl in her class who could take anything apart. Melanie herself had donated a cassette player she thought was ruined and an alarm clock that she had dropped leaving part of its guts exposed through the chipped plastic shell. This girl returned the cassette player—reassembled and working—but pronounced the clock a goner. She did not really care so much about fixing things; she said she liked to understand how they worked.

Melanie thought if she got this girl to help her take the house down board by board, they would not find the same answer, like a malaligned gear or dented soldering.

In the living room, there was an end table that had not been packed and on the bottom shelf there was a bowl of restaurant matches. Melanie selected one of her favorites, a blue cover with match heads as silvery as snow. She squeezed the rest of the leaking mineral oil onto her father's things and struck one of the phosphorus tips until it flamed. Her hands were shaking, but she managed to ignite the entire book and launch it onto the pile, the sheen of petroleum caught quickly. There was a whoosh as the oxygen sucked away from her.

She inhaled heat and wondered if her father's breath ever caught like this, ash on her face, ash in his lungs.

When the smoke detector sounded, her mother came running, a torn philodendron vine laced through her fingers. There was a fire extinguisher still in the hall closet, and it took just a second to dampen the flames. They stood there for a minute while the foam settled around them. Melanie could see that the wall was stained black.

The girl at school was not really her friend, but sometimes they ate lunch together, and when Melanie had gone to her birthday party that year, she was the only kid who showed up. The girl told her that day that her parents sometimes got angry at her, for example, when she had smashed the panel to the microwave to get inside. They thought she was violent and odd. They thought she should just use the buttons to heat up food, like everybody else.

"Are you okay?" her mother asked. She held the cylindrical red can like a weapon, out in front of her, fingers gripped tightly. The smell of burnt synthetics was deadly, but her mother's face looked more tired than anything.

Melanie nodded, and she apologized. "Do you have any more boxes?" she asked. "We have a lot left."

"Sure," her mother said. She tossed the extinguisher onto the smoldering heap and led Melanie to the garage. "You do the living room, and I'll finish the kitchen." She said there were a few things in the bathrooms, and then the movers would come, and they would be done.

"I'm sorry about the wall," Melanie said. "I could paint over it."

"It's your father's problem now," her mother said.

When the truck and the men came, they took their boxes and some of the furniture and all of the plants and left the rest in a mess.

In the newspaper that came early, before the movers, her horoscope had said to "embrace change," but she wanted to feel anger when she got into her mother's car, driving away from the house for the last time, though she did not. She felt sad and in-between. They all loved the way the place had held them. Melanie was sorry for the scar up the wall, sorry for all the projects they would never finish. She was sorry for the way the light fell as they followed the bumper of the moving van, the house shadowed under a canopy of clouds.

Chapter Thirteen

Irene

Summer, 1974

Irene started with Sammy the summer before her freshman year, at the river, where all of the high schoolers met. Colorado was a dry place, but there were a few bends where water licked the shore. She wasn't supposed to be there, or at any of the mid-July parties, but her father was working swing-shift again and she figured if she got home before he did, he'd be dead tired and not notice anything. She wasn't sure if the other kids were there by permission or by lies, and she wasn't sure who had found enough beer to fill a cooler. On foot, it took her a few minutes to cut across town and then another twenty alongside the highway before she dipped down to look for them. When she got to the place where the banks were broader, the group wasn't hard to find, a ring of headlights and someone's radio was going.

It was an accident that she'd heard about the party. She had walked to the city park with its old, leaking pool, and then she had realized she was too old to swim there—it was only little kids in the water, so she looked for some shade to cool down in before she went back home. Sammy was eating his lunch at a picnic table. She knew him from junior high when she'd had a locker near his. Because the school was so small, everyone had classes together.

He saw her too and called her name and waved her over, and she sat down across from him. Out of the direct sun, the sweat on her face started to cool.

"I'm working at the stockyard this summer," he said. "I lied to them, though, because I'm not sixteen yet, and you're supposed to be sixteen. Just a couple more weeks and I don't have to worry about them finding out. I think my birthday is the day after the job ends," he said. He laughed and took a bite of his sandwich.

"It's probably nice to make money," she said. "I wish I had a job. I'm bored." There was a light breeze that blew against the damp of her shirt.

"It's not much of a job," he said. "But I'm trying to help my folks."

"That's good," she said.

Once, when she was in junior high, they'd been at a dance, and she wasn't sure why she'd even gone. She'd attended the school her entire life, but she still hardly had a friend there. While she was trying to disappear into the wall, Sammy had asked her to join him for a slow song. It had been the first time she'd ever touched a boy, though a lot had changed since then. In the two years that had passed, she saw how boys saw her differently now. She saw herself differently, too.

"Some people are getting together at the river tonight," he said.

"South of town?" she said—she was guessing. There were two main party spots she knew of, though, she'd never been to either one while anything was happening. She liked to walk and sometimes found smoldered out fires or beer cans floating in an eddy.

"No," he said. "North. Just past the Larimer's place. You know it?"

"Yes," she said, and she did. The water hardly ran there, but there was a frontage road that came down off the highway and broad, well-packed dirt in a cluster of trees.

"See you then, okay?" Sammy said, and he smiled at her, crumpling up the waxed paper from his sandwich and putting the ball in his lunch tin.

By the time she arrived that evening, she was damp again from walking through what was left of the day's heat, and her favorite jeans felt too tight. Most of the other girls were in shorts or skirts, and she felt soggy and self-conscious, scanning for Sammy and wondering if anyone would notice if she snagged a beer.

She waited until it seemed like everyone was looking somewhere else, and then she lifted the lid of the cooler, though just as she did, she heard a male voice.

"Hey," he said.

"Oh, sorry, I thought it was for everyone," she said, and popped the top of the can quickly and took a drink so he couldn't make her put it back. When she turned, though, it was Sammy, lopsided grin and the same T-shirt he had been wearing at the park that looked like it needed to be washed. He was in jeans, too, ripped at the knees and frayed. All around, headlights were on, and from how many cans were already crushed on the banks, she thought it was good that the lights were on draining the batteries, and that no one had enough room to roll start, hopefully ensuring no one would drive drunk.

Maybe it was the backlight from the cars or maybe it was the smell of the water and the way her shoes sunk gently into the ground that was softer towards the shore, but Sammy was more present than she'd ever noticed, eyes full and his posture open.

"Did you walk here?" he asked.

"Yes," she said.

"We could have picked you up," he said.

"It's fine," she said. "I've walked a lot farther than here before."

He nodded, just as someone killed the lights that shone behind him. There were other headlights blazing, but it took her eyes a minute to adjust, and when they did, Sammy was next to her, reaching for her free hand. His fingers were rough and warm. She felt a pressure on her foot and realized that he had accidentally stepped on her.

"Sorry," he said.

"No problem," she said. She drained the last of the beer and tossed the can into the brush like everyone else seemed to be doing. Tomorrow, she would walk here again and remember to bring a bag with her to pick them all up.

She leaned closer to him. She might not have any real friends, but Irene still knew how to be bold, and she got one arm around his hips. He was slimmer than her, she thought, and feeling the press of his pelvis against hers, she said his name.

He was tall enough that he had to tip his head down to kiss her. More of the car lights had gone off, and she could hear the Platte, trickling. In the hazy dark, he led her to a place that was grassy and dry enough, and quickly, she felt his hand at her zipper, and then felt his bare chest against hers.

She hadn't expected to go so fast, but she didn't mind. Afterward she curled into him while they listened to threads of conversation from the party, and then she said that she had to go, she had to get home.

"I'll walk you," he said.

"Thanks, but you don't have to," she said.

"I want to," he said, shaking his shirt out before pulling it on.

She felt even stickier when she wriggled back into her jeans, and she needed to pee. By the time they made their way up the frontage road and back to the path of the highway, Sammy had put his arm around her, and he kept it there, all the way home, walking her to her front steps. The lights were still off, and she wanted to ask him to come inside, but she didn't dare.

"See you around, Irene," he said.

"I'll meet you for lunch tomorrow," she said, as he was turning to leave, and he looked back at her. "That would be nice," he said.

Inside the house, she lay on her bed in the dark, breathing grass and mud and him.

Chapter Fourteen

Melanie

Summer, 1987

In their apartment, her mother still cooked, even if it was cheap stuff like bulk frozen chicken breasts and canned sauce that she boiled down with leftover wine and garlic because buying six pounds of tomatoes was too expensive. Melanie would sit and fiddle with her schoolwork while her mother sautéed. There was a gray light over the kitchen table and a gray light over the stovetop. The walls were gray from all of the fat that had smoked off of all of the meals that had been prepared by them and by previous tenants, and Melanie's eyes were gray from the drudgery of school.

Sometimes she went to her father's. So far, it was during school breaks. He started traveling more, and he said his job made it too difficult to watch over her, though she was almost thirteen and she did not think she needed much watching over. He also said that he had to work more to pay child support, but Melanie knew this was not true because she had found his un-cashed checks tucked into an envelope in the kitchen junk drawer when she needed some batteries.

His house was much nicer than the apartment, but the time passed very slowly. He had a small outdoor pool, and she liked to sit by it, the aqua reflected back at her, the water very still and stinking of chlorine.

She liked to watch the shine when a small breeze came up, the tiny ripples when a wasp landed and broke the surface. In her bathing suit, she read magazines, the pages curling in the heat, and she studied the horoscopes—she was a Cancer, the crab, and she thought a lot about walking sideways, between her two parents, between the life she had now and the home they had before.

Sometimes that first summer after the divorce, her father wanted to get out of the house. That was how he would put it; *Let's get out of the house,* he would say. He bought her a horseback riding lesson on a mangy, overworked pony. He took her to the park by the river, where they dutifully licked ice cream until there was nothing left of hers but a mushy cone. Once they went to Denver and he sent her up in a carnival hot air balloon while he stayed on the ground. She knew she was supposed to pretend that she did not know why her mother had left her father, but she saw the gloss on his eye when he looked at the girl taking tickets for the ride, she had on a dirty shirt and did not seem that much older than her. The carnival girl's father operated the balloon, and Melanie did not want to go up in the air with him, but she did anyway, peeking over the basket as the man worked the burner and her own father became small. It was a sunny day, and the heat and the propane made her woozy.

Her father lived in his house alone, mostly. Occasionally there was a woman just leaving when her mother dropped her off, or someone pulling up the back drive when she was being picked up. Once Melanie had found a fresh lipstick in the hall bathroom. She put the lipstick in the refrigerator, right by her father's half-and-half, so he would know she had seen it.

In the balloon, she wondered what would have happened if she had asked the carnival girl to come with her, if they had left their leering fathers on the ground to distract themselves, swapping stories, while their daughters sailed up until the rope was taut. What if the carnival girl had a penknife in her pocket and she sawed carefully through the tether, slicing the twists of jute one by one, until the balloon loosed and the two girls floated away, just another bright spot in the blinding sky.

* * *

Sometimes on the way home from school to meet her mother at the bank, Melanie would walk by their old house. It was not exactly on the way, but if she was quick in the library and skipped her trip to the park, she could get to her mother and not be late.

From the outside, the house looked almost the same to her. There was new siding, but the same old eaves buckled under the weight of leaves that hadn't been cleaned out since last autumn. There were brown circles on the grass from dog piss. The compression arm on the screen door had lost its snap, so it was always half ajar, like a warning.

She never saw anyone come in or out of the house, but the drapes had been changed and her mother's climbing rose knocked from the trellis. The house as she had known it had not been perfect, but she thought it could have been, if there had been more time.

* * *

The apartment was the first place they had come after the split, and Melanie figured they would be there for a long time. Her mother did not ramble. In school they were studying the history of the Oregon Trail, and Melanie could not say that she preferred the politics of Westward Expansion to her mother's. They had been instructed to choose one stretch of trail and draw a detailed map of it. Melanie picked the last miles leading to Oregon City, the end of the line. Her map had a little key to mark points of interest—clean water, wild onion patch, blackberry grove. Her teacher thought this was very clever, so Melanie did not tell her what she had really been thinking: *dead horse, poison oak, dysentery.*

Her father was more like the pioneers than her mother. He was the one who looked out across the horizon and wanted more than a small place to live and a tidy routine. The thing about the divorce was that her parents did not seem any happier apart than they had together, just older.

In the balloon, she had thought about jumping over the side. She did not really want to do this, but she liked the idea of a freefall and the wind holding her, the look of shock on her father's face when she landed a few feet from him, hair windblown and eyes shut. The operator probably would not have stopped her, though his daughter might have.

Once, not very long before the divorce, her father was supposed to come home on a Tuesday, but he did not. Her mother was making coq au vin, and it smelled like a miracle, chicken and wine and bay leaf. Maybe that was when she felt the first groan in the house. While the rooster stewed from tough to tender to tough again, her mother waited for lights in the drive.

On that night, Melanie selected the record—she loved Kim Carnes—and she sat in the dark with her mother while their dinner burned.

Her mother had a story about how she had met her father when he was fresh off his military service after he had been drafted in late 1971. In this story her mother was a brunette girl with legs up to there, and her father was handsome in his tattered green coat. They married quickly. Her mother had saved some money from her job working the food line in the hospital kitchen, and they put a down payment on the car her mother still drove, and they found the house. Melanie knew she was born immediately after they got married, maybe a little too quickly for the math to add, but she was not sure, exactly, when their anniversary was. Once in a while on a long night, like the Tuesday her father did not come home, her mother would have more cocktails than was customary, and she would tell Melanie that it was better to wait. It was better to see some of the world on your own first, because marriage was hard.

Her mother had not waited when she was nineteen with blue eyes wide, so she waited with the stereo shouting love ballads and the oven sizzling. Melanie wanted her father to come home too, maybe even more than her mother did. She did not know what was so hard about getting back to the house before dark; she did it all the time. She did not know what was out there that could keep him.

What is better than the candlelight on the mantel, she wondered, *the leaves on our vines?* She would have drawn a thousand more maps with reliefs shellacked in glitter, roads demarcated with more precision than the best cartographer, if any would have led him to them.

Chapter Fifteen
Jenny

Fall, 2005

Even after the children were born and had gotten well into growing, Jenny did not go back to work. She missed having her own money, but other than economics, it seemed to her that jobs were just something people did because they didn't have something better to do. She understood she was looking at it from a place of privilege—she'd grown up poor—and sometimes she did think about going back, especially after Connor, the second, who would not stop crying. Stella was only two when Connor was born, and she was constantly sneering at her brother and pulling the pans out of the low cabinets. Finally, Jenny cleaned out one of the bottom drawers and told Stella it was just for her, filling it with old kitchen things: an apple corer long gone dull, a silicon coated whisk that was chipping, a set of cracked measuring spoons. Then, at least when it worked, Stella would sit on the tiles and open and shut her drawer, taking everything out and putting everything back in, over and over again, and Jenny could simply step over her while bouncing Connor.

Now that both the children were a little older—Stella was five and Connor three—it was easier to keep them busy, but still the days felt very long. She prayed, sometimes, that was the closest word for it, for her husband, Brian, to not work late. With Stella in Kindergarten for half days, Jenny was calmer, but she still watched the clock as she started dinner, making some small negotiations.

If he is on time, I won't mention the hall toilet is running. I will fix it myself.

If he is ten minutes late, I will smile. I will ask about traffic.

If he is beyond an hour, I will remind him he is missing time before Stella and Connor go to bed. Gently. I will be gentle, and I will ask him to read them their stories.

If he does not come home at all…

On occasion these tiny bargains saw Brian sloping through the doorway in a suit crumpled from sitting all day at his desk and spending an hour in the car, but usually there was no sound of tires gripping the concrete of their driveway, no key scraping the lock.

In those loops where he did not arrive at all, she felt ragged and worn-out, but mostly frustrated, and she didn't see how going back to work would change anything. They'd have more money, but she didn't think they needed more money. Brian had suggested that the kids would benefit from being around their peers in daycare or aftercare, but Jenny didn't think either of them would like it all that much. The half-school days were hard enough. They were mostly solitary children, and prone to colds. He didn't know them as well as she knew them, how could he, gone all the time, though she never said this to him.

Her own father had left when she was a child, and she knew he wasn't anyone worth measuring against, but she couldn't help but to compare. Brian was doing better: at least he provided.

Part of his working long hours had to do with Brian being in line for a promotion, though if he got it, he would also have to travel. He worked in software sales, and when her mother had asked her to explain what the program was, as she called it, did, Jenny was at a loss.

"It's something with banks, like processing transactions," she had said, because she did not really know either, and because she thought this would make her mother lose interest.

Jenny did not feel good about the prospect of a travel schedule for Brian, when the stretch of highway between home and office already seemed longer than a transcontinental flight. She wondered what it would be like when he had a real reason to be gone. She conceded it had been her idea to move to the suburbs after she had gotten pregnant with Stella, and she conceded that she had willingly quit her job, because she felt like she could. Her belly had bloomed, a halo around her, and she saw a chance to sink into the circle and disappear there for a little while. He had been angry about it at first, but that had passed.

She took care of everything. She made his life easier. She had always wondered about women who had careers, like she once had, leaving work and not going back, but now she understood the appeal of a space where she was the absolute authority. It did not even matter that her children did not always listen to her, and it did not matter that they misbehaved and that sometimes she got angry with them for fighting, or that they demanded to follow her into the bathroom. They were hers. They belonged to her, and the world they inhabited belonged to her, and now it was Brian who had something she could not understand.

By the time Connor was toddling, there were spans of weeks that she could count on her husband not coming home on weekdays at all, and in these times she tried calling him at work in the day, and the administrative assistant sent her to his voicemail. She called his cell direct, and he would not answer, and she would be angry, because at home, he was always on his phone, or checking for the red blinking lights that meant he had a message, sprinting across the house if he had left the mobile on a countertop out of immediate reach. Sometimes at dinner, she would ask him to put it away, and sometimes she would be talking and he would look down at the screen, and she would just stop and wait for him to finish what he was doing as he scrolled or typed or frowned.

Once she told him that she did not believe he had so many meetings that he couldn't call her back.

"I've seen you take calls everywhere," she said. "Everywhere we go you take calls and text." She listed some of the places where she had seen him do this recently. At Stella's dance recital, his phone went off while his daughter was in mid-twirl, and he took the call. Before dinner, two nights ago, with everyone at the table, just as she was about to serve, they waited for twenty minutes while he took a call.

He said that they did not have to wait for him, and she said that she was trying to teach their children manners, to wait for everyone to be present.

Or at the indoor swim park, last Saturday, where he was visibly annoyed at the presence of so much water, so dangerous for the electronic workings of his phone.

"Those were all work calls," he said.

Now, when he called her, he called to tell her he was staying in the city with one of his friends, and he acted like they lived in New York or London. Like *the city* was hours away. She wondered if it was the effect of the suburbs, creating distance, built to create distance. They were just outside of Denver, a big town, a town she liked, and major to the region, but not a metropolis. Their house was thirty minutes from his office with no traffic, and by the time of night he was finally checking in with her, the roads would have cleared. She would even offer to pile the kids into the car and come get him—when he drank too much at a company happy hour, or if he felt too tired to drive safely after a long day, or if he pushed it, saying, *Well, if I come home now, I won't get back in time in the morning to get decent parking, so I'll just leave the car in a good spot overnight*—and every time he said no.

"Okay," she would say. "So take a cab," but he refused this as well, as an unnecessary expense, a hassle. It was tempting to pinch Connor, who cried easily, to try and sway Brian, to try and make him feel some type of fatherly compulsion, or to say Stella had a burning fever, but she always decided she should save these measures in case she really needed him.

He told her that he was working so she did not have to.

"I'm fine," he would say. "Don't worry about it."

She was not worried if he was fine or not fine.

He said she didn't understand the pressure of being the bread-winner, even though he had to know that she did: she had taken care of herself for a long time before she met him. They were both already thirty when they married.

Once she asked him to explain to her exactly where he was sleeping when he stayed out, and he said, *Gary's.* He said he had clothes there.

She remembered Gary, and she remembered his small apartment downtown next to the state capitol, in a building with a perpetual sign that read *1 Beds: Inquire.* She was not exactly sure what Gary did, but she did recall the patina that blanketed the apartment, dirt and hair and moth dust, the cabinets crammed full, one greasy towel in the bathroom—she could not imagine there was anywhere for an extra shirt of Brian's, clean and pressed like he would need for work, and she could not imagine that Brian was really so organized that he had a full set of clothes at a drinking buddy's house. She had not seen Gary in years, and once she asked if he had moved or if he had changed much, and Brian dodged, saying that Gary was the same as he had always been.

In these days, she took deep breaths. She put the children to bed, reading to them each from books they liked. She missed when Connor was still small enough that she could hold him while she read to Stella. It was easy to focus on and finish the books. The slim bindings and the sometimes intentionally clumsy artwork paired with straightforward sentences comforted her. After their tiny snores had started, and she had successfully closed their doors, she focused again on breathing, poured herself a generous glass of wine, and wondered if she was happier with her husband or if she had been happier without him. She wondered if it had been a mistake to have children so early in their married life—they had waited two years, but that still felt like nothing, like she was still getting to know him, even as he pulled away from her, slowly, like cream from milk.

Chapter Sixteen

Irene

Summary, 2007

As the summer fires started, Irene felt the pressure from the heat and the smoke had bled down into everything, like a low hum, like it was not only the charcoal in the air making it hard to breathe.

Over three decades ago, Irene had given up her baby girl, and she thought of her every day. This, she figured, was not so unusual.

She'd be what they called a "bio-mom" now, but it was different in the 70's. She and Kathleen had worked it out, Kathleen's mother had helped. The father, Sammy, Kathleen's brother, was dead, and Irene had been only fourteen. She'd not turned fifteen until after Melanie was born.

She didn't think Melanie could ever understand the shame they all felt then, how making their plan seemed so reasonable, and how they never really thought of it as lying. It seemed ridiculous now, that they'd gone through so much trouble to keep Melanie secret. Times had changed.

When she was bitter she'd think that Kathleen had only wanted her brother Sammy's baby, but keeping the secret had linked her and Kathleen. They'd been made sisters, and Mel belonged to both of them. Irene knew this.

Her own mother had left when she was ten, the same year her father lost his only sibling in the accident with the chicken truck. She knew what she had done was better, staying close, even if shadowed.

Irene had to admit that she wanted, just once, to hear Melanie call her "mom," but after so much time, telling the secret seemed even less possible.

When Mel was small, folks would remark on how much she looked like her mother. And she did look like Kathleen and Kathleen's side of the family. Still, Irene saw her own face reflected in Mel's as well, and if anyone noticed, they'd never mentioned it.

Sometimes she'd bite the inside of her check so hard the skin broke, and remind herself that as much as that hurt, it would hurt Mel so much more. How it would seem like a lie to her. Sometimes she whispered *daughter* to herself, and sometimes she wished that Mel would guess it.

When Andy and Kathleen divorced, Kath had come to her in a panic.

"He never adopted her, formally," Kathleen said. "What if he says something?"

"He won't," Irene said. "He's turned out to be a real shit, but what would he say, really? *I raised her as my own and now I don't care?*"

"If he gets mad enough, he might," said Kathleen. "I can't read him anymore."

When they'd met, Kathleen had told Andy the baby was hers, that her husband had been killed in the war. Andy, was himself just back from Vietnam, and the story of the young widow with a newborn had been enough for him to make his own promise, to raise the girl, to keep the devastation from her. Perhaps he thought of it as his final act as a soldier, in service to another soldier.

Irene had never been good at reading him either.

For years, missing Sammy had sustained her, but it was harder and harder to miss him, because she didn't know the type of man he would have become. He might have stayed close, he might have drifted like Kathleen's other siblings, or like Andy.

When her father was dying, she spent time with him, in the cramped house she'd grown up in. She had questions for him, about his brother, about her cousin Lucy Estelle who'd she'd not seen in years, but again, she bit the insides of her cheeks. He was an old man. The longer she kept her own secrets, the more she realized how others had to keep theirs.

Upset by the divorce, Mel used to pine and pine for Andy, and Irene wanted to tell her, *You don't have to be so upset about it, you know, he's not your real dad.* She wanted to tell her, *I picked your name, I named you.*

But what good would that have done? She should know as well as anyone that's not how family worked.

Chapter Seventeen

Melanie

Summer, 2007

There was a time in Melanie's life when she could barely imagine living beyond thirty, and as she approached thirty-four, she reflected on the feeling of being sure she would die young, and how the feeling had sometimes motivated her, but how it had mostly made her live her younger life as a fatalist.

All through her twenties, she went to the shows of great and horrible bands, installation artists, and drama troupes; she worked jobs, and she visited her parents, but she did it without purpose frequently. Occasionally, she would catch a few lines at a reading or see a performance that was inspiring—the smooth vowels of a poet with a practiced voice, or shreds of old linen draped on a dressmaker's dummy and shellacked in glitter displayed in perfect light—that would make her want to create, or write, and after work sometimes she would pull out her old notebooks and scribble or sketch in them self-consciously, the way she had when she was in college, when it was enough just to be young and optimistic and feel time stretched out in front of her. What she admired about amateur painters—or anyone whose work might be very bad but was still being shown, even if it was just at a never-busy coffee shop—was that they had finished something. Starting was not so hard. Sustaining through lines and lines, strokes and strokes, seemed impossible to her, and then she would tuck the notebooks away again and read magazines.

Years ago she had drawn maps, which her mother had saved. The travels of Ponce de León, the Oregon trail. She wouldn't call it art, but she remembered liking the work.

Maybe her email, her constant, ridiculous email, had saved her. Some direction, in ones and zeros. Salvation through a server.

* * *

Another part of the dying-young fear—there was a time when she would have called it a premonition, but now she was sure it was only a fear—was the flashes of the fragile nature of her own body, imagining being knocked flat by a stranger who hurled, punched, stabbed. Moments would come when she thought it was finally happening, like when a strong-looking man bumped her outside of the bank, just as the security guard ducked out on break. The man excused himself, and that was all, but she was left staring at her shoes, waiting for a blow or some pressure at the neck that never came. There was the time when she was in college that a man who was on the same bus as she was suddenly jolted up and got off at a neighborhood stop, following, it looked like to her, two pre-teen girls. He was tall, rumpled looking. Stringy hair. She remembered looking around at the other men on the bus and none of them moved, so she pulled the stop handle and ran after the girls, passing the man who was shuffling after them. *Do you want me to walk you home?*, she had said, and the older one holding the hand of her little sister said, *Yes.* She looked behind her, and the man was there, watching them, she thought. *Let's walk fast. Don't run.* And she led them through the quiet streets to their front door. There was a light on in the house, and she heard a television, but no one appeared when the girls called. She breathed for a second, and she told them to lock the door.

Her own apartment was not so far away, so she decided to cut through the houses instead of going back to the bus line, and when she came around the next corner, the man was there, like he had been waiting. Smiling, she remembered he was smiling, he tried to loop his arm around her shoulders, and she thought she should scream, but she was mute, as if in a frustrating dream. It was not hard to break free of his grasp, and then she ran in the direction of her building but keeping close to the more well-lit streets, the early spring air pushing her, giving her speed, and when she got home her key shook in the lock, but the door opened easily, and she closed it behind her and turned the dead bolt. She lived in a corner unit, and she kept the lights off and peeked through the blinds, but she did not see the man anywhere, so she flipped on all of the switches and made a cup of tea. She pulled a chair to one of the windows and opened it, leaning outside so the smoke from her cigarette would curl out into the night.

Then, she wondered about these girls and who was letting them ride the bus after dark. Her mother, or her father, or even Irene—none of them would ever let her do that.

Chapter Eighteen

Jenny

Winter, 2005

The first time Brian left on a trip after his promotion, she thought maybe it would be okay. He packed a small bag, folded his shirts carefully, and he kissed her good-bye. He let her know his progress, a connection in Chicago, a landing in Baltimore, and when he got back to Denver, he seemed ready to be home. The car dropped him off in front of their house, and he hugged her when he came in and later that night he sidled up to her in bed, kissing her mouth and yanking at her underwear. In that moment, she thought his promotion could be very good—it would give them a chance to miss each other. That night, she enjoyed their lovemaking, and she told him so. It gave her the feeling that they were new, and she thought he would start to understand why he should come home.

Yet, as he grew into his new role, Brian started to spend more time "on the road" as he called it, but it was not the road as she thought of it, not a station wagon packed to the gills with sandwiches and a cooler of sodas, it was him, spread out in business class, a slim leather carry-on tucked into the overhead with his laptop at his feet. The purser would offer cocktails, but he would have water, pretending to be disciplined.

The first time, she worked at being flexible. She was doing laundry when she found a business card in the pocket of his jeans, a woman's name imprinted on the heavy paper. She panicked, thinking she should have been checking his suit pants before they went to dry cleaning, but then she calmed herself with a breathing technique she had learned at yoga and simply set the card on the desk that he had eventually hauled into their guestroom, directly in the center, so he would know that she had seen it. It was not the card itself that bothered her, it was the ballpoint inked across the back: *Call my cell!* with the digits and a smiley face. She could not remember ever personalizing her business card when she worked at the law firm like this, she only thought of Brian's old friend Gary, slipping his number into her coat.

Then she did start to check, every pocket. She found receipts wadded into his trousers—she had been an accountant after all, she understood that the slips she discovered were the ones he could not submit for reimbursement to his company—and more cards with notes. She wondered why he was not being careful, because if it were her, she would be more careful. A hundred dollar's worth of cocktails on a Wednesday or, for example, an itemized slip which included two entrée salads, one dessert, and several bottles of wine; this was the way people ate when they were courting: booze, lettuce, chocolate. She recognized it from having been there, sitting in a padded booth, eating lightly, before sharing a sweet, and then drinking too much.

She wadded up the dry cleaning and put it in the bag. She did not ask him about the crème brûlée nor the cabernet. This was when she thought the most about going back to work, about having both spaces. One where she was Mommy, and the other where she had her own tipsy dinners with the board or some new junior partner who might remind her that the years of yoga and Pilates had paid off.

At home with Stella and Connor, she brooded sometimes, and she remembered when she said she would never do this: move to the suburbs, organize herself around naptime, and pay such close attention to bowel movements and laundry, but she also liked her life. While she did not like what she saw as the evidence in Brian's pockets, she appreciated what it afforded her. Her mother had worked twice as hard as him to just barely pay the bills, and even now, when her mother Lucy Estelle was scraping by on Social Security, if she needed something, Jenny wrote her a check, deducting it from the register without thinking about it. They did the same for Brian's parents, and they both liked being able to help them all out.

When she thought about it, she was not entirely sure how things could be different. If she was the one at work and Brian was the one at home, would she be able to say no to flirty business trips and long hours? Would she even want to? She did not know if he had slept with anyone, she reminded herself, and she did not know how much it would really bother her if he had.

Sometimes she thought about what would happen if she packed up the children into the car, grabbed a few personal things, and started the long drive to her mother's. Her mother was still in the tiny home she had grown up in. In her hometown, out on the eastern Colorado plains, there were poor schools and few jobs, and everything was dusty, always. But she remembered how close they felt. Once they were sitting at the kitchen table when the lights flickered out, but Jenny could see a beam coming from the neighbor's porch—it was only them.

"Damn power company," her mother had said, but they both knew it was the unpaid bill causing the blip in service. "I'm sorry, girl."

Jenny remembered saying it was okay, that she was almost ready for bed anyway, but her mother had suggested they go outside and sit awhile. It was summer and there was still some dim light from the long dusk, so they moved to the porch, Jenny with a glass of lemonade made from powder and her mother with what was probably the last cold beer, and they sat in the gathering dark, rocking chairs creaking, and watched the red taillights from the cars on the highway in the distance.

There was a sound that her mother said was a sound like cicadas, but she said she hoped that she was wrong, because they did not need a pestilence along with everything else. Jenny agreed with her, and she reached out to hold her mother's hand.

They had many nights like this, sitting on the porch or at the kitchen table. Lucy Estelle taught Jenny to play cards and cribbage, the games a way to mark time. They had a rain barrel that they checked the level of every morning, and except in spring or after a late snow, it was usually dry, but they kept to the ritual of it. Her father had been gone so long she was not sure she would know him if she saw him in the street, and even as a child she understood how lucky she was that her mother was not bitter. They were a girl and a woman making their way.

She did not worry that her own children were growing up without love, even Brian, as distant as he was sometimes, doted on them, but she worried they would not know this feeling of quiet togetherness, when life feels mean and hard, but still cannot break the family.

Chapter Nineteen
Kathleen
Winter, 1974

Irene's belly grew in the space of a few months, and all Kathleen did was spend time with her, skipping basketball practice to meet her in the library, shadowing her almost. She brought some of her sisters' old clothes in case she finally began to put on weight, she told her she should stop with the smoking, and she made an appointment at the small public health clinic for a checkup. They ditched school to walk the few blocks through the crunchy snow to learn there was nothing irregular, as far as the nurse practitioner could tell.

Kathleen quit the basketball team for good and got a job in the hospital kitchen standing on the concrete floors until she thought her legs would give out. She molded tub after tub of Jell-O, and after the chickens were roasted, she picked the carcasses clean and boiled them for stock for endless bowls of soup. The other kitchen ladies asked her about her boyfriends—her long legs, her long hair, she must have a steady—but she ducked her head and focused on water coming to a boil or on perfectly cubing potatoes.

"You should learn to type and get a job where you don't have to wear a hairnet," said one of the women. She lifted her dress to show Kathleen her web of purple and blue spider veins visible even through the compression hose. "These floors will wreck your pretty calves."

After work that day, Kathleen went to the drugstore and purchased orthopedic shoe inserts and a jar of witch hazel. She soaked a cotton ball and rubbed her skin to ease the tension and strengthen her vessels, because she had heard this produced results. Her mother sighed and said she wished Kathleen were still on the basketball team—she had her whole life to work, and anyway, she thought castor oil and elevation were better for veins. She brought Kathleen a pillow and massaged her feet.

* * *

The money was adding up very slowly, but Kathleen was thinking of Sammy. She was thinking of Sammy when she pulled tendon from the bone, when she dressed salads of nearly translucent iceberg lettuce with grated carrots, when she broke down the wax-covered produce boxes and fed them to the trash compactor. Irene's grades had improved, and Kathleen had brought her home several times to study—the first time, Kathleen saw her eyes shine at crossing the threshold of her lover's home, not a bride exactly, but welcomed. Her mother asked, *How do you know that girl?* Kathleen said, *From school.* Her mother said, *She's got a baby on her*, and Kathleen said, *I know.* Her mother said she liked Irene, and she thought she knew her father. She said he was mean twenty years ago, and he was probably meaner now.

Kath wanted to say, *That's Sammy's baby.* She wanted to say, *Can we take Irene to live with us?* But she could not yet, so she smiled at her mother and made Irene a cup of tea, the mug chipped from Sammy's clumsy dishwashing and the water steaming.

* * *

The school counselor called Irene into his office, and she refused to talk to him until he called for Kathleen. He said that Irene could not stay if she was with child. Irene denied she was pregnant.

"I've gained some weight," she said. "I'm not happy about it either." Her jaw was set in the lie, and Kathleen thought she looked believable. The counselor shook his head, and he referenced school policy. Kathleen wondered if it was a bad idea for her to be there, if perhaps he remembered the uniforms. The girls' basketball team was at the district finals, though the boys' team had failed to qualify. For a moment she recalled being on the court and how she had loved the finality of the rules. The parameters of the game were very unlike life. Steady. Refereed.

The radiator in the counselor's office was making a popping sound. It had been painted bronze once, and the color was coming off in small chips, sparkling on the dull tiles.

"She married my brother before he died," said Kathleen. "She's widowed."

The counselor did not look convinced. The radiator burped, and Kathleen felt in control. She knew she could not change what happened to Sammy, but she could change what it meant. When she said that she had been their witness, the glow in her eyes was real, thinking of her brother, too small for her father's one good shirt, walking proud toward his lover in a collar that was permanently crumpled, the loaned fabric stiff from starch and bluing. Irene would have borrowed a dress from one of his sisters, a dress that had already been remade several times, so the stitch marks crisscrossed like quilting. Even low heels would have sunk into the soft grass in her parent's yard as Irene walked the aisle made by splitting the family into two lines. In the absence of anyone to play the wedding march, they would have rung bells from her mother's Christmas pile, glass and pewter, copper- and brass-plated to look like gold.

They would have barbequed afterward and drunk beer all night, and when the water took Sammy, he could have thought of the late autumn sun and his wife and the smell of charcoal and the heat of their lips pressed in matrimony.

The counselor frowned and straightened some papers on his desk. He referenced the policy again, said that he'd need to see the documentation. He said he had never had this situation before, and even if she was married, Irene might need to leave the school. He would have to check with the board. In his admitting that he was not sure what to do, Kathleen saw an opening.

"We'll go to the safe deposit box today," she said, knowing she was only bargaining for a little more time.

When he excused them, they walked out into the narrow hallway, waxed tiles and rows of grubby lockers.

"If he would have asked me … " Irene started to say, and Kathleen put her arms around her where they stood, flanked by the lessons happening behind closed doors, squeaking shoes in the nearby gymnasium, and the smell of dust, until the bell rang and the other kids spilled out around them.

* * *

Her mother was mending socks at the kitchen table, and her father was staring at pounds of ground beef, calculating how many patties to make. It was only the five of them now. Once they had been almost twice as many, and out of habit he had thawed too much. He asked Kathleen to chop an onion. It always made him cry. Her work in the hospital kitchen had given her some expertise with a knife, and she sliced quickly after washing her hands. She helped her father form the patties and walked with him to the grill. The light above her mother in the kitchen glowed yellow. She could hear her other brothers in the house. Mikey had just started sleeping again in the room he had once shared with Sammy.

One thing that Kathleen remembered about Sammy was that he liked to barbeque, because he liked to be outside. He was not good at it, he was not precise, but he enjoyed especially being under the fall leaves, just when the first bite of cold made the air smell amber, face against the heat of the charcoal, and the stainless tongs flashing.

She had not talked with her parents about what she would do after graduation. She knew she could go full time in the kitchen, and as awful as the work sounded, she did like having her own money. All of her sisters had moved right on from their father's home into someone else's, to the home of another man, to a shared apartment with a girlfriend; Darlene, even, had gone to live with her then fiancé's parents. Kathleen did not know if this was the expectation or just how it had worked out.

Her father was scraping the grill, and even this small motion showed the muscles at his back and across his neck. He was handsome. He had never hit any of them, but Kathleen thought that if he had, it would have surely hurt. Once her mother threatened her with a belt, but she never wore a belt, and by the time she found one, her anger had quelled, and Kathleen's punishment was to organize the hall closet and the closet she shared with her sisters. She spent the rest of her summer afternoon going through old shoeboxes and re-hanging crooked, mostly worn-out shirts and shaking the dust off their winter coats and checking the pockets for change. She found thirty-five cents, a stick of gum, and a handful of crumpled cigarette butts. She also found an attachment that had gone missing from the vacuum, but no belts, and when she closed the closet doors, she liked the clean feeling, everything neat and contained, so she took the sponge from the kitchen and scrubbed at the brown marks around the doorknobs that had built up from being touched by so many hands. In school, she had learned that finger grease was from the eccrine glands, but she did not remember what the real purpose was.

When her father put the burgers on the grill, there was a sound like a can opening, a hiss. She thought to ask him about staying on after graduation. He was nudging the meat with the spatula and kicking at a piece of snow. It had been sunny that day, and there was some low cloud cover that had come up at dusk, so the air was warm for the season, but the ground was still frozen in the places that had stayed shaded.

Maybe she would not stay. Maybe she would talk to the counselor about taking early graduation so she could get on full time before the baby came. Maybe they could find a converted garage or a mother-in-law somewhere, and Kathleen could get a job on a night shift so she could be home during the day when Irene was at school. Being poor did not scare her, and she knew it did not scare Irene either.

What scared her was slipping. Her sisters had slipped from the house into lives that did not seem that much different to Kathleen. Sammy had slipped on the ice, and away from them. Her father turned all of the burgers and asked her to go inside and set the table, and she did. She put the plates out on the worn tablecloth, sliced a tray of pale wintertime tomatoes, and took a new jar of mustard from the pantry.

On the basketball team, she had liked the idea of them all as moving parts. At first, they ran their plays poorly, but when they started to get it down, the moves felt sure and fluid. At work, sometimes all the kitchen ladies synced into a perfect rhythm of grating and stewing and plating, the clatter of crockery and cutting boards being flipped was percussive against the stainless steel countertops, as order after order was loaded up onto the delivery carts, smoothly and quickly.

She wanted this sureness, this feeling of doing things right. As her brothers and her parents sat down at the table, she understood why her sisters had left. The chance to change. The chance to have their own table, something that belonged to them. Like when she had lied to the school counselor about Sammy's betrothed, the chance to take the story and bend it as much as the facts would allow—not always to a happy ending, but a better one.

Chapter Twenty

Melanie

Summer, 2007

Monday at work after Kyle's funeral, Melanie was shy. She was not sure what to say to Alex. She had spent the rest of the weekend vaguely shocked she had let him into her house. This was not a good thing, she reminded herself; she was breaking her own rules about *What Happens In… Stays In…* It did not have to be Las Vegas to be a good idea.

He must have felt the same way, because the whole day he did not swing by her office or email her anything. She thought she saw the slope of his head for a minute by the server room, but when she turned the corner, there was no one.

The last thing on her calendar was an all-office meeting. By the time she got to the conference room all of the chairs were taken, and so she leaned against the wall just outside and wrinkled her nose at the administrative assistant, who incorrectly dialed the number for the telephone bridge three times in a row, until finally one of the developers took the speaker phone, shaped like a star with its five points of sound, from her and tapped out the digits in perfect precision.

"Do you think it's going to be bad?" asked the person next to her, and she turned to him, Alex, jammed into the other side of the doorframe.

"No," she said. "There are no snacks. Usually when it's bad there are snacks." She said this with authority, though she could not tell if he believed her or not.

They listened to a recap of the quarterly earnings call from the publicly traded parent, and then they learned their business unit was dramatically underperforming. Not to worry, said the voice from corporate—she thought it might be her boss but she had not caught his name—there would be some cost-cutting measures that would get them right back on track.

Melanie looked around at the room.

"Are we on mute?" someone whispered, and the developer who had dialed the numbers shook his head and stabbed the red button.

"Now, yes," he said, but no one had anything to say after that.

The voice asked for questions, but there were no questions. The voice implored; he really wanted them to ask some questions. He covered the targeted 20 percent budget reductions, explained that all nonessential travel would be suspended, and assured them that he understood most of them would do more for the company than to simply abide by these minimums.

The call ended, and the employees filed back to their desks. At her laptop, Melanie waited for the follow up email that would give her the details of the reductions.

* * *

When the company had first been acquired, she had met with a local contract auditor from the legal firm Chicago headquarters had hired. Her name was Jenny, and she had said she was only looking at individual department budgets, mostly for mathematical errors, so they could be sure about establishing a baseline.

Her hands were beautiful, Melanie noticed, with her ring finger circled by a studded platinum band and the other digits slim and unadorned.

"You know, I've been out of the workforce for a while," she said, by way of explaining, Melanie thought, why a woman who was at least mid-thirties had been sent to do what was essentially a beginner's job. "My kids are four and six."

"Oh, those are such fun ages," Melanie said, which is what she usually said about people's children, no matter how old they were.

Jenny had smiled and agreed that they were fun. She said her husband was extremely busy with work, and she thought she would try it again, to get out of the house. She said she was on the wrong side of the mommy wars, with a light and nervous laugh, because she thought it was harder to work full time.

"Still, I think this is going to stay temporary," she said, looking to the side. "Okay, shall we get to it?"

After their meeting, Jenny said her report would reflect that she had found no issues with calculation, and that the distribution of funds was sound.

Her hair was very fluffy and curled around her face.

Yet, even though there was nothing to flag, Jenny said, she estimated the parent company would still ask for at least a one third reduction. Then, Melanie had shaken hands with Jenny—she liked her, despite why she was there—and chatted with her on the way to the exit. For a moment she thought of asking her to coffee sometime, but figured it might be seen as a conflict of interest, and she opened the glass door into the cold of late winter, and then went back to her office and shopped online for something to wear to the holiday party.

It had been almost a year and a half since then, so she figured she should have expected this next round of cuts. At 5:10 p.m., there was still no message, so she started working again on her report of the industrial marketplace. She wrote phrases like sales velocity and *HVAC ecosystem* without irony or pause. She had never imagined herself as someone who thought the way she thought now, in percentages and acronyms, pitching, more than actually figuring anything out. At 5:20

p.m., there was still no message, and she wondered for a minute if her budget had been zeroed out. She had actually always been very careful, with detail given down to the penny and inflations built in so she could come in under her number consistently, because that was the kind of fake successes she had learned were noticed. She logged into the company travel account and saw that none of her upcoming trips had been flagged for review. That was good, she thought. Or maybe corporate was just being slow. She watered her potted palm tree from a glass of water that had been sitting on her desk the entire day that she had not quite managed to drink, and she switched off the repti-lights. At 5:35 p.m. her BlackBerry buzzed. She anticipated that it was finally the budget email, but it was Alex.

Subject: *I'm still in the office. You?*

Instead of replying, she walked across the thin, dirty carpet, past the conference room and the kitchen, past the servers whining even though it had not been a hot day.

"Hey," she said, through the open door.

"Hi," he said. "Did you get a budget email?"

"No," she said. "You?"

"I don't have a budget," he said. The overhead lights of his office were blaring, but she could see his laptop was packed up and that he was finished working.

He did not say anything about the funeral, but he asked her if she would like to come have a drink. She trailed him in her car to a suburban neighborhood that was generally in the middle of where they both lived. When they arrived, she parked several spaces away from him because it seemed presumptuous to get too close.

The bar was dim and smelled like old cigarettes. Alex ordered beers for them both, and the clack of balls from a game of pool was like awkward punctuation. Her hair felt a little greasy and her clothes rumpled, but she ignored this and concentrated on the brittle sound of plastic against plastic, and sometimes the chalky smoosh of a stick's tip.

They had a table midway between the curve of the bar and the door. As Melanie wondered if someone they knew might walk in, she took a long pull of her beer, and she heard a pool player break. The beer was hoppy and cold, the pressure against the cue ball sharp.

She asked Alex what was going on with him, and he said that he just wanted to see her. She considered his sheepish look in this strip mall bar, and she remembered again the way he had thrown his jacket down over the peanut shells back in San Antonio. There were a lot of things she wanted to ask him, about his life, his spouse, but she did not say anything for a long time. She noticed how the felt on the pool table was worn, showing board underneath. The lamps swayed, multicolored and strong on their chains. She felt a little woozy, but she wriggled her chair around the edge of the table so that their knees were touching, and she flagged the waiter down for another beer.

"I thought it was strange they didn't say anything about Kyle on the call," she said.

"What would they say?" Alex asked.

"I don't know," she said. "Maybe, Sorry? They must be sorry; they're going to have to pay his life insurance."

"There are eight thousand employees at corporate," he said. "People die there every day. It's part of their cost of doing business."

"That's depressing," she said.

The light in the bar was murky, and the place was filling up, more people were hanging around the tables, some of them starting to make bets.

When Melanie had first started working at the company, it was just another job in a line of jobs. She was young enough that she did not have a true sense of loyalty to an employer, but she was old enough that she tried not to bounce around too much because she thought it looked bad. It was not the life she had imagined when she was growing up, tethered to a smartphone and constantly purging her small condo to make room for anything new, but she thought it was working out all right.

She remembered, in her final year of high school, getting the college admissions notices. Her father had said he would pay for her to go anywhere, but she chose to stay close to home, because of her mother, she had thought then, but she understood later it was because of herself. She was scared to go too far, because even then she had seen how even a little distance could bust people apart. Now, because work had taken her out of Colorado, she thought a lot about how life would be different in different cities. What if she had moved to New York, L.A., or Chicago? Denver had been easy to stay in, big enough that she could move out of the suburbs to a more urban neighborhood when she left her mother's apartment, making life feel different for a while, though there was still the familiar view of the brief downtown skyline and the mountains poking at the clouds in the distance. She lived close to both of her parents, and occasionally, if the weather was nice or the wind was not blowing too hard, she would take a long bike ride to her mother's.

She looked at Alex and gave him a half-smile. Something dropped in the bar's kitchen, a clattering of glass and steel, laughter. The right advice would be to stop seeing him outside of work, and she told him so.

"I'm not happy at home," he said. "You know that."

There was more laugher, the sound of plates being stacked, and he had a look she had seen before, but not on him. They didn't have much in common besides what had happened after the peanut shells and their shared work email domain, but if the timing were different, maybe they could figure things out together. Maybe his wife was another right person in the wrong moment. How to account for that, she did not know.

After they had paid the bill, he walked her to her car, with his arm at her waist, and she liked the way his hand felt, resting at the band of her pants. For a moment, her father flashed in her head, and it was the first time that she had thought it: she was just like the women her father had been drawn to, women who he stayed out late with, plied with a vision of life that was less complicated—no kid and no years of marriage with all the hurts and resentments and disappointments to bog them down, just a smooth sail of after-hours cocktails and the courage that comes from being away from home. It was not the women's fault, she was sure of this. Her father, like Alex, had to make his own path. They were the ones with the most to lose, while people like her would float.

In the parking lot, at the door to her car, he pulled her close so that their chests were pressing.

"I really am not happy at home," he said, reminding her, and she wondered if her father had talked like this to a relative stranger, saying to her what he could not say to his wife.

"I know," she said, but did not pull away.

When he kissed her, she could not stop thinking of her mother on the stepstool, pulling the philodendron vines from the ceiling, cursing and crying. The half-emptied rooms of the house, the ashen pile they had left in the entryway.

Melanie took a step back, though she felt how her body had warmed to him without her wanting it to. She liked the way he felt, the way he tasted. She liked the way he was open to her, and she had drunk just enough beer that she felt inclined to fold into him, to not be practical. Still, she said she should go.

Alex was watching her and clasping at her hand. She knew he was thinking that he was ready to give up his life, not for her, particularly, but in general, and she wondered how she could convince him that he was wrong. He might get better sex for a few weeks or even months, but he would still be lonely, and at night he would pad around in his slippers, wondering why it was so quiet, wondering why there was no one to talk to. It would be difficult to move on. It would be difficult to commit again. Or, at least that was how her father had been. When Melanie went to stay with him, he was always restless once the sun went down, overfilling his cocktail glass and pacing.

"What if I stayed over at your place?" Alex said.

"You can't," Melanie said. She almost said *sorry*, but she was not sorry, and she was glad she caught herself.

He looked deflated for a second, and as he pulled his fingers from hers and turned towards his car, she wanted to tell him to try and remember everything he had ever loved about his wife, not just the obvious, like a first date or the birth of their children, but everything— the way she might be a desperate snorer and deny it, or the way she might leave her shoes and stockings in a trail from the door to the sofa, like breadcrumbs, for him to find her.

What if she's the best person you have, Melanie wanted to say to him, *but you're ignoring her?*

She clicked her key fob to unlock her car door. She got inside and buckled up. From the side mirror, she could see Alex was still standing in the parking lot, and he was looking at her bumper or something else low to the ground. Backing out of the parking space, she was careful of the other cars and of him. When her vehicle was parallel to where he stood, she rolled down her window and looked up towards him.

"Get in your car," she said, but he shook his head and said that he could not.

"Yes you can," she said. "You just don't want to." The radio was switched on very low, and she heard the sound of the newscast like a hum. He was looking away from her.

Putting the car into gear, she was not sure she was being fair. He was hurt, she could see that, but it was not something she could be responsible for. Slowly, she let the clutch out and, slowly, she maneuvered away from him. When she checked the mirror again, he was in the same place on the asphalt, eyes turned down and head hanging.

Chapter Twenty-One
Lucy Estelle
Summer, 1970

The night Jenny's father left, Lucy Estelle had turned in early, taking the baby with her. They both woke at the same time in the morning. Jenny opened her tender brown eyes to the new light in the bedroom, and her mother said, *Good morning, honey girl.* Lucy Estelle hadn't put Jenny in the bassinet, and it was clear to her that her husband had not touched the other side of the sheets. She scooped her daughter into her arms and lifted her shirt. She left the room with her daughter content on her breast and she checked the house—a small, tidy house; a modest house—and she found no trace of Larry. She checked again; it did not take long to look twice, but still, no one. She checked a third time, stepping out into the yard, peeking into the backseat of her car while noting that his truck was absent. She swept the shower curtain aside, just in case he had drunk too much and, in the dead heat of summer, fallen asleep against the cool of the porcelain tub. She checked the closet: a duffel bag, gone. She noted a few swinging hangers that she was sure had held shirts the night before. When she finally popped the tin where they kept the grocery money, there was only the silver bottom. Jenny was still at her breakfast.

In fact, Lucy Estelle had always known better than to keep much money in the tin, because Larry dipped into it so often for beer. One day not long after they had married, she had been wise enough to move most of her money from her regular bank to one a few towns over. Her family had always been customers; the branch had given them mortgages and auto loans and had helped her greatly when she had to sort out the life insurance policies after her parents had died in the accident. The teller had even called a manager to the floor, trying to convince her to stay, and Lucy Estelle had said she was sorry. All she could think of was what would happen if Larry drained her savings. He was her husband. He could do that. Now she kept most of her spending cash and her checkbook in an envelope in the bottom of the box of laundry detergent, a place where she was sure he would not look. The rest of her savings, which was not much, but it was all she had, she kept in a branch thirty miles away. When she handed over the bills at the gas station or wrote out a note in the market, her transactions smelled of manufactured scents like Mountain Fresh or Spring Rain or whatever had been on sale.

She had not loved Larry when she signed her name on the paper-work, and she had not loved him when Jenny was born.

Lucy Estelle missed her own mother. Her mother, canning cherries. Her mother, brushing her hair until the shine came up. Her mother, giggling when her father pinched her tush in the kitchen. Her mother, holding her daughter's hand on the porch on nights when the moon was not out, saying, *We named you Lucy Estelle, girl, because Lucy means "born at daylight," and Estelle means "star."*

* * *

It was Saturday. Lucy Estelle sat at the empty kitchen table. She looked at the phone on the wall but it did not sound. She looked at the beer cans in the bin, but there was no rustling, no message for her. She had not known Jenny's father long. They had met at a party on the riverbank that she had gone to with some of her friends from school; it was the summer of their graduation. After that, he had come around some.

Lucy Estelle worked at a construction company, in the office. She did paperwork for permits and the field-crew schedule. They had given her the job out of pity because her parents had just died, she was sure, but she was good at it.

After she had told Larry she was pregnant, they went to the court-house. She had worn the same maroon dress she wore on her high school graduation day, because it was her only good dress. Her aunt had bought it for her. It had come in the mail from JC Penney. He wore a shirt borrowed off of a friend.

She looked again at the beer cans in the bin. He had been working his way through a case when she went to bed. Usually, she would have heard his truck—the low, rumbling motor, the exhaust rattling, and then the way he drove the diesel, with his foot to the floor, squealing down the dirt drive, rutting the grooves even deeper. This was not the first time she had awoken to find him gone, but it was the first time he had taken anything.

Lucy Estelle whispered to her daughter, *We'll be okay,* and rocked her until she went back to sleep.

She thought about Larry being gone and how the tiny house had a little more space. Maybe she was meant to not wake up. She was not sure she would have tried to talk him out of leaving, but she knew she would have insisted that he say good-bye to their daughter.

She had grown up an only child in a quiet house—her parents found each other late, and even one baby was a risk, but they tried it anyway. Her mother had been frank with her that she, Lucy Estelle, was not the first one, but she was the first one to have been born whole. On certain days her mother had a quiet, low sadness, and as Lucy Estelle grew older she could only imagine her mother was thinking about the others. She knew two had been miscarried very late and were buried in the garden under a carpet of iris and phlox, but she was not sure about the rest.

Lucy Estelle had told her mother almost everything, but she did not tell her that sometimes she dreamed of them—she was not sure exactly who they were, except that they were her siblings. She had dreamed she was out in the garden and their parents were calling to all of them. Their shared mother was shouting their names, she knew this, but the actual syllables were just out of reach, like listening underwater, or sometimes the syllables were slightly clearer, like when she would build a fort of couch cushions and blankets and the adult voices on the other side were muffled through the quilting and cotton batting. In her dreams, there were creatures around, a sounder of pigs or a brood of chickens snorting and clucking at the children. It was the swine who were the most urgent, nudging and rooting at Lucy Estelle's feet while she tried to kick away their snouts, the jabbering of her brothers and sisters fading into the forest, the sows circling her in a chain, some of them a ton or more, their teats dragging against the patchy lawn. She understood that to avoid being trampled, she had no choice but to stay in the center of their ring, so she let them herd her along. She understood she was supposed to feel safe. When she dallied, their bristling skin scraped against her calves. The hens pecked at the fresh ground turned up by the heavy hooves, the roosters would not stop their hooting, even in the afternoon light. Both the barrows and the boars kept a sly eye turned toward the chickens. They were not nimble enough to hunt, but they were keen to get a taste of poultry if one of the birds was disabled, or better, crushed.

In the dream, she would reach the door to the back porch, and the swine would get fuzzy then, starting to depart. She smelled of feather and mud, her face streaked with tears and her dress torn, tufts of down in her hair. She would know that if she stepped up and opened the screen the barnyard would dissolve, and it would be only her and her mother. She would have forgotten she was calling to the others, and the nicks left from the sows nipping Lucy Estelle's ankles would close in an instant. She worried for the other children left alone, sheltered only by the ragged edge of trees and the low shrubs in the garden. Still, she lifted her foot up on the homemade stairs and reached for the screen's latch, every time.

* * *

The house had belonged to her parents. The car accident had happened when she was a junior in school. That had been hard. She had never wished for a sibling more in her life. She was glad both sets of grandparents were gone, though, because even as a young person, and even before she was a mother herself, she understood how it was worse to bury a child. She was not sure how to approach the arrangements; she was not sure how to handle everything. Her aunt was a great help then, asking questions and sitting with her through the long nights and helping her clean out the house. She did not want to erase her folks, but she could not stand to see her mother's empty dresses in the closet and her father's mud boots by the door, crumpled and leaning sideways.

There had been a wreck on the road, and her father had swerved to avoid it. The rolling of his small pickup was lost in the larger commotion of a crumpled passenger car with a child inside and crates of chickens upturned on the asphalt, their light bones crushed on impact.

That day she had come home from school and the door was locked. Lucy Estelle—without a key, because she had never needed one since someone had always been home—waited for them on the steps until a police cruiser turned and came slowly up the drive, dust pooling with the gentle exhaust.

When he reached her on the steps, she stood, and he took off his hat.

Her parents had turned the latch against their own not coming home, and while she could have broken a window, it did not occur to her that this might be necessary.

"I'm sorry if you were waiting on me," he said. He was a regular cop, not a Stater, but an officer from a few towns over whom she did not recognize; his forehead was white from always wearing the uniform cap. She had not caught his name, but she didn't think she would forget his pinched face. He had other words on his lips, but she dropped the backpack she had been clenching the whole time and fell toward him.

He smelled like aftershave and nervous sweat. He put his arms around her, warm in the already warm air. She thought she heard him say, *Your parents*, but maybe she only felt it.

Then, she heard the stamping of the hogs, the low braying of the cattle, and the peal of the cock's crow in the dry air.

When she tried to move her legs, she could not, so the officer carried her to the backseat of the cruiser and hoisted her inside; he turned on his lights for the short drive into town, the flash of red and blue reflecting against the road, like a beacon for nothing.

* * *

There was some money, her parents' savings, which would carry her for a while, but as soon as she graduated, she took the job at the construction company anyway. The house was paid for, and the small life insurance policy arrived before she even had time to wonder. Her mother had a dent in the side of her head that was large enough to nix an open casket, but at the service Lucy Estelle had kept her face neutral. Her father's sister and her father's brother were there, her uncle was with her small cousin, Irene, and she remembered worrying for the girl, only ten. Her parents had always paid special attention to her, a child without a mother, and Lucy Estelle knew she would not be able to visit her the way her folks had, making the drive across the eastern plains and bringing biscuits wrapped in a tea towel to keep them warm.

Later, she overheard that an off-duty officer had found her parents, had tried CPR, had torn his clothes to tie their bodies, had ridden with them to the county hospital. She had heard he was nearly naked when he trailed them to the emergency room, his uniform shredded and even part of his undershirt torn to strips. His boots streaked the tiles red. The details did not matter to her. One truck on a single lane road erring on a turn, or a pile of metal on the highway flattened by a semi: the outcome was the same.

* * *

Even if the house was small, Larry had been impressed that it was hers. She did not even try to make him understand what she had lost for it, or explain that she did not care about property. He walked the perimeter of the yard and speculated. She sat at the table and pined.

In time, she hoped, the baby would change them. It had happened quickly, and she could tell he did not want to propose, and though she did not want to accept, either, they both agreed. The same doctor who had seen to her pregnancy had done their bloodwork.

And when Jenny came, she came fast. It was spring, and the driveway was pitted with mud. Larry was not at home—he was never at home—so Lucy Estelle drove herself to the hospital, breathing deeply as she worked the pedals. *This is the clutch*, she repeated to her left foot as she navigated, and to her right, *This is the accelerator, and this is the brake.* Still, the car jerked down the road, and she squinted until she realized that only the parking lights were on, but in the dim twilight, the brights hardly made a difference.

Before she left the house, she wrote a note: *Baby coming. See you soon?* and left it on the counter. He still had not turned up hours later when Jenny was born, early in the morning, and was still not there that afternoon when a nurse came with paperwork. She gave Jenny her own maiden name, and she said she was married but that she did not want to list the father.

The nurse shrugged. She'd been a few years ahead of Lucy Estelle at school. "Doesn't matter to me," she said. "If it matters to him he can go to the records office and make the correction."

Lucy Estelle looked around the empty room. "He won't."

"Sorry," the nurse said, and started pumping on the blood pressure cuff.

At home with Jenny the morning Larry left, she missed her mother. Her mother, who peeled peaches for her because she did not like the velvet skin. Her mother, who plaited her hair into tight French braids and fishtails. Her mother, who probably never wondered if her husband would come home, and probably never thought about changing the locks just in case he did.

Lucy Estelle kept Jenny close, the baby's skin warm on her skin. She had milk for her daughter and a solid roof. She had some money still, from the life insurance—the accident was only two years ago, but how time had passed—and she had the job at the construction company that was waiting for her on Monday. They had been nice when she had taken a few weeks off when Jenny was first born. It might have been pity again, but pity didn't bother her. She was working part-time, and Jenny stayed with a woman down the road who had three children of her own and was grateful for a few extra dollars. If she had to compare Larry vanishing to her parents vanishing, it was nothing.

"Nothing," she said, and the sound of her own voice startled her.

She decided she would change the locks, and she got up carefully so as to not wake the child, and she washed her face and combed her hair with one hand. Anything more would have to wait. She found her car keys on the hook and eased Jenny into the passenger side, milk-drunk and swaddled. Lucy Estelle drove slowly—she had wanted to get a car seat but had not yet.

At the hardware store, she recognized the clerk, Roger, from her class in school. She told him that she wanted to get new door handles, that the old ones were always loose.

"I'd try tightening the screws before getting all new," he said. "Larry could do that for you," he said.

"I don't think Larry is going to be doing that for me," she said.

"He's not so handy, huh?"

Lucy Estelle avoided his eye, but nodded. There was a row of packaged knobs, their latches like tongues.

Roger looked at the baby. Jenny was still asleep; her head rested on Lucy Estelle's shoulder and the top of her shirt was a little damp from the heat and a fine thread of drool.

"You got a dead bolt?" Roger asked.

She said she did, and he suggested she might change that too, if it was from the same key.

Lucy Estelle thanked him and paid for the merchandise and drove home, a little more quickly this time, because Jenny was awake and fussing. She took a deep breath as she came up the driveway, and didn't exhale until she could see there was no one parked in the carport.

When she stepped inside the house, she had Jenny balanced on her left arm with her shopping dangling from her right, and on the counter, glinting against the scratched laminate were Larry's housekeys, which she had not seen in the darkness of early morning.

"I guess we don't have to change the locks, baby girl," Lucy Estelle said to her daughter, and Jenny gurgled and kicked her legs.

She checked the clock, still before noon, and she drank a glass of water. She nursed Jenny until she was asleep. She put her own milk-stained shirt in the soaking pail, for now permanently kept by the diaper pail, and took the laundry off of the line. Her father, though not wealthy, had long been a believer in conveniences, but her mother had always refused a clothes dryer. They used the line most of the year and a clothes horse in winter. Inside or out, her mother had always hung everyone's private things between the folds of a shirt or under a tea towel for modesty, and for years Lucy Estelle donned underwear damp at the crotch and bras with a moist back, even when her skirts had gotten crispy.

She checked the baby and the time again. Without the ticking of the punch clock at work, the hours moved unevenly. There were a few dishes in the sink, so she did those. Jenny was content in her bassinette, so Lucy Estelle took the garbage out, and bagged the aluminum cans. Always between jobs, Larry would have taken them himself to the scrap man, but she had always just left them on a corner in town for someone else to pick up. She thought of making herself some lunch, but she wasn't hungry. Jenny's diaper was fresh, and she wrapped her tightly in a blanket so she would not fuss, and returned to the car. She was low on gas, and when she stopped at the filling station closest to her house, the attendant refused to let her pump it herself even though she had pulled up on the self-serve side. *No ma'am!*, he said, and he also washed her windows. She tipped him fifty cents and continued towards town.

First she returned the dead bolt and lock to the hardware store, and Roger counted back her bills to her and offered to come out to the house and help her if she needed it.

"Haven't seen Larry today," he said, trying to be casual.

"Is he usually in?" She was a little startled. She did not know what her husband had done during his days, but it was not house projects.

"No, Lucy. I was only saying." He closed out the sale on the old manual register.

"Thank you," Lucy Estelle said, accepting her refund and sorting the bills into one compartment of her wallet, the change into another. She took a deep breath and left the store with its smell of fertilizer and dry goods, bleach, and packaged teakettles.

* * *

The other thing that happened in her dream was that she would be in the vegetable garden, and she would find something, like a tiny toe, a bit of hair ribbon, or a lock of blond curl scattered there among the roots of an azalea. This caused her to dig carefully, wishing for bristles and tweezers rather than a spade. She would rummage in the boxes in the carport for a discarded paintbrush or an old ice pick, and with the makeshift tools for her personal archeology, she unearthed a velvet dress and a fire engine, a stuffed bear—matted and maggoty—and once a full crib complete with yellow trim and tiny, downy sheets, the pillow imprinted but empty.

Always, the pigs, the cattle, and the sharp beak of the chickens at her heels. Always, her mother's voice in the distance.

Sometimes, when she woke, she would wonder what would have been different if she were not an only. A tall sister to take her hand, a small brother to protect. Like the hens, she would guard the clutch, and even without her parents, feel sure.

Chapter Twenty-Two
Melanie
Summer, 1988

The apartment building they lived in was flanked by impenetrable juniper bushes and was between her mother's job at the bank and Melanie's school, and sometimes when she flushed the toilet the water knocked through the pipes in an unconventional way.

One day when Melanie checked the answering machine there was a message from her father about his child support checks. He was reminding her mother to cash them. He said he did not understand why she had not cashed a single one—almost a year's worth. He said he did not think it could be that hard to just take care of it, since she went to the bank every day. He said he was not sure what to make of it, since cashing checks was what she did for a living.

It was not his business, Melanie thought, but she could see his point. She deleted the message.

She knew where the checks were; crammed in the junk drawer in a repurposed solicitation envelope, with two plastic windows on the front. This was unlike her mother, who was organized and saved receipts and kept records. The junk drawer itself was not even that junky. Melanie wondered if her mother was ashamed to take her father's money, since she was very good at making do. Her mother had come from a large family, and she was the last of four girls—her three younger brothers followed her. Sometimes when Melanie complained, her mother told her that she should be grateful that she never had to wear hand-me-down underwear and that if she had a cavity she got to go to the dentist instead of chew aspirin. Melanie did not actually believe that the dentist was all that great.

"I don't have any cavities," she reminded her mother once.

"Because I had your teeth capped, and you get your teeth cleaned," her mother said.

That night, when her mother came home, Irene was with her. Irene had high-piled hair and Melanie adored her—she smelled like cigarettes and lemon and was once widowed and once divorced. She never talked about either man, but Melanie's mother said she would have liked Irene's first husband, and when Melanie asked why, her mother thought about it for a little bit before she said because he was like them. He was young, and his name was Sammy, and he would have loved her.

* * *

Her mother didn't get the paper, but she brought home week-old news from the branch. Melanie read the comics, the lifestyle section, and the horoscopes.

What meticulousness, Cancer! You may feel a sudden, urgent need to take a close look at your financial situation, wardrobe, cupboards, or car. List the things you need to do in order to fix them over the next few days. You're going to spend this time taking inventory in your life. Why not? It's important to get a really good look at the reality of things, occasionally.

* * *

Irene lived in a nicer apartment building nearby, with aqua siding and a small pool. She always wore heels, which she almost always took off as soon as she was in the door, padding around in her stocking feet, sparkle or suede waiting to clack home with her. Irene and her mother worked together at the bank. Her mother had gotten the job for Irene, because they had been friends for a long time. There was no part of her life that Melanie could remember without Irene. When she was young, Irene would come for Thanksgiving and stay the night and stay up late with Melanie whispering in the dark—Melanie would tell her everything: crushes, the teachers she hated, and the ones she loved, the things that drove her crazy about her parents. Irene always listened to her, nodding and sometimes squeezing her arm. *You're a good girl, Mel*, Irene would say. *Your folks are so lucky to have you.*

For dinner, Melanie's mother made an egg-drop soup, the wisps of white like lace through the broth, with slices of fried tofu on the side and a sprinkle of scallions. She was branching out, she said. Experimenting. Melanie thought she and Irene were dieting again. The apartment was warm from the stove, and they had gotten tipsy from wine. After dinner, Melanie spread her homework on the kitchen table, and Irene insisted on doing the dishes since they did not have a dishwasher.

"I won't argue," Melanie's mother said.

"Because you're not stupid," Irene said, and they both giggled.

The pans clattered in the sink as Melanie worked through her figures. Her mother had taught her fractions with recipes as a guide long before they got to them in school, and algebra had worked out all right for her, but now she was struggling with geometry. She liked the neat graph paper, and she liked the ragged sound of her mechanical pencil along her protractor, but she did not care about triangles. Equilateral, isosceles, scalene, her teacher had written on the board, with examples. Melanie cursed Euclid and looked out the window.

Irene finished the dishes and went to the balcony to smoke, and Melanie's mother opened another bottle of wine.

"I love you, honey," her mother said, pulling the cork and dropping it into the garbage can.

"I love you, too," Melanie said. "I liked your soup."

"You're so polite."

"That's what Irene always says," she said, flipping to a new page in her notebook.

"You should listen to her," her mother said.

"I do. Can I have some wine too?" she asked. She was almost fifteen, she reasoned.

"Half," her mother said and poured it for her. "My European daughter," she said, laughing and clinking Melanie's glass. She liked her mother like this, in one of her easy moods.

Irene and her mother stayed up talking until the second bottle was drained, and Melanie listened to them from the sofa, thinking about the checks and wondering how much her mother cared if she failed geometry.

When Irene went home, and her mother closed the door, the apartment was quiet. Melanie helped dry the remaining dishes, and they made lunches for school and work—a sandwich for Melanie and leftover soup for her mother.

"I like that Irene still visits us," Melanie said.

"She's one of the good ones," her mother said.

The telephone rang—Irene confirming that she was home. They always did this—and Melanie and her mother went to their respective rooms. As she closed her eyes, she wondered if her mother also waited in the dark, for something.

* * *

The next day, Melanie took the child support checks out of the envelope, and she heard her teacher's voice. *A rectangle is any quadrilateral with four right angles.* She had her own account at the branch that her mother had opened for her when she was in elementary school, but it seemed like a lot of work to deposit her allowance into it then record everything in the register, so she pocketed her weekly twenties, and when her money was gone it was gone, or if she had some leftover, she put it into an old mustard jar that she used as a piggy bank. Once in a while her mother would bring home coin wrappers from the bank, and they would sit at the table listening to records and roll Melanie's change and bundle the one-dollar bills, while her mother would compliment her on learning to save. Then they deposited everything so she would earn interest, but she didn't like how the mustard jar looked when it was empty, like clutter.

Many of the checks were expired, going back years, and she was pleased with herself at understanding to look. She separated these and wrapped them in a piece of her lined notebook paper. She could do her mother's hand very well; being in her first year of high school, she was old enough to have to forge a note once in a while. *Got your message*, she wrote to her father, *these need reissue.* She did not sign her mother's name even though this was what she could do best because she thought that would be a little like showing off, and she wanted to keep it all very businesslike.

Carefully, she addressed a clean envelope. She put two stamps on it to be sure. She dropped the letter in the outgoing bin in the apartment hallway immediately so she would not have time to change her mind. She checked twice to make sure that not even a corner peeked out of the slot.

For a week straight, she rushed home from school to retrieve the mail. In those days, she noticed that they did not really get much besides bills and grocery store circulars, and she was not sure what she had been expecting, other than that she was surprised how frequently the box was crammed with announcements of a sale on beef chuck, addressed to *Or Current Resident.* When correspondence from her father finally arrived, it was the only thing that was personal, made out in his square hand. Her heart pounded for a minute. Maybe there was something besides money; maybe her forged note had meant something to him. She wondered if she should have tried to write something emotional, like *I miss you*, or better, and less of lie, *Melanie misses you*. The envelope was heavy, cream-colored stationery from his job. She liked the texture of it, and she liked the gray marks left from the sorting machines where letters skidded through rubber wheels. They had been to the post office on a school field trip, so she had seen how it all worked.

When she picked the seal off carefully and slid the contents out, there was no message beyond the glue, just her own name, *Melanie*, made out on a single check's subject line, with the range of dates it covered. It was the largest sum she had ever seen. There was another check, new, for the current month, and she understood that this was what was left of her parents' lives together, a transaction.

She was not sure what they thought, but Melanie was not happy with either one of them. Her mother did not ever talk about him, except out of sheer practicality, like *Remember you're going to Andrew's tomorrow*. Her mother never called him *your father* or *your dad* or *Andy*, which is what he went by, always *Andrew*, and sometimes Melanie had to remind herself that her father did have a given name, just like she did. Her mother used to call him *Toots*. Her father used to call her mother *Kath*, like most of her friends did, and now, he did not refer to her at all.

When her mother came home from work that day, she kept asking Melanie what was wrong, and each time Melanie said, *Nothing*, because she could not really name the disappointment. She had put the check back in the drawer, but she could not stop thinking about it. She had also folded and torn her father's stationery until she could not get it any smaller and thrown the shreds in the trash. Then, when she was worried her mother would notice the confetti on top of the garbage, she took the whole bag out to the dumpster at the back of the apartment building and put a new liner in their kitchen can.

When a week had passed, there was another message on the answering machine. *You should have received the check by now*, he said, *but still nothing has cleared*. She played the message over and over again.

Was there not something else he wanted to say? Was there a part that had been cut off? The beginning of the answering machine tape always made voices sound scratchy and warbled, since it had recorded and deleted messages over and over again so many times. She listened again and again until the cassette jammed and part of the tape came spooling out. Then she unwound the plastic from the heads of the cassette, untangled it, and cranked it back into its case with a bobby pin. When she tried to play it again in the answering machine, her father's voice was even more distorted and the message would not erase, so she took a quarter from her mustard jar and went to the pay phone on the corner and dialed. She waited for the machine to pick up, and then she stood there, recording the sound of the traffic in the background and her own breath, until she heard the *beep* that meant the machine had cut her off. Inside, she deleted her call successfully and sat in the kitchen with no lights on until her mother came home.

As a child, before they had moved to the apartment, she had dreamed of finding treasure in the attic or in some forgotten cubby under the stairs, a box of tarnished silver waiting to be uncovered in the yard. The envelope was tucked neatly back in the junk drawer, and every time she looked in that direction, the handle wanted to be pulled.

Melanie knew her mother took lunch from eleven until noon, so the next day she faked sick to get out of her classes, dodged the nurse's office, and hurried to get to the branch. She knew almost every one of the tellers, but she picked Irene, who was glowing bronze with self-tanner. She thought of Irene on their patio, cigarette smoke curling like a halo around her, and Melanie did her best to approach her with confidence and calm.

"I have a money problem," Melanie said, firmly, and she told Irene about the checks and the message from her father, the new envelope, and the second message.

"Sounds like a man problem to me," Irene said, and her penciled eyebrow was arched high.

Melanie thought she might cry, and Irene explained she could deposit them all into Kathleen's account, because anyone could make deposits to anyone else, or she could just tell her.

"She'll be angry either way," Melanie said, and Irene agreed, so Melanie decided to deposit the checks, and she asked Irene if she would please come over after work.

"Sure, honey," Irene said. "Sure thing."

Melanie was not sure what to do when she got home, so she did what her mother did when she was agitated and lit the stove. She dug into the freezer, through the crisper, and dashed to the corner store with the four dollars she had left from her allowance. She came up with enough food to make three turkey burgers and a salad with lemon dressing.

When her mother and Irene walked in the door, she saw by her mother's face that Irene had already told her. Kathleen went to the junk drawer, fingered through it, and shut it hard.

"It's actually a lot of money," she said, to neither of them. "Dinner smells good, Melanie."

"I told you, you should not be ashamed to take it," Irene said. "It's for Mel."

"Your perspective might be different," she said. "But I don't want Andrew's money."

"Not so different," Irene said, and bowed her head a little.

Finally, they decided that because the money was for Melanie, she should choose. She could return it to her father if she wanted, or she could put it in her savings.

Melanie had not thought beyond getting her father's voice off of the answering machine, but she remembered her mother had told her about going to the ocean once when she was a teenager. One of her older sisters had moved to Portland and invited Kathleen to visit. This was before Melanie's mother met her father—she was sixteen and took the Greyhound from Denver to Oregon, and she was scared for most of the way because the bus was populated by so many men, and she was not used to being on her own. She kept her bag in the seat next to her but at certain times the bus would become full, and someone with a gritty chin would sit down next to her and ask her name, and she always said, Cathy, even though no one ever called her Cathy.

Her mother had said that when she arrived on the shores of the west coast, she had been surprised at the constant, grainy drizzle and her sister's damp apartment. She had spent forty-eight hours on the bus, and when she took a shower she did not feel clean, closed in by lumpy mushrooms sprouting out of the tiles and tufts of peachy mold around the windowsills.

Melanie wanted to see the water, but she did not want to go to the cold Pacific. When she thought of the maps she had drawn, and when she thought of the travels she had traced with Ponce de León, Florida was like a finger pointing to her.

Chapter Twenty-Three
Lucy Estelle

Fall, 1970

In the nighttime, Lucy Estelle feared Larry's homecoming. She worried he would cruise up the drive, tires spinning, and burst through the window to take Jenny and leave her alone. Not that he would want the child, just that he was prone to poor decisions. She kept her daughter in the room with her—it was easier if she fussed, anyway—and her father's pistol in the nightstand. She had checked to make sure Larry had not taken it, but he had not taken anything other than the money and his clothes. It was not like there were caches of jewelry and other weapons around the house, but she guessed he was just not ambitious enough to even open a drawer and check. The pistol was old and may not have ever been cleaned. It was unloaded, and there were no bullets anywhere, nor had there ever been. Her father had always believed the threat of a firearm was enough. He had grown up with guns, and had been to Korea, and never wanted to hear the sound again. *If they won't go away with the barrel pointed at their face,* he had said to her once, *they aren't going away.*

* * *

From the beginning, she had not thought that she could keep Larry.

When they had met, the river was high, so the kids crowded onto a narrow flat of mud below where they had parked their beater cars and borrowed pickups. The riverwater had never cleared and still churned with the fecal smell of spring. Hardly anyone had swum or fished all season.

Back then, Larry was handsome, in old jeans and a flannel shirt. He had high, delicate cheekbones, and he had been out of school for a couple of years. Lucy Estelle had heard a few things about him, like that he had been to county jail because he was rowdy.

At the river party, when Larry approached her, Lucy Estelle was talking to her friend Maureen, her best friend, she supposed, now that her mother was gone. He came to her with a freshly popped beer and a crooked smile; one side of his teeth were perfectly straight and the other side, the left, zigzagged. Maureen nudged her forward, arching her eyebrows and turning towards another girl who was with them. Lucy Estelle returned Larry's greeting when he said hi. She liked his hazel eyes and the way his widow's peak divided his forehead. He was not the kind of guy her father would have welcomed, she was sure of that, but she had been on her own for a year now already, without them, and it had made the world harder and sharper. She was happy her parents had given her chores like cooking and laundry and chopping wood, happy they had taught her to balance the checkbook. Especially in the first weeks, even when she did not feel like living, it was a comfort to realize she could take care of herself. Her father's one sister had come to stay with her for some time; her mother was an only, like her.

It was the last time she ever saw her aunt Dot, and Lucy Estelle had heard later that Dot had not even gone back to her family, her daughter Irene and her husband Don, but had just lit out to Kansas, where her people were.

The beer was warm, but she sipped it anyway, and it did not take long before Larry laced his fingers through hers, his hand hot in her hand. When they sat down on a patch of grass, she felt the damp seep through her jeans. She had not ever really been allowed boyfriends, but had always liked boys who paid attention to her, even the bad ones.

That evening by the river, even then, she saw how he kept one eye on her and the other eye on the rest of the world. When they had taken their clothes off under the dim summer stars, she had never seen a man's body in full, so close. She had never felt so much skin on her skin. They moved to the back of her car—her mother's sedan, her parents had been driving her father's truck when the accident happened—and she could hear the party continuing on around them, the clinking of bottles, the low gurgle of the river, and the humming of some other car's radio. She wished they had a little more space, but they did not, and she eased into being comfortable, with Larry on top of her, with Larry cradling her head against the glass of the wing window.

I think I'm in love with you, Lucy, he had said.

Okay, she said, because she knew he was lying, but she didn't know why. Later, she collected her clothes and drove home alone, back to the empty house, and took a shower, her body still warm with him.

* * *

On the day of their wedding at the courthouse, Larry was not paying attention, so she signed her maiden name on the paperwork and walked away from the recording clerk before any name-change forms were produced. For a moment she thought about turning back under the guise of having to pee and demanding that everything be shredded, but she did not. They had a reception that was mostly his friends and Maureen, and when Maureen turned to go off with one of them, Lucy Estelle grabbed her elbow. *Don't*.

* * *

The day she returned to the courthouse, it was not busy. She was not sure if she needed an appointment, but the clerk told her to wait, and another clerk led her to a room and handed her a clipboard of triplicate forms. She bounced Jenny and said in her nicest voice *Please don't poop*, and Jenny smiled the smile that Lucy Estelle was sure was gas, and she set to the forms directly.

The petition for divorce had only a few more questions than the one for marriage, minus the blood test, and the clerk told her they would try to serve papers, and if they could not in six months, everything would finalize with no other action, no custody, no community property. The clerk asked for a last known address, and Lucy Estelle hesitated at first, and then she told her about the keys and the money tin, and the clerk nodded and instructed her to leave it blank.

"It'll make it easier if we can't find him," she said. "It's better. Sometimes they can get weird."

* * *

The morning her parents left forever, she had gone to school. When she thought about it, she believed it could have been worse. Her mother had made her a lunch. Her father was already off to work at the feed store, and she remembered him, she was sure she remembered him, kissing her good-bye. He always did this, tiptoeing into her room, smelling of shaving cream and shampoo. He worked the early shift, so later he would have come home, and he and her mother would have had a snack of something from the garden, and he would have had a cold beer. Sometimes when Lucy Estelle would arrive home from school they were not hungry for dinner, and she would rummage in the cabinets, and her father would have a second beer, and her mother just a tiny sliver of pie.

She could not say that there was anything different about that morning. She and her mother did not have words like they occasionally did, and she was grateful for this. Maybe her mother had kissed her, too, one small, wet peck on the forehead. Maybe she folded her in her arms as the school bus pulled up, so that Lucy Estelle was embarrassed in front of her classmates but really wanting to stay nestled between her mother's elbows and against her soft chest.

That day, her father would have come home and they would have done errands like they always did. The store, the gas man, perhaps the dump. They would have been driving together in his truck, close on the bench seat, and Lucy Estelle hoped her mother's hand had been on her father's knee the way it was when she was in a good mood. She hoped that when the last turn came, they were not thinking of her, only each other.

In the house, she turned the dead bolt. Jenny rolled some but stayed asleep. Lucy Estelle had let the garden go, but she still heard the animals, especially at night, scratching and grunting. This was what Larry could not know about her, her secret family, her parents who went off to join the beasts and the other children.

In the mornings, before Jenny would wake, she went to the garden, weedy and overgrown, and looked for the traces of any of them. Her mother's embroidered handkerchief, snagged on the lilac, her father's cigarette ash, dropped among the failing peach trees. She was not sure what she believed about the afterlife, but she hoped they all walked there together, hand in hand.

Chapter Twenty-Four
Melanie
Fall, 1988

The first time being on an airplane was like nothing Melanie had ever experienced. The power as they took off was sheer and amazing, and the bumps as they ascended into the sky were terrifying. She held her mother's hand. Melanie had the middle seat, between her mother and Irene, and while Irene would not trade with her, she did not complain about Melanie leaning into her lap for most of the flight so she could watch the plane's shadow glide across the tops of the clouds.

It was early October, and Melanie was surprised that her mother had agreed to the trip and surprised that she allowed Melanie to skip school. They deplaned in Fort Lauderdale and took a shuttle to a beach resort, Irene leading the charge. Melanie was overwhelmed by the shimmer of heat coming off of the concrete around her and the rows of stucco apartment buildings, layered like birthday cake along the highway. Their hotel was pretty and cool, and there was an uncorked bottle of white wine sweating on a chrome tray. Irene immediately poured herself a drink, while Melanie's mother told her to change into her bathing suit. Irene went to the balcony to smoke, and Melanie undressed as wisps of tobacco blew into the room.

"See," Melanie heard Irene call to her mother. "This is what I'm talking about."

The resort was all-inclusive with restaurants and bars dotting the property. Melanie thought it was amazing that she could go into any of the shops and order a soda and they would give it to her without her having to pay. Ditto for an order of French fries. Her mother and Irene seemed to be spending most of their time in lounge chairs by the water, oiling their bodies and sipping frozen drinks. They looked good in their bikinis. Even Melanie could tell they still looked young. They had grown up in the same small town together, but now that Melanie's grandparents and Irene's father were gone, they never went back there.

There were some kid activities she had been signed up for, and she resented these. She was almost always the oldest in the classes. Doing crafts and taking ballroom dancing lessons was not what she had in mind for her vacation. In dance, she was a head taller than any of the boys, and when the instructor told them to pick a partner, she was the only one left without a mate. The rented shoes pinched her feet and her skirt was sticky across her thighs.

The man who taught the class was named Joseph, and he had light brown hair and strongly developed arms. He was different from the guys at Melanie's school, with their scraggly facial hair and slouching socks, and different from her father, whose hair had begun to recede from his head and sprout from his ears. She was thrilled when Joseph saw her there, uncoupled, and bowed, just barely, his hand extended.

He twirled her in front of the class, using her to help show the other students how to follow the line and follow the music. When he dipped Melanie toward the polished floor, she felt his arm strong at her back, and his face was close enough to feel his breath. Joseph said she had a knack for the steps but Melanie did not think she was actually doing anything. He was leading, and she always felt a half-second off.

On the fourth day, her feet finally felt loose in her shoes, and she almost slipped backward on the waxed hardwood, but Joseph stepped behind her so that she fell against him instead of the floor. Her spine was awkwardly against his chest, they were both warm from the music and the motion, and as he righted her, his lips were on her ear, *Stay after class.* She was not sure if she had heard right because in the next moment he had her spinning away from him as the song ended. Joseph was clapping for the other students, *Good job, good job*, and Melanie was breathing hard, her feet sore and her chest pounding. She went to the showers with the rest of the girls, and she washed herself carefully under the pressure of the nozzle and fluffed her hair as best she could. There was mouthwash and deodorant in the locker room, so she used this and then she went to the center of the studio floor and sat down with her legs crossed, and waited.

It was not long before Joseph came. He had counted the children and sent them back to their sun-soaked parents, and he was wearing a fresh shirt. He went to the PA system and selected some music that Melanie did not recognize as one of the songs they had already danced to, but she liked the lush swell of it and the way that the sound echoed in the empty room. Joseph had taken off his shoes, and he padded toward her. He sat down in front of her and moved her hair away from her face.

"How old are you?" he asked.

"Why?" she asked. And then, "I'm sixteen," she said, even though her fifteenth birthday was not for another nine months.

Joseph seemed to be thinking. "You look older," he said, and she understood that for someone her age this was a compliment, though for someone her mother and Irene's age it would not be. She blushed and thanked him.

The music sounded like it had gotten louder, and Joseph scooted a little closer to her on the floor, so their knees touched.

"How old are you?" Melanie asked, because she did not know what to say.

"I'm twenty," he said. "I want to study dance in college, but I need to save so I'm working here."

"That sounds cool," Melanie said. The place where her skin touched his skin burned.

When he leaned in to kiss her, she was not sure what to do. She felt his tongue in her mouth, she felt his body lift and push her flat onto the shiny floor. She felt his hand climb beneath her skirt and his chest flatten against her breasts.

* * *

There were only two days left in Florida, and Melanie was floating on her back in the pool wearing the new bathing suit Irene had gotten for her at the gift shop, when Joseph swam up next to her.

"You okay?" he asked. "I didn't see you yesterday."

She treaded water. "It's too hot to dance."

"It's never too hot to dance," he said. "I missed you."

She considered this. She had not known how to feel so she had skipped the lesson.

"You're too old for me, Joseph," she said, but she felt his hands reach for her, through the turquoise water. He shimmied as he held her hips, keeping them both afloat.

She could hardly see his face for the glare of the sun.

* * *

On the last day of class, Joseph was not in the ballroom. A young woman with tight calves and slim pants explained he was ill and tapped her shoes. The music came on. *And, one-two-three-four-five-six.* Melanie wondered if this was what her father's money had paid for and followed along, without a partner, her feet tracing the boxy steps, making a parallelogram, a rhombus.

* * *

When Melanie got home to Colorado, she was wondering if she should send Joseph a message, and when she checked her horoscope, it read:

If you have been feeling particularly hurt or rejected by someone whom you have not been able to forget, then take heart from today's planetary alignment. It will begin to defrost your heart and melt away the pain. A particularly pleasant meeting may just inspire you to start thinking of the future instead of the past, and none too soon!

She picked out a pretty postcard from the drugstore, with a view of the mountains, and sent it in care of the hotel. *I am sorry you were sick on the last day,* she wrote. *I hope you are feeling better.* She left her telephone number, and from the minute she dropped the card in the post, she eyed the phone, but the postcard came back to her a few weeks later, marked undeliverable.

She asked her mother to use some more of the child support money to move, and they got as far as Irene's building. In the courtyard the small pool was circled by mesh lounge chairs, and she would recline and watch the boys her own age clown on the diving board, doing flips and cannonballs and making the sunbathing ladies like Irene and her mother shriek at being splashed. All of the boys were tall and tan, but none of them, she thought, had moves like Joseph. Sometimes she would dive into the water and float for a minute and imagine the way his hand had come through the water to her. She would waltz in her flip-flops in her bedroom, keeping three-four time alone, like the last time in class, with her shadow creating a constant, perfect partner.

Chapter Twenty-Five
Simon
Winter, 1974

The townie cop, Simon Stevens, had been spotlighting the river. No one saw his face when he grabbed the boy's arm, a cushion of ice, to drag him from the water; no one knew what he had been thinking of. Simon had never wanted to go to Denver, so he had stayed on in the same small constellation of towns dotting the plains where he had been raised, mostly because he did not like trouble. He was generally lenient with the kids, making them grind out their joints and dump their beers, never taking any of them in unless they got nasty or seemed set on driving. The automobile, like the flu, was dangerous, especially to the young and the elderly, he had learned.

As soon as he could get the boy partway to the bank, he started CPR. It was the first time he had done it on his own. He'd been through trainings in his three years as an officer, always with an instructor looking on, coaching. He counted, blew twice, and then again: counted, blew. The boy's lips were set with chill, and Simon pushed his clasped hands deep into the frozen chest, trying to move the air. Only a little water expelled, murky and cool. In his trainings he had learned a rib could fracture and the heart could bruise during artificial respiration, so he focused on being forceful enough to be effective but careful enough not to hurt, and he kept counting. Between breaths he radioed for help. The boy was not responding, but he thought he remembered that working toward resuscitation could prove useful for up to thirty minutes. He had only been through five cycles, so if his pace was correct, it was only just a little over five minutes. The boy was cold, very cold, but he had been in the water, Simon reminded himself. Surface blood vessels would have contracted to keep the core organs warm. Listening for a siren and the crunch of tires on the crisp gravel by the bank, he thought he recognized the boy's face, but he put this thought out of his mind. Counted, blew.

The ambulance came, finally, at eight cycles. He knew both EMTs, who rushed with a respirator, and Simon helped them get the boy to the back of the ambulance while one squeezed air and the other took over pumping his chest. Simon still tasted the boy on his lips, metallic.

He hurried to his cruiser to follow. Though the winter sun had not been down all that long, the dark was already deep. He turned on the patrol lights and raced toward the hospital, his siren calling across the broken ice.

He wondered if he had just experienced his first time really touching a dead person. Police training had prepared him, in a way, for certain realities, but it had not prepared him for what it would mean to him, fishing a slight boy's frame from the water, putting his own breath to the boy's mouth. From an angle, he thought he could see how the river ice might have looked crossable. Simon was sure someone would ask why the boy had not used the bridge, and though he was still young himself, he could imagine his even younger self taking a shortcut despite the risk. It could have been the boy was angry, or in a hurry, or not being careful, though it seemed more like plain bad luck.

At the hospital, the boy was the only person in the single bed of the emergency room. The doctor had tried defibrillation to start his heart by electric shock. His wet clothes had been stripped. It had been over thirty minutes now, maybe, Simon thought. He had meant to check the time on the dash of the cruiser but he had lost track. They kept trying.

Simon counted with them silently. The boy looked better, he thought, but it was only the heat and the lights of the hospital—the sense of safety, the feeling of not being alone. Finally the frantic wheeze of the respirator stopped, and they pulled a blanket up over the boy's head, his damp hair soaking the edge of the hem.

* * *

Simon was not the first Officer Stevens in his family. His father, Frank, had been another small-town patrolman, and as a child Simon had waited up nights, when he was supposed to be sleeping, for the scratch of the key in the lock and his father's boots thudding up the hallway. He often thought of the man and how, on those long nights when he had only wanted him to come home, he worried for him, even in their little, safe town. His mother waited too, and she must have known Simon was not asleep, but she never fought him on it, not even when he dozed, exhausted, through his school alarm. Though he did not like that his father was gone in the night, he understood it was important work. He made things safe. Sometimes people had problems with themselves or one another, and his father solved these problems, he knew, or at least he thought he knew. That had unraveled when he'd joined the force.

Simon checked the dead boy's pockets for identification, and he made his calls from the payphone in the lobby as he picked through the sodden wallet. The driver's license not even two years old, the picture lit too brightly but still hopeful looking. The name was familiar: Samuel Henderson. He knew some Hendersons, but he could not place this one. There were also four dollars and a picture of a girl with dark hair, waterlogged and colors running. He noted the address on the ID and put the wallet in the bag with the boy's clothes. He would have to go to the house, he knew, and tell them. It was 7:30 p.m. and he imagined this boy's family cleaning up their dinner dishes and wondering about their son. He did not want to knock at their door and take off his hat. They would know before the words were even out of his mouth.

He had his own boy, Brian. The child was just a toddler. The pregnancy had been hard on his wife, Bonnie, and her doctor had cautioned against having more children. For now, Simon was happy they had a son, though it felt selfish to him. They had tried so hard for a baby. Never had he been so focused on a woman's cycle as in those early days of his marriage. It was something he'd not given much thought to. Bonnie had been his first girlfriend, and he did not have sisters or any girl cousins who were close. Their mothers knew each other from school, and it felt natural to Simon when he started to think of Bonnie as the woman he would be with for life. There was a photo of them as children, covered in mud, while their mothers drank beer from the can at an outdoor table in the background. It used to hang in Bonnie's childhood home, and now it sat on their mantel. A neighbor, long dead, had taken it by accident. She had gotten a camera as a gift and was crossing the yard to ask one of them to show her how to use it when the flash went off.

It was not until later, when they were a year into their marriage and wrestling to conceive, that he learned how his own mother had struggled—he did not know she had held on to the pregnancy that had become him only barely, and that even after months of bed rest, he was still premature. It was out of necessity that he was an only child, like his own son might turn out to be. Bonnie said he should have told her all this before they took vows.

"I would've still been with you, but I might have wanted to start sooner," she said. "In case it would've made a difference."

He hung his head then, because he would have told her if he had known, but he had not, and he was not sure they really could have started trying much sooner than they had. After he proposed they had married quickly in his parents' backyard, on the last warm day of autumn before her senior classes started again for the fall. They used paper plates left-over from his own graduation party in early summer to serve the cake his mother had made, a pretty sheet of white ringed by the last chrysan-themums of the season.

The doctors always said it was on the woman, pregnancy troubles. He'd heard enough from them to keep his mouth shut, but he couldn't deny his own experience, the experience of his father. He'd never been that interested in science, but one day, Simon thought, the science would catch up. People could believe it was the woman or it was God making a baby, but he knew it took two people, a man and a woman.

They lived with his parents the first year, and he started his police training, while she finished up her final year of high school.

Bonnie's own folks had been gone since she was girl, and he regretted he did not have the chance to ask her father for her hand. As much as she was a woman who lived her own life and knew her own mind, she would have liked that. Her older brother had given permission. She was the youngest of three, and she and her other brother had lived with the eldest, who had just left home when the accident happened. It was not long before the middle brother quit school and moved to the mountains, where he worked sometimes in the mines and some-times in a mobile sawmill. Simon knew him by sight but little more.

He hoped it was a comfort to his wife, knowing that her parents had gone together, hit by a poultry farmer who made a bad turn. Even though it was early afternoon and fully light, the driver's rig—an eigh-teen-wheel truck that belonged to his son-in-law, and that he should not have been operating at all, much less driving on the highway packed with cages of fowl headed to the processing plant—swiped the rear of their sedan with one of the front tires and then barreled over the pas-senger and driver with the rear wheels. When Bonnie told it, there were feathers like hail across the asphalt, the broken glass shining like crystal. She was eleven, in the backseat, and when the paramedics came with a halligan bar, they found her father reaching to her mother, their arms crushed in place, and a girl curled into a ball in the one corner of the car that had not crumpled, with only the lightest touch of bruising.

She hadn't seen it, but she had heard there was another car, carrying an older couple, had swerved off the road to avoid the car Bonnie was in, and they had died too.

Every day Simon saw how Bonnie was right for him. She made his mother coffee in the morning before homeroom, and she cooked their evening meal as well. If his father was on shift, she saved a plate for him, covering it with waxed paper in the refrigerator.

It was not his expectation that she would do these tasks, and he spoke to her, quietly, in the room they shared, his childhood room, about how happy it made him that she looked after his parents so well, but that he had not brought her to his family home so she could wait on them. It was only that he could not afford their own place yet.

"I've been looking for a job," Bonnie said, "but there's nothing that fits around school."

"I know," Simon said. Their town was small, and sometimes, when things had been tight, his mother, and Bonnie's mother as well, had taken part-time jobs at the processing plant again, driving an hour through the dry plains to sit on hard stools with the smell of wet bird. Simon would not have his wife there, after the accident with the chicken truck, when even a tuft of down would smell like death to her. Also she did not drive and did not want to learn, and he did not want to have to drive her.

She said being with his parents was better than at her brother's, that his parents were kind, that his mother was too old to do so many chores, that the work was less than living with her sister-in-law's four children, all girls, the youngest two still in diapers.

"I've been living on other people's kindness for a while," Bonnie had said. And, "Your folks are easy. Your momma always thanks me, and that's a hard thing to say to a woman who's in your kitchen."

He was proud to have been offered a job by the time she matriculated. It was his father's job—his back was finally bad enough that driving the cruiser pained him enough to admit it—but Simon applied for it just like anyone else. Going to the interview was the single most nerve-wracking day of his life. It meant everything. After he got the offer, they found a rental in town, with bad carpet and dented paneling, and they made their home there. It had a wood stove, and after his shifts he'd go to the shed and split log after log, working the muscles in his shoulders and thanking the world to have a strong body.

He loved his married life. They had his parents over on Sundays, and Bonnie's brother's family came once a month or so, or they visited them in their home. The children tumbled into his wife's lap, and she would braid their hair and slip them chocolates.

When he had thought about it, which was not often, he had always thought he was an only child because his parents were older when they had him. He had never wished for a sister or a brother; he was happy being a single to their couple. As a child, some of his friends got beat up by their siblings and then had to bunk with them. It did not seem so great. Also, he thought his parents were too tired for more children. They were always worn out.

It was after Simon got his father's job and his father moved to a desk at the station that they started trying for a baby. He knew that he knew hardly anything about sex; he understood all the mechanics, like anyone who lived so close to livestock ranches would, but the act of being so close to Bonnie was thrilling. He wondered if she might be more experienced than he, though he could not think of any boyfriends she might have had before him, and he did not ask. It did not matter, because they were married now and she was his.

Those were long months in their first house. Simon on the night shift, Bonnie bored with no one to look after, her studies finished, and every cranny of the house already scraped clean, curtains sewn for the windows, her summer canning long done. She went to her brother's and helped with the children, and she went to his parents' and made casseroles to freeze, ironed the sheets, and sat with his mother.

Only once did she bring up the processing plant, that maybe she could try for a job there.

"No," Simon said. "We don't need the money."

"It's not about the money," she said. "It's quiet here all day. I don't know what people do."

* * *

It was autumn when they had their year anniversary, and still no baby. His mother had packed a piece of their wedding cake in powdered sugar and had frozen it, and they thawed it out and ate it for breakfast. To celebrate, they went to Denver, where they stayed overnight in a hotel. Bonnie said she felt like a bumpkin, she'd never seen a bed so huge or felt sheets so soft. They had dinner in a downtown restaurant and then came back for cocktails in the lounge. It was his first time in a taxi, but he did not say so. He felt very sophisticated and very proud. He was an officer of the law. He had a beautiful wife, and he loved her, and he pulled her chair out for her when she sat down and stood when she went to the restroom. He had been raised right, and he was a gentleman.

Toasting one another with a glass of sparkling wine, she was even prettier seen through the effervescence and amber.

* * *

Simon went to his patrol car. The lights had been on, but it started just fine. He took a deep breath and felt cold. His boots were wet and his sleeves still damp; he could not feel anything but the boy. Slowly, carefully, he drove to the address on the ID. When he pulled up to the house, he realized he'd been there before. He'd dropped off one of the older girls—Darlene, he thought her name was—once, when they were in high school. He remembered her being very drunk, and he'd just happened to see her walking. She was a year ahead of him in school, and she had several sisters. He always got them confused.

The porch was dark, and he heard footfalls coming to his knock. The father answered.

Simon had not practiced the words, but he wished he would have. When he took off his hat, the father's face blanched.

"What is it?" the father said forcefully. "What's wrong?"

Simon asked if the man was Samuel Henderson's father, and the man said he was, and Simon could barely remember what happened next. He knew he stuttered and stumbled over the words—the river, the attempt at CPR, the cold. *He was so cold when I found him*—but the man understood, and he collapsed to the floor, still holding the handle of the door, one arm stretched out.

Another of the boys passed by the entryway, and Simon searched for his name. His face was familiar, but he was not sure if it was because it was the same face as the father. The boy called to his father, and his father let go of the door handle. Simon heard the man's sobbing, deep and throaty.

Simon said he needed one of them to come to the hospital, to identify. He felt his stomach turn over. What if the wallet was stolen, what if it was not this man's son? He'd have to do this over again.

The man took a deep breath. The other boy, younger, a shag of brown hair, was helping him off the floor. *Goddammit, Sammy*, Simon thought he heard the man say, and he blushed. Who was he, to deliver this news? People expected his father. His father would have known how to talk to the man, who had half closed the door to open the adjacent closet. He was putting on his coat, his boots. The other boy was putting on his coat as well and calling into the house. Another boy appeared, the same face, the same shade of auburn hair, but cropped short.

"I should drive you," Simon said.

"Goddammit," the father said again, but one of the boys told him to get in the cruiser, and so he got in the passenger side while the boys climbed into the back, where they were separated by thick glass encased with mesh.

Simon drove to the hospital, wishing his own father were with them. He was not sure which entrance to go to, so he took the man and the boys to the emergency department, where the single bed was now empty and the puddles from Samuel Henderson's dripping clothes had been mopped clean.

* * *

He had not really known the story of his birth until he had a late-night conversation with his father about how much Bonnie's condition was weighing on them, the stress of it. His father had snorted at this word, condition.

"It's life, son." And then, "Simon, I got to think it might be you, not her, from your mother's side."

Simon remembered touching his gun then. He had just gotten off his shift, and there was a note on the pad by the kitchen phone telling him that his father had called. The hours were getting on, but his father had kept the habits of a man who had worked nights nearly his whole grown life. Simon's grandfather had done graveyards at the refinery and his great-grandfather had been in the dark of the mines. He guessed they had all learned to be happier when the sun was not pushing into them, and Simon was proud to be following them, so he rang his father when most folks would be settling into bed, but when the Stevens men were just waking up.

Before the conversation, he had never thought it might be him, and after, he thought of little else.

Simon made an appointment with the doctor, asked if there was some test he could take. The old doctor shook his head.

"My dad—he had this problem, too," Simon said.

"I wouldn't be so sure," the doctor said, "This is not something that comes from the father."

But Simon was sure. He didn't have so much education, but his police training had taught him to look for patterns, in both expected and unexpected placed. What he saw seemed clear: despite what the doctor said, it wasn't the women, who had married into his family, it was the biology of the men.

A few weeks later, his father had come over and had too much beer, and that was when he told him everything about the others. *We got used to the ones who left quick, his father said, but I can't forget the children who were more. Their faces. Your brothers, and a sister. We buried them by the lilac that marks the property line to the Phinney's orchard. We had our number, of how many times we would try. We almost got there.*

Simon only nodded through this story. His parents had always seemed so old, and now he thought he knew why. He and Bonnie were not getting any younger either.

When he went to bed that night, he was resolved to stop trying, to not put his wife through any more. The unfairness of it struck him like a blow, and he was terrified of the idea of multiple miscarriages and buried babies.

He got into the sheets next to Bonnie, and she was naked, her ponytail matted at the pillow. He tried to wake her from her deep sleep, and she smelled like she had been drinking as well, sitting alone at the kitchen table, while he and his father paced the yard.

"We don't have to have a child," he whispered. "And I'm sorry."

When he was younger, when he had told his father he was planning on going into the police academy, his father took him to the same spot on the riverbank and passed the light from bank to bank. His father told him sometimes he came here to think and watch the water and the halogen shine. Together they listened to the scanner.

Simon always went to that place when he missed his father or when he was confused. Until he found the boy, Sammy, he had always thought of it as looking into nothing. Another Stevens man, tending the beacon for no one.

They had conceived. There was one miscarriage first, but Bonnie said she wasn't sure, maybe she'd been wrong, but Simon bit his tongue.

One more time, only, he thought, *And then I'm getting that operation a man can get.*

What Simon knew, when he found him, was why his parents kept trying, navigating through heartbreak after heartbreak. It was better to have a short time with a child than no child at all.

He felt sure of this, even if his own boy, Brian, was just barely out of diapers.

He was not ashamed to admit that he had been scared to see the dead boy's face, lips purple and hair tangled, and to see how he was so young. Even frosted at the lashes, there was youth at his face.

Simon was still eligible for the draft when Brian was born, but he did not say anything to Bonnie. He thought it would be hard to get an exemption, and he was not sure how it all worked. She did not like to have the television on, so he kept an eye on the newspaper for the announcements, and he thought of what his father had said. *We had our number,* and Simon prayed to no one in particular that his number had already come up, decades ago in a cramped house where the wind howled off the plains and his mother hoped for him, or someone else, when he was everything to her.

After he took the man and his other sons back home, Simon went to the station. He wished his father would be there, shuffling through his paperwork and making coffee, but there was only the other patrolman, waiting for Simon to return the car.

"I guess you heard it on the scanner," he said to his colleague, and his colleague nodded.

"Go home," he said. "Do the paperwork tomorrow when you have a clear head."

"Not sure my head's going to clear about this anytime soon," Simon said.

"It will. Maybe see Frank? He's good on these things. He always helped me."

Simon nodded. It didn't think it was fair to go to Frank, his father. He thought of the dead boy's own father and how he had fallen there on the threshold to the house, the light from the living room shining onto the porch where Simon stood, and the two other boys circling, helping the man to the cruiser and making sure he had his gloves. The man was lucky to have more than one, Simon thought. The others would help him. His own parents' others could not. The boy Samuel would rest too soon. The man and his remaining sons and his wife and the sisters would mourn him. Simon would go home and clutch his wife and child and wait until the morning to call his father. His mother would secretly watch the papers, too, for Simon's birthday, there in black and white, but the number never showed. Every spring the lilac would bloom, like a gift.

Chapter Twenty-Six
Melanie
Spring, 2007

In her office mail, Melanie got a brochure for a conference called *Doing More with Less—The RIGHT Way*, and as she read it, she was sad about Alex, sad that she had sent him away from her in the parking lot of the strip mall bar, sad they had been there in the first place, sad that he was unhappy in his marriage, sad that she was more like her father than she might have ever imagined. To distract herself, she read the brochure again, an entire three days devoted to cost cutting, the apex of corporate efficiency.

That afternoon she would be leaving for Cincinnati, a quick overnight to an industrial buyers meeting that she had put into the travel system before the latest austerity announcements, and as it had not yet been flagged, she had brought her slim carry-on to work and it was perched upright next to her desk.

She liked to travel. She liked the hum of the planes and the disconnection, out of range from her ever-beeping email and her body tucked in snugly to the worn seats. It made her feel aware. *Here are my arms, tight against my sides. Here are my knees, clamped together to avoid the knees of my fellow travelers.* She empathized with the families who struggled with their over-packed luggage and their cranky children.

People complained about screaming toddlers, but she put on her head-phones. *It's their ears, plugged from the pressure*, she sometimes muttered, or *They can't control it, they should chew gum.* Even without kids of her own, she was sure they were generally not crying for the sole purpose of being annoying, and if they were, she tipped her mini serving of vodka to them in acknowledgment of their success.

She did not see Alex before she left the office, but as she was in the air, the miles ticking by, she knew they needed the separation of a few states.

The ride was a little bumpy, making people who did not fly often nervous. Wheels down, the dusk was just coming up, and the plane taxied to the gate of the airport balanced on the Ohio-Kentucky state line. She powered her BlackBerry on, and she started scrolling. In her personal inbox, coupons and announcements, including three reminders to change her refrigerator water filter from the company that she had ordered her last water filter from. In her work folder, notices for upcoming performance reviews, a thread about the budget reductions, and the usual all-company updates, but nothing she wanted to click. At the bottom was also a message from Alex. Subject line: Hey.

She opened the message while a taxi driver navigated the twilight traffic. *Hey, I'm sorry about last night. It's hard. I don't think you know how much different this is for me than it is for you, is all. Let's have coffee when you are back.*

Tomorrow she would be a participant in a training conference, badged and coiffed, ready to learn about market conditions and perhaps even the parent company's favorite, market penetration. She shuddered some. She reminded herself that she was good at what she did, that she had health insurance and a nice place to live. She reminded herself how much harder her life could be. She thought about things in a way she had not been present with in a long time, like, *If my car is going to career out of control and slam into a wall... if I am stuck outside on some cold night and then in the morning my body declines to wake against the crystalline ground and the clear air...* There were so many different ways to die. Once she had read that sometimes the terminally ill experience an almost manic productivity—when they know it is happening, but still have a little time, they start working in a new way, stop caring about their jobs, stop caring about replacing their flooring in the entryway, for example, and focus on what they want.

It seemed like a hard way to get to some kind of clarity, and she wondered how people who were in less dire scenarios kept their urgency from fizzling.

Chapter Twenty-Seven
Jenny
Winter, 2005

Stella had not exactly been perfectly mapped out, but she had not exactly been an accident, either. Frustrated with the idea that family planning was all up to her, she had flushed her birth control one night and then entered their marital bed with abandon. Weeks later, when she sat over the toilet, late, with the two blue lines, she wondered at first if she had made a horrible mistake. She had terminated once, years before she had met Brian, and she did not regret it, but then, flushed with love for her husband, she did not think she could do it again.

She had been surprised it was so easy to conceive, and especially surprised that it was so easy for her and Brian to conceive. There were whispers on both sides. Brian was an only. She was an only. Her mother and her father were only children as well. She got the feeling not all of it was by choice.

She remembered a time after she had first met Brian, when the sky was snowing one of those first, early rushes of soft, sloppy flakes that chills autumn out of the air, and the remaining fall leaves come down, wet and gloppy. In Denver, sometimes it was possible to watch the weather coming in off the Front Range. That day, the sky above the Rockies had been streaked gray, so Jenny went digging in her closet for a pair of boots she had not worn since the last spring had broken, and she polished out the grime and salt stains until the leather was plush and soft. The boots zipped snugly around her calves, making a pretty arc. She wore heavy leggings and a wool skirt, a sweater, and mittens, because she thought mittens were funny.

Brian was taking her to dinner, and she was warm inside, dressed for outdoors, or maybe it was from the wine. They had a nice time, and later, they had met Gary—the same Gary her husband said he was always with now—for drinks, and she had liked him. He had a certain kind of unflinching charm back then, when they were young and compliments went a long way.

A few days later, she was digging in her coat for a tissue and found the business card he had slipped into her pocket. He had written out his home number on the back and circled it. Though she had never called him, she still had the card, saved just in case.

* * *

When Stella began, before they knew she was Stella, Brian had noticed something about her, but she could tell he did not know what it was.

"You look different," he said.

"I've been doing yoga," Jenny said, but her heart jumped.

"I'm not sure that's it," he said, but he went back to what he had been working on, and she practiced calmly inhaling and exhaling, waiting for the courage to tell him.

* * *

The other time she had been pregnant, it was a pure accident.

When she had gone to her old college boyfriend, he was watching television on their small sofa. They were in their last year of university, both a little worried for what would happen next, but neither of them talking about it. She did not think people had to get married to demonstrate commitment, but she also knew that sometimes people did not get married—even after cohabitating and planning out joint budgets and doing laundry and all of the other everyday life things—because the commitment did not seem right.

Over ten years had passed since that afternoon, but she still remembered the even balance of the test on her palm. How she tried to hold it still as she waited for it to reveal the results, even as her hands were shaking. Though the instructions said it could take up to a minute, once her urine had passed the control line, there was no waiting. The indicator was clear.

"Hey," she had said. "Can you pause that for a second?"

Irritated at being interrupted, he had narrowed his eyes. It was the middle of the day, but he did not have classes, so he had a cocktail, and he swirled the ice.

She lowered her hand so he could see.

She told him it was a relief to her actually, to be only pregnant; she had noticed feeling off a week ago when they were out. She had ordered a beer that she had to choke through, her guts moving in an unusual way. She had worried she had stomach or throat or gland cancer. Or diabetes. Or lupus. She had not thought of conception immediately because she took her birth control every day at 7:15 a.m., a time she remembered very clearly, because it was the hour and minute the school bus used to pick her up on the dry road in front of her mother's house.

She flashed to the literature: *Even with perfect use, hormonal birth control still presents some risk: the only fail-safe method to prevent unplanned pregnancy is abstinence.*

The look on her boyfriend's face told her he did not agree that being with child was a better option than illness. This was another time where she practiced deep breathing.

She was scared, but he was angry.

When they had met, they had been at a birthday party for one of their mutual friends in a stuffy apartment, home to several cats that she never saw but whose fur clouded the air. After the cake, people crowded onto the small balcony to smoke cigarettes and pot and brush their arms against one another. They had liked each other then, meeting the next day for breakfast and drinking mimosas with their waffles to soften last night's hangovers and laughing loud enough for the other people in the diner to turn. At his apartment, the one they now shared, he'd taken off her clothes slowly, in the full light of day.

And now, so quickly, her body had turned into a wedge.

She saw how he was sure that she was ruining his last year of school, maybe his life. How unprepared for any kind of consequences he was. How he could not believe this was happening to him.

The apartment was a duplex that had been quartered, and she had moved in with him at the end of the last school year because she was there all the time anyway and his roommate was moving out. The unit was old, but in a charming way, in a half-restored building that had a dirt yard in the back, pitted and packed hard from some past occupant's dogs. There was a pile of dusty bricks from a demolished chimney scattered in one corner near the chain-link fence. The summer she had moved in, Jenny had dug the yard and arranged the bricks until she made a terrace of red. By the time autumn came, they had a perfect spot to put a fire pit, and they sat outside burning leaves and drinking whiskey from the bottle. There were a few stubborn patches of grass that had responded to her watering can and shrubs she had pruned to look a little more intentional. They hosted one early autumn party where even when the breeze became cool, no one wanted go inside.

A baby was not in her plans, then. She still punished him for a few days, because it hurt her, the way he reacted. She let him go sleepless, let him call his friends in a panic, let him think that she would turn two blue lines into a child that would bind them forever, like magic.

The power of it was intoxicating. She could change everything.

Later, when she finally told him she really had no intention of going through with the pregnancy, he came to the clinic with her and held her hand, and he did not blanch, or at least he did not show it. After, he had given her his coat when she could not zip her pants from the swelling. She had been surprised that her middle was bigger coming out than going in.

When nine months had passed, though, she felt a panic. She felt an emptiness in a deep part of her, like an abandoned wasp's nest, delicate paper curled around nothing. She held her belly sometimes, and she was constantly at her breasts, checking for tenderness. She monitored her cycle, even though it had always behaved evenly. Sometimes she was sure she felt the same catch in her insides, or she smelled something so strongly she believed it was happening again.

He did not understand her sadness, when she would have been full term. It was harder to remember, she supposed, if it was not taking place in your own body, but for all the big deals men made about their sperm and their dicks, she thought he could have at least tried to think about how it might feel, months later, when something was supposed to happen, but did not, and she could neither talk to him about it nor forgive him.

When they graduated, and she got her job at the law firm, she waited for two pay cycles, and then she rented her own apartment. It was almost amusing how hurt he was. After his protests about what it would have meant to have a child together, when she told him she was leaving, he looked like he had been punched, and stood half collapsed on the red brick cradling his own gut.

And then she met Brian, and with Brian, her world orbited on a different axis. The red patio was a long time ago. Once or twice she had talked to her old boyfriend, but now it had been so long that even thinking about the hardest thing that had happened to them did not make her feel much of anything. The last time she saw him, he was passing the window of a coffee shop where she was meeting a co-worker, and she simply let him go by. It was strange to think she could go from sleeping with someone every night to not even knowing what part of town he lived in, or if he even still lived in town.

* * *

A few times after the kids had been put to bed, and she had gotten the call from Brian, she thought about dialing the digits on Gary's old card to see if her husband was really there, splayed out on the undersized couch, sleeping toward a hangover, but she never did. She thought, *Maybe his number has changed, maybe he would not tell me anyway, maybe it's better if I just trust my husband*, even though she was not sure if she did trust her husband. It was hard to tell if she was noticing something or if it was just that being with children—people who were not that great at using words yet—made her pay too much attention to every small signal, like pooping or a poor appetite or mussed hair.

For their part, the children did not seem to care. When he came home, they rushed him, toddled towards his legs and added greasy finger marks to the creases around the knees of his suit pants. When he did not come home, they shrugged, ate their macaroni and cheese and begged for a movie, which she indulged. She had not grown up with so much television—she had chores. She also had not grown up with a father in the house, but it was different knowing that he was gone for good. When she was young, Jenny and her mother would sit at the table and giggle and chat, and when she was honest, she remembered that they ate a lot of beans, and it had been a long time since she had put a dipper into a bag of bulk pintos to make a meal. She remembered how they would laugh about their farts, and how it was not until Jenny got to college that she understood that not everyone had grown up this way. In fact, few of the people that she met in school had any idea how to cook, even functionally, or how to be poor and happy at the same time.

There were waves, she supposed. He came home, he did not. She was sad, she was not. The children bothered her, they did not.

She did not have many friends left who were still childless, and even fewer who were still single, but when one of them called, she had found herself going on long diatribes about potty training or when to switch to solids and complaining that her nipples hurt. There would be silence on the other end of the line, or distraction—more than once she was sure she had been put on mute while someone vacuumed or ground coffee.

When she was first pregnant with Stella, and also when Connor had been young, she cooked constantly, but now she never wanted to cook. Sometimes she would organize vegetables and cheese on a tray, and she was the first to admit that while it looked nice, it was not exactly dinner. She could not tell if it was because Brian did not come home that she had lost her motivation, or if it was because she had lost her motivation that he did not come home. She knew that it only took a few times of laying out a perfect roast and carving it herself while the children demanded chicken nuggets to stop putting in the effort.

* * *

When Brian's promotion came through, her heart jumped for a moment—maybe he really had been working late all those nights. Maybe he had been squirreling away extra hours saved from not commuting and putting them towards reports and finishing his email. She called a sitter and dressed a chicken to roast. She opened a bottle of good wine and wiggled into a pair of pantyhose, and she stood in the full-length mirror, her legs skimmed in black nylon as she pulled a dress over her head. She still looked good, she thought, and stepped into the pair of heels Brian had bought her many years ago. The last time she had taken them to a cobbler, he had told her that he remembered the shoes, and that it would be the final time he could do anything with them. She had been having them resoled, re-heeled, and generally refurbished for years. The shoes were gray suede with a stacked heel and a square toe. They were less in fashion than when Brian had first gotten them for her, but the arch was still shaped perfectly, and they brought her to a height she liked, and she loved the clack of them against their tiles.

The day of the promotion, when he called her, and after she had said her congratulations, she added, *Can you please come straight home after work,* and he did, rolling up the drive just after six, as the chicken finished to a perfect brown as she tossed lemon onto an arugula salad.

He kissed her on the cheek, but if he noticed the shoes—the first gift he had ever gotten for her—he did not say anything. He asked after the children and told her that the kitchen smelled good, that she smelled good. He looked tired, not excited, and she poured him a glass of wine.

"Sit down," she said, and took his laptop bag from his shoulder.

Brian climbed onto one of the bar stools at their eat-in and sipped his Pinot. Jenny swirled her wine in her glass and took a big gulp, congratulating him again.

He said that it was going to be different, and she said that she was proud of him and topped off her glass. She had on an apron over her dress, and she was stirring water and flour in a ramekin so she could make gravy.

"The travel," he said. "I hope that's not too hard for us."

She heard the hesitation in his voice, and she wanted to say it might be easier on her, since she would not be using up so much of her time hoping. She kept mixing the flour and the water and then stirred it into the pan drippings, attacking the lumps with her fork and turning down the heat.

They talked about the trips, domestic and international, and Jenny understood she'd underestimated it. Already, he had a new language, pretty words like Benalux, EMEA, and the harder sounding APAC. Later, she had looked these up and realized they were acronyms: Belgium, the Netherlands and Luxembourg; Europe, Middle East, Africa; Asia Pacific.

He drained his wine and lifted the bottle for another glass, but it too was empty. "More?" he said, shaking the bottle. Jenny nodded yes, and he went to the rack, made a selection, then loosed the cork.

She poured the gravy into a small serving dish, and she pushed the chicken toward him. He sharpened a knife and sectioned the meat expertly, breast for her, a thigh and a wing for him. He told her he loved the salad. She said, *Oh good*, but she had already known he would like it, because it was a popular side at one of the restaurants they used to go to, and he had always eaten all of it. She had found the recipe online.

They sat next to each other at the counter. Jenny wondered why she had not set the table, but she had not, so she got up to dim the lights in the kitchen. At least the dishes would not be shining so hard in the sink. She felt silly in her dress. Brian was still in his button-down shirt from work and trousers, but crushed from the day. His forehead was greasy. She hoisted herself back onto the stool and put her napkin in her lap. Less light helped.

The room was silent other than the sounds of their cutlery on the white stoneware. She thought of saying something, like asking how much the pay raise was or inquiring after Gary, but she kept her mouth busy chewing. She thought of the last time they had sex and ticked off the days in her head. It was after Connor's final day of soccer, forty-eight days gone, if she was adding correctly. She startled some at this, and her fork clattered onto the granite countertop.

"What?" Brian asked. He looked tired.

"Nothing," she said. The band of her pantyhose was cutting in to her belly.

When she had worked as an accountant at the law firm, she had been very young, she realized. Sometimes she did long hours, but mostly, she focused on her tasks and tried to get out early. The fresh JD's who were trying to make partner sat at their desks to be seen—they could just as easily do all that reading at home—and she glided past them, in the same gray suede shoes, and went off to a happy hour, where she would walk into some low-lit bar, shake the snow off her coat, and feel every eye on her. Ignoring the old men nursing their whiskeys and the law grads, who were not going to make partner if they insisted on leaving the office early, she would beeline for Brian, his hair always sticking up a little, his smile bright and wide. Then, she would scoot into a booth next to him, and say, *Hey, darlin'*, clink a glass with whichever friend he had brought along and slide into another long night in what was a series of long nights back when she could not believe the luck of her life.

Chapter Twenty-Eight
Melanie
Winter, 2007

A few months before Alex in San Antonio and Brian in Chicago, Melanie had left the man she was seeing. Josh was a lot like her, and she liked the long afternoons they spent together, and she liked when the daylight drifted into dark and they cooked together, boiling down bones for stock or waiting for bread to slowly rise.

They had been talking of moving in, getting him out of his cramped apartment and into her townhouse, where they could split the mortgage. He asked her if she might travel less, and she said she didn't think so. He asked her if she wanted children, and she said again that she didn't think so. Sometimes he had a puzzled look, and she would ask him what he was thinking about. *You,* he would say, and she would frown, not sure what was so confusing.

Also, her mother's voice, in their old gray building, making dinners with Irene and sneaking puffs of her cigarettes, echoed. *Wait to marry,* they had always said, though Melanie felt like she had been smart about not getting tied down too young, and marriage was not top on her list of life goals.

One night, it was late, and Josh was suddenly angry with her. He was watching a movie and she was on her laptop.

"Stop with your email," he had said.

"It's just work," she had replied, though she did not have that much to do. She was only organizing things into folders, but she did not like hearing what sounded like a command from him, when she was only trying to put some order to her inbox. He said that she was too serious about her job, and she felt a rage come up in her that she had not expected.

"Who?" she had said. "Who will take me seriously if I don't take myself seriously?"

"Is that your goal?" he had asked. "I think people take you pretty seriously."

He did not know what it meant, she thought, to self-sustain. He did not know the power of it.

She thought of her father's home, the gleaming pool, the polished floors. She thought of the women who filtered in and out around him, lipsticks and crumpled tissues left behind for Melanie to find like the offerings of tide pools. A single black stocking. A dropped earring. If she collected everything she could find and arranged them neatly against the cool tiles around the pool, she could not make a picture of one single woman. Maybe her father was chasing her mother, in his way, and it was her Melanie wanted to be able to build out of the debris. Her mother was at the apartment, always at the apartment, and her mother was not waiting for her father to come back. She thought of a shoe she had found once at his place that could have belonged to Irene, strappy with a stacked heel, and a napkin with her oxblood shade of lipstick on it.

The morning after the fight, Melanie had felt wetness on her palms, but her hands smelled of sweat, not chlorine. Josh was there, in her bed, lightly snoring. He was an okay guy, she thought, but she knew already she would wake him with coffee and ask him to come downstairs, and she would tell him that she thought they should wait—*wait*—for him to move in, because she was not ready. He would ask her why the sudden change, and she would not be able to tell him that it was not sudden, it was cumulative. There were many relationships that could take these half steps forward and full steps back and still get somewhere, but she was increasingly sure theirs was not one of them. Movers would never come for his things, and she would never clean out part of the closet for him in her condo. Josh would stay in his little apartment, doing whatever it was he did there, and staying static for Melanie. She had not spoken to him. Neither of them had tried to get in touch.

It had been Josh's number she had left for Brian to call after she had spent the night with him in Chicago, because she had thought it was funny, if mean. She remembered Brian's trendy, too-stylish glasses that he must not have been used to yet, because he had a habit of adjusting and readjusting them, like he was trying to find the clearest, most exact place to look through. She remembered how she had snuck out while his face was smashed against the radiantly white sheets.

* * *

She was not sure she missed any of them, her father or Alex or Brian or Josh, but she wished she was at her mother's apartment and that they could meet Irene down at the pool. Even though years had passed, when they met in warm weather, they still wore their bathing suits, though the suits had gotten much more modest. They would open a bottle of wine, even though it was against the rules, and she would lie out on a chair between them.

The late spring air would be cool still in Colorado, but the pool was always filled by May, even if it was not warm enough to swim. Melanie thought if she stayed still enough, positioned perfectly in a patch of light sun, she could stay out without a cover-up or a towel, under the heat of the least distant star.

Chapter Twenty-Nine

Irene

Winter, 1974

It must have been the same fear she had now that had pushed her own mother to leave. She'd been told it happened quietly and without warning, her mother heading out for work one day and never coming home. Irene was not sure she had any true memories of the woman, only scraps and fragments she had pieced together from a handful of ragged photographs. There was a rumor once in a while, like that her mother had gone back to her people in Kansas, and Irene thought of her pointing her empty, rusted car east on interstate 70, gunning through the flatlands of the plains until she reached her other family's door.

Her father had done his best, she was sure. Her mother, too. She understood her mother more, the closer and closer she got to becoming a mother herself. People said they could not imagine how a woman could take off like that, but for the first time in her life, Irene could feel for her, finally. Maybe her mother had felt as alone with her father as she was feeling without Sammy. Maybe her mother saw her whole life about to unfold, but then there was a catch at her belly, the quickening. Maybe she felt alone, and then felt alone with her husband, who she would have married in haste.

Irene's mother had come to Colorado with some friends, headed towards the promise of the mountains. Her father had told her this. They had planned to find a rental in the Rockies and learn to ski; they would take odd jobs and double or triple bunk to make ends meet. It was unusual for a group of girls, but there were six of them, a family of sorts, all strays in one way or another. Her mother never made it to the slopes, and she wondered if her mother had ever really loved her father, or if she was simply lured when she was out on the road by the steadiness of a man with a job, when maybe her own money, meant to last through the winter, might have already almost run out. Maybe her mother saw in her father the kindness Irene knew he held. Maybe her mother had held onto it just as long as she could.

Chapter Thirty
Melanie

Summer, 1988

Her father's pool, the smell of chlorine and juniper, the lipsticks on his bathroom counter.

Her mother, searing a roast and drinking wine with Irene.

Her mother had been left, but she seemed the happier one. Melanie thought this was another thing people did not understand. When one person goes, even willingly, they give up everything, and they lose their rights to the life they had been working at. When someone is left, there is the shock of it, the feelings of betrayal, but they get to keep hold. They get to be wronged. Her mother got Melanie, and her father got his bankbook, but it was her mother who really got her freedom. Her mother's days were not so different with Melanie's father than without him, but there was less worry, about where he was or when he would return, so when her mother was at home now, she was peaceful. She was waiting for nothing, for no one. Irene would swing by and they would sit on the balcony and do one another's toenails in sparkling colors, the acetone polish remover wafting around them. Irene smoked furiously even though the labels on the polish bottles clearly cautioned against this, and they cackled at each other's jokes and spoke in an innuendo so unsubtle Melanie understood it even when she was young. She missed her father, but if it came to having someone around, she would pick Irene, who was more like her.

Chapter Thirty-One
Brian

Spring, 2007

Brian came home from work, and nothing much had changed since that morning. After Chicago, he would be home for a week, at least, so he had been heading to the office every day to get some quiet. His daughter was twirling in a tutu in the living room where his son was watching television. Neither looked up at the sound of the latch in the door, nor at the sound of Brian shuffling his things into the closet, just as they had not noticed when he had left, when he did this in the opposite order. He was both a little hurt that they did not notice him and relieved that he did not have to talk to them yet. He made sure his jacket was hanging properly, and then he continued on. It was Wednesday, and when he was not traveling, he was increasingly less and less glad for the middle point of the workweek, getting closer to the weekends, which dragged on and in which he found himself scrolling through his BlackBerry and thinking about the office. He checked the device while he was still in the hallway, even though he had just checked it when he had gotten out of the car, but there was nothing.

In the kitchen, Jenny was deciding what to cook for dinner, and she was standing in a way that terrified him, with her hand cradling her belly—when she was pregnant with their children she was always in this posture, and he had come to fear it.

"Jenny," he said, maybe a little sharply, and she looked up from her cookbook. When she turned a little toward him, he could see in the other hand a glass of wine—a good sign for baby watch, a bad sign if he wanted to get laid later—and he thought that perhaps it was just the angle; perhaps she was not doing the belly cradle at all.

"Hi," he said. "I'm home."

"Hi," she said. "Chicken or pork, do you think?" She swirled the wine and tipped her face into the stemware. The wine looked cool and golden, suspended in the crystal.

"Chicken," he said. "Just that and a salad is okay for me."

"The kids won't eat salad," she said.

"I'll make salads for us then," he said. He was still not sure about her right hand—it was lingering just at the top of her pants. *Maybe she does not know yet*, he worried, *but the hand knows.*

He loved his children. He reminded himself of this frequently, when he was frustrated at them, or frustrated at his wife, whom he thought should go back to work. Their children were beautiful, even he could admit this. Like most children they did strange and wonderful things and expressed themselves in a way that Brian found pure, but he did not find them satisfying, intellectually, and he did not quite understand how Jenny could either.

"What if I just made some pasta for all of us?" she said. "I'll put broccoli in it for you, and they can pick it out."

"Make whatever they want. It's fine," Brian said. "Is there more wine?"

She nodded, and he was relieved when she flipped the cookbook closed and poured for him, tipping out the last drops. He was more comfortable when her hand got busy—she was rummaging for pans and chopping vegetables. She drained her glass and suggested they open another bottle. He looked at her closely, for signs of the pregnancy glow.

When Jenny was pregnant, she always said her fingers were swollen and took off her rings, but when Brian looked, the rings were on. Her fingers were circled in silver and in their platinum marriage band. He went to the pantry and found a decent red, took it back to the kitchen, and removed the cork.

After their son Connor was a year old, Brian had gotten snipped, but she could still get pregnant from some other man, and he had heard of vasectomies reversing. Connor was four now, just starting to get fun.

The vasectomy had not been one of Brian's best moments. There had been a clinic on the lowest floor of his office building, and he had made the appointment for the end of the day, and taken the stairs down so no one from work would see him. He was on his way home in forty minutes; he felt very efficient.

There was little pain, at first. The after-care instructions specified he should ice his groin, and by the time he arrived home and the local had worn off, this seemed like a very good idea. He took a magazine and a cold pack that he had sneaked out of the freezer to the master bath and lay down on the plush rug. He set his watch timer. He realized, there on the bathroom floor, that he would need to wear the dressing to bed. He realized this would go on for several days. It was not like he and his wife had sex every night, but they were still intimate, even with two children down the hall.

The situation suddenly seemed very difficult. Brian understood he could not hide from her through the entire weekend, and he wished he had done this when he was out of town or when Jenny and the children were visiting her mother. He thought for what seemed like a long time, and he wondered if he should just get up, but that seemed impossible. His BlackBerry was still in his pants' pocket, and so he called the home phone. When she answered, she sounded puzzled; she would have seen his name on the caller ID. *Please come upstairs*, he said.

When Jenny opened the door, she gasped. *What the fuck?* He understood how it must have looked to her, his clothes in a pile and a wound on his crotch, so Brian told her about the clinic and how he had thought this would be something that he could have taken care of, without bothering her, but now he realized there was a little more work involved than what he had anticipated.

"Can you bring me a glass of water?" he had asked her.

"You want me to bring you water," she had said.

"Cold water."

"Say please," she had said, and Brian knew that she was very angry. He accepted this.

"Please."

He had been relieved when she turned from the bathroom and he heard her padding down the stairs. The pain was picking up. His eyes were closed. It had been such a small incision, and they had shown him what they had done—two tiny pieces of his vas deferens on the stainless steel, he'd not known the name, but they told him, and it looked like bits of overcooked macaroni. They also told him they had put titanium pins in to close the holes, and in a panic he asked if he would now set off airport metal detectors. The nurse said that he had no idea, since she never flew and offered Brian a Valium. They had not wanted him to come on his own, but he had told them he just lived around the corner, and he had paid cash so they had worked with him.

Jenny had come back, and he heard ice clinking. He was grateful for even the thought of coolness. Maybe she would get him an aspirin, he hoped. She was talking, but he could not really hear her, even though her voice was raised. The ice rattled in the glass, and he wished she would lay on the floor with him, her head in the crook of his arm like they did at night, her breath hot on his neck.

When he blinked his eyes open into the light, Jenny was above him with the glass, and the water poured across his face. For a moment he thought he might cry, but the cold was so perfect. It calmed him.

* * *

When Brian was young, he had been a very average child, and an only child. He was not really sure why his parents never had another baby, and he could not say that he had ever wished for a sibling or that the topic had ever even come up. Some of his friends at school had brothers and sisters, and they mostly seemed annoying. They seemed like they made things crowded.

Brian's parents had not gone to college, and they were very keen on him having an education. He could say that if he had done one good, sacrificial thing in his life, it was putting himself through university. His family did not have money—his dad was a small-town cop and his mother a homemaker—and he was not really ambitious or bright enough to go after scholarships, so he worked full time and lived in a ratty studio apartment in a part of town that he was not sure his class-mates even knew existed.

Once when he came home, there was blood on the stairs of his building's entryway, and when he told the building manager, the building manager said that he would get it cleaned up. Brian had said then that while he believed cleaning up the blood would be helpful, the building manager should consider their conversation to be Brian's notice that he would be moving out.

"I need it in writing," the building manager had said.

"Okay, I'll get it to you tomorrow," Brian had said. He was very tired. He had classes during the day and after that he worked in the stock-room of a grocery store, breaking down pallet after pallet of trucked in cereal and watermelons and mustard jars. The job was not as interesting as working at a coffee shop or a club, but it was union. The extra fifty cents after nine p.m. and on Sundays made a difference.

The building manager thought for a second, and then he asked Brian if he would stay if the rent was lowered.

"By how much?" he had asked.

"How about fifty bucks?" He was a direct man, and Brian had no complaints about him. The building was horrible, but he did not actually think it was the manager's fault.

"Okay," Brian had said. Fifty dollars was more than half a shift.

They shook on it, and Brian stayed.

That night in his apartment, he made sure that the dead bolt was engaged. He checked it several times. He was not sure whose blood had been on the building steps, and he reminded himself that it did not necessarily mean violence—maybe someone had sneezed and busted a capillary of terrific size. Maybe it was not even from a person. His grandmother, before she died, would sometimes get a jug of pork blood from the butcher's and cook it down to make the black pudding her own grandmother had made. He could just as easily imagine an old woman with a recipe in her head tripping up the stairs and creating a spill similar to someone getting their face smashed in, so he tried to focus on this. He remembered that he had not really liked the pudding, but he had not disliked it either. He was not sure that he had ever really put it all together; if he had, he was sure as a child he would not have touched it.

That night was a very long night. He was not a fearful person by nature, but there were sounds in the apartment that made him jittery and restless. He wondered why the building manager had not heard anything or noticed anything on the steps until late at night when Brian came home. He wondered if he had just missed whatever had happened, and even if it was just a grandmother stumbling on the stairs, shouldn't someone have come to help her?

Sometimes Brian was depressed by living alone. He thought if he fell in the shower and hit his head, his brains dashed into the tub with the soap and the water, the first people to notice him missing would be work, and the second maybe one of his professors who actually took roll. But they would not do anything—his job would give him a pink slip for a no call, no show, and his professors would scratch him from the class list. He had no friends who would report his absence, and while his mother would be upset if he did not call her from a payphone on Sunday, like he almost always did, the almost meant he was not regular enough that she would send some kind of squad. She would only keep close to the phone until Monday and have hope for the next weekend, Brian immobile in the tub, until the water ran cold.

In the morning, he could not exactly say that he was grateful to be alive, but he was relieved. His dreams had been restless, and his sheets were wadded up around him. He thought of the fifty dollars.

While there continued to be loud noises late at night or early in the morning, Brian resolved to stay in the apartment until he graduated. On that day, his parents sat in the stands of the school gymnasium, and he could have sworn that when his name was called, he heard them clapping through all the other chatter and applause, and for just a minute it was only the three of them, swelling with pride, for him.

* * *

The pasta Jenny was making turned out perfect, how he liked it, just a little al dente. He made his salad and watched his children pick around their vegetables. He felt his son and daughter were becoming stranger as they got older. They were either oblivious or hyperaware. He did not remember being like them. At his parents' table, he would not have been allowed to make a pile on his plate of the things he did not like. He would have been told to eat it. It puzzled him how Jenny indulged them. He did not think this was the best way.

Frequently, he thought back to what life had been like for them in their downtown condo, when he walked to work and Jenny boarded the train, her pretty shoes clicking down the pavement. He liked the shine of her hair and the way her skirts fell across her ass—her ass was still lovely; he was happy to have a wife who had stayed pretty—and he would watch her walking until she turned the corner, and he would think how much he loved her and loved their life. He would think that he could not imagine waking up next to anyone but her, the mole on her cheek, the sour of her breath when she had been drinking wine all night.

In those days, when he would come home early from work, he would ramble through the condo and wonder when Jenny would get in. He would listen for the train and miss her. He would make sure there were fresh ice and limes. Now, whether he was early or late, when he came home from traveling or when he was leaving, she was always there, with Stella and Connor. Sometimes when he swung his car around the last corner, he would hope that they were all out on an errand, but they never were. He would turn the key in the lock, hang up his coat, and disappear into the house to join them.

This was why sometimes he didn't come home at all. He told Jenny he was staying with Barry, an old friend from their past, but usually he just worked very late and then slept in his office. He had an inflatable bed, and he got up early and went to the building's gym and then showered. He needed the space. Sleeping in the office reminded him of his old college apartment, the feeling of always being alert, and this helped him at work, helped him stay on an edge.

Those years ago, he had his reasons for wanting to get the vasectomy on his own. He had been scared it would open up a conversation about a third child. He was scared Jenny would simply not like the idea. He was scared that at some point in the future, he and Jenny would divorce, and he would meet another woman who wanted children of their own, and if he had not already had the procedure done, he would give in to her.

If he could do it over again, Brian wanted something different. He wanted to vacation in places where there was no kiddie pool reeking of pee and to live in a home that was not a tripping hazard from all of the plastic and plush toys scattered through the halls. He wanted to work late and call his wife from the office and suggest she get off the train a stop early and meet him for a drink.

He wanted to see her walk into a downtown bar, in the deep of winter, steam coming off her hair, shaking snow from her coat, and watch every other man in the place look at the woman who had just rattled the door, the woman making a beeline for him, just like Jenny had, when they were new.

Chapter Thirty-Two
Melanie
Summer, 2007

I t was June, and the summer had just started to open while Melanie typed in her office—she thought she felt it move, even, the almost imperceptible angling of the earth a smidge closer to the sun. Her budget email had finally arrived, and she had decided not to fight it, initialing each line-itemed reduction and returning the scan to her boss's administrative assistant with no additional comments.

* * *

Alex had stopped by her office, but she had waved him away. Brian, from Chicago, had left her a message on her work line. She did not remember telling him where she was employed, but she figured he must have tried her ex-boyfriend Josh's number first, as that was the number she had given him, and she wondered why he had called now. It had been three months. Maybe she had told him where she worked, or maybe Josh had said to try the office. *Because she's always there*, he might have said. She had deleted the message and kept typing.

Her mother called on her lunch break and asked if Melanie wanted to come to dinner with her and Irene, and she had told her that sounded nice. They were going to make pasta, so her mother was checking to see if Melanie was dieting.

"I'm not going to change dinner," she said, "but if you are doing that low-carb thing you might want to bring something for yourself."

"As long as there's wine, I'm okay," Melanie said, and she could feel her mother nodding.

"Between you and Irene, I think I should invest in a vineyard," her mother said.

Melanie smiled. "You should," she said. "I'll go in thirds with you two. We can call it *Triple Threat*."

"I know this is what you do, honey, but the name needs a little work."

"Brands are not really what I do, Mom," she said. "It was a joke."

At her desk, her report on the industrial marketplace was starting to really take shape. The conversations in Cincinnati had been helpful, giving her insights that she had not found through Internet research and by reading trade journals, and she had actually had a lovely time with a group of ageing rust-belters who liked cheap whiskey and classic rock. The report had some pretty graphs that she had built herself from different data points and were arranged in the document to break up the longer stretches of text. Each one was labeled and then indexed. The report was getting close to thirty pages. She was sure after she turned it in she would hear nothing, or next to nothing, and her hours of work would sit unreviewed on her boss's desk, and the company would expand or not expand, and her charts would make no difference, though like her budget, she had decided not to care.

In the bottom left hand of her screen, her instant message was flashing, Alex again.

Coffee?

No thanks, she wrote. *But thanks.*

I want to see you.

She ignored this and logged out. She was tired. She was tired of work, and tired of negotiating, though she did want a coffee. She was tired of men who were married talking to her, though she admitted that she talked back. Stopping would be easy. The easiest thing. *Think of your mother*, she thought. *Think of what your dad did to her.*

The report was in its final stages. She sent it to the printer and then waited in the hall as the pages spooled out, crisp ink on the white paper.

* * *

The last time she had seen her father, it had not gone well. There was more distance between them than ever, now that she was grown up, now that there was no custody agreement. He still had the house with the pool, and he still had rounds of women who came by, but the house was sadder than ever, with dated carpeting and cracked concrete on the walkway. Now, he did not even try to hide his girls—his word—he either introduced them or told them to leave. The women were sadder too, older, more desperate, and less frequent. The house was like a monument erected to something important that had then been forgotten, the base of it getting rough and crumbly, and the curb overgrown with dry weeds.

Once on a Tuesday, Melanie had come by after work, still in her business casual, her armpits a little damp and her face greasy from the day. Her father embraced her, lightly, the way a certain kind of co-worker might. He smelled like he had been drinking, and the wine spills in the kitchen proved it. She got some spray and a rag and went to work on his granite.

"Leave it for the cleaning lady," he said.

"It will soak in and stain and then you'll be pissed about it," Melanie said.

"Fine," he said.

They ordered dinner, Thai takeout, and Melanie picked through her rice as her father set to demolishing his noodles. He did not look good. His face was getting a deep drinker's cast and his hair was nearly gone, though he seemed to be refusing to simply shave his head and accept it. There were some smooth spots and some tufts. He would be fifty-five this year—not really old yet, but past the point of pretending it was not happening.

He wanted to know what she was up to, so she filled him in on the changes at work, how the acquisition required some adjusting. She told him she was traveling more, for now, and she told him that she sort of hated her job, but that it was also okay, she was an adult now, with a mortgage, just like everyone else.

"How's your mother?" he said, with his mouth mostly full.

Melanie shrugged. "She's the same. You could call her."

Finishing chewing his bite, he swallowed. "There's a lot you don't know, Mel," he said.

She thought his face looked a little soft, and his eyes, even if droopy from wine, alert, and she was not sure if she should push him, saying *Like what?*, or *There's a lot I do know*, or *I'm sure Mom already told me whatever you think you have*, but then she did not say anything. Her father went back to his noodles, she back to her rice. *Like what?*, she wondered, but it did not matter. His home phone had rung at least four separate times, and he finally answered it.

"Sure," he said into the handset. "Whenever you want. Yep, she's on her way out."

It was hard for her now, in her thirties, to remember how they had been, the three of them, in the house on the street flanked by trees, her mother's flowers ringing the lawn and her mother's cooking making the kitchen smell warm and perfect. When her parents met, he must have been different, he must have been kinder and he must have made her mother feel something she could not get anywhere else. Where was that now, she wondered? She could not find the part of him that her mother had fallen in love with, even as a shadow.

* * *

Though the summer had just begun, there was fire across the Colorado Front Range. Melanie fortified herself by drinking water, by giving her tiny yard an extra shot with the sprinklers. She was not in any immediate danger, but the smoke streaked the sky a sinister gray-brown and through the particulate of charred tree and deer and incinerated homes, the sunsets blazed hot orange and pink.

At the office, her co-workers were agitated. Her place was in central Denver, edged by pavement, a brick warehouse, and another row of townhouses, which were mostly unsold and empty. There was little to burn besides dirty glass and chipped asphalt, so she was safe, even if the municipal trees were drooping. Her neighborhood was still coated in spring pollen because they had mostly had dry storms where the wind picked up and hurled gravel, while the clouds cracked with lightning. The dry air sizzled the rain before it reached ground.

* * *

Once when she was a child, Melanie went with her parents to watch the Fourth of July display at the park. Usually the celebration fell during the week of her birthday, but even when there was no ban, her mother would not allow fireworks in the yard in summertime. Still, she and her father would drive the seventy-five miles to the Wyoming border where he would purchase shrink-wrapped flats that he stashed in the garage until the New Year, when he would light them off over the brittle snow, the icicles on the eaves shining from pyrotechnics while Melanie spelled out her name with a sparkler.

They took a cooler, chilled white wine for her mother and beer for her father, a carafe of lemonade for Melanie. They spread a blanket under an elm tree, and her mother ran her finger down Melanie's cheek to check she was properly greased, even if the light was fading. Her mother was fair and demanded everyone wear sunscreen long before it was popular. They had some sandwiches and peanuts. A band played in the gazebo, the gold horns reflecting the whitewashed boards. The night fell fast under the shadow of the Rockies, the sun disappearing more quickly than it did in the low country, obscured by the pearl of mountaintop.

When the dark deepened, the band packed up their instruments and the first tracers of saltpeter and sulfur appeared, ascending toward the moon, bursting into aluminum white and lithium red, like glass broken in a sunny room. Melanie loved the splash of metallic across the sky and she loved the speed of sound—slower, yes, than light, but as the crystalline bloom fizzled, the sonic leftovers punctuated the fading glow, and she felt it in her core.

When she was struck by a piece of debris that came hurtling towards her, it hit her chest, and even in the dim she could see it was black and crumbly at the edges, to the touch still a little warm. She brushed her shirt in surprise. She thought the firework would disintegrate—it was only cardboard. She liked this bit that had slipped through, and she saved it in her pocket.

The night air was warm and sometimes just in advance of the sound of an explosion, she could see her parents' faces, fully illuminated. They were smiling as they held hands on the blanket, the crumpled beer cans next to her father flashing. The sky above them smoked. Melanie saw a boy from her school a few blankets over, looking at her, but she ignored him. When the last of the rockets burst, her mother packed the remains of their picnic and the air was heavy. They folded the blanket into a neat square and her father dumped the melting ice from the cooler onto the grass. Melanie trailed them to the car, her ears still ringing. At home, when she closed her eyes, she held the piece of cardboard between her fingers and the afterimages were bright behind her lids.

* * *

Everyone at work kept the news open in their browser tabs, and a few, at certain developments, grabbed their lunch bags and lit out for home in the suburbs. They received all-company emails from their corporate parent in Chicago about out-of-state fire crews who had been flown in from Idaho, Kansas, and Utah. Then the power went out, and the lights across the entire office park were gone, the substation either zapped from the heat or was consumed. They all knew it was only a matter of time before the grid was rerouted, but they packed their things anyway, sliding laptops into slim shoulder bags and rubber-banding file folders they knew they would not look at but took anyway to make their desks appear clear. The entrance to the highway was clogged with everyone else who had the same idea, but when Melanie came slowly around the last little curve before her exit, she was shocked at the quantity of smoke billowing from the foothills.

At home her yard was dry again, but the electricity was functioning. She charged her computer and set the sprinkler. The news said tens of thousands of people had been evacuated from Colorado Springs, a sprawling, heavily evangelical and military town to the south. Homes had been foamed and pets had been counted. One photo showed a family gathered on the waxed floor of a high school gymnasium, their clothes crumpled and their necks bent in prayer. As she continued to click through the news, she found another version, where the same family were only a few in a larger circle, a hundred butts against the hardwoods, legs crossed, heads tipped so deeply as to touch their chests.

Alex texted her. *Are you okay?*

She did not reply.

She hoped for rain and sat on her patio, pecking away on her laptop, constantly refreshing her browser. The all-company emails increased in frequency, broadcasted from a perch in the Midwest. The charitable foundation committed to a donation of Gatorade and batteries. Someone with enough rank decreed the Denver offices officially closed. IT announced that backup power was on the ready should it be needed, and her battery was already running low again.

When Melanie looked to the sky, there was a hail of ash.

* * *

For years, while her mother had lived in dreary apartments—first in the gray building walking distance from Irene, and then in Irene's building with the aqua walls—her father dated, progressed in his career, and sometimes disappeared for months, only to resurface when one fling or another had ended. All that time, her mother kept her same job at the bank, counting other people's money, helping seniors learn to use debit cards, and explaining the general policy on overdraft charges to those who needed it. Her mother, Melanie knew, was a favorite among the customers, Irene a close second. Her mother was patient with people who came in with a jar full of pennies, rolling them expertly while the line grew; the other tellers said to go use the coin machine at the grocery store. The rolling machine took 10 percent, or roped people in to taking a voucher. Ten percent was a lot, Melanie's mother said, when someone was counting coin. A thousand pennies made only ten dollars.

The little branch her mother worked at had been absorbed by a national chain, and after work, when Melanie came for dinner at the apartment where she had lived between fourteen and eighteen, her mother was telling Irene about how she had not expected television cameras to show up to cover the few fascinatingly disorganized protesters who had been gathering outside on the steps. She was saying that she smiled at them.

She hugged Melanie hello, offered her a glass of wine, and continued saying that she had just wanted to make sure the people protesting knew that she only worked the bank's window. That she did not have a great job, she was just close money. That the big bank had not done anything for her, either.

Melanie sat, Irene squeezed her, and they clinked the rim of their glasses.

What Kathleen had definitely not expected, coming back from her lunch break, was the young woman with gummy braids to scream at her, *How can you work for these animals!*, and the camera to pan awkwardly to Kathleen holding a doggy bag, with the heel of her shoe caught in a crack in the pavement—she had not really been listening until the boom mic was in her face. The camera caught her just as she dropped her leftover lunch, while trying to wedge her foot back into her shoe, and she said, in her broadcast debut:

"What? Do I know you?"

On camera, the woman with the braids approached her. "I said, 'How can you work for these animals?'"

Kathleen, bent towards the sidewalk, her skirt riding up a little, said, "Well, I guess I need a job."

It made the evening news, and they watched it from the kitchen, peering over the half-wall that separated the living room in which the small television was perched on a table that Melanie knew was scratched and battered, though her mother had draped a well-ironed runner over it.

The story led with *Bank Executive tells Protester to Get a Job.*

"I wish there were better work for the kids," Melanie's mother said later, while they had their pasta and more wine. "They aren't wrong to be angry, but what can I do? You're one of the lucky ones, Mel."

Melanie snorted. *Lucky.* "I hope your boss gets the memo that you are now an executive, according to Channel 9. You should put that on your résumé."

"Already did, baby girl. I got the phone turned off because I couldn't stand the ringing," her mother said.

Her mother and Irene cackled, and Irene went to smoke on the patio, and even though Melanie wanted to join her, she did not. When

Irene came back inside, she smelled not just of tobacco but also of the fire from the early summer blazes.

* * *

Finally, the sky did break, with a deluge that soaked the smoldering forests creaking with smoke until mud sluiced down the hillsides and through the suburban alleyways. On the radio, Melanie had heard an interview with evacuees returning to their homes. One family stepped into a foundation of ash and sifted for anything left. They found a chipped ceramic coffee cup, whole in the debris. *Even after the rain, it was still so hot*, the woman said, *I could not hold it in my hands.*

* * *

Her desk was the most constant thing, with the background noise from her co-workers and the heat of the building. As a follow-up to her budget email, she finally got the notice that all of her travel, categorized as nonessential, was suspended, and she sighed, but was happy for a stretch of being at home.

She checked her phone and saw she had four missed calls, *Goddammit, Alex,* she thought, but when she scrolled through the menu, it was Irene. Four messages.

Call me.

Call me back now.

Mel, you need to call.

Fuck!

Irene picked up on the first ring. Her mother had done an errand at lunch, and in the blazing heat of day, had been struck by another woman, driving drunk, driving her son-in-law's car on her own errand. They had both been taken to the hospital.

"I'm on my way," Melanie said.

Irene emphasized that Melanie should be safe, and Melanie said that she would, but Irene made her promise, and so she promised before hanging up and tossing her phone into her bag to run across the parking lot to her car.

She wanted to return to the time when the cardboard had fallen from the sky, just trash really, but felt like a treasure to her, when light shattered against the low clouds and the booms were so loud her ears rang for days. If she closed her eyes, she could feel the night-damp grass prickling through their picnic blanket and even with the breeze, smell the last bit of smoke, curling through the air.

Chapter Thirty-Three
Irene

Winter, 1974

I rene and Kathleen decided to swear, and once they swore, they could never go back on it. When Irene asked—*Would you think of taking the baby?*—she saw Kath startle some, not at the suggestion, she thought, but at one of them having said it out loud. Irene was sure her friend had already been planning the same thing, because as true as sisters bound by blood, they knew each other's minds.

Irene took her hand then. They were at the park after school, and the weather had turned brittle. They both had old but good coats. Even though the child inside of Irene was still very small, she had been feeling warm all of the time, warm like she had never experienced. Thin her whole life, she had always felt chilled, but the new belly wrapped her, and the baby quilted her, and she loved the closeness of the child because it was like being with Sammy again, the tight feeling of two bodies fitting together.

The night of the ice, when Sammy had come to her room while her father was at work, he had told her he wanted to watch his sister Kathleen's basketball game, but Irene had not wanted to go back to the school. Now she wished they would have crouched together on the bleachers and cheered on the girls' teams—she had been afraid, she could admit it now, to meet his mother. She was sure his mother of seven children would see immediately that she was pregnant, even though she was hardly showing, she was sure. She was scared to be out with him, a high school girl with her high school beau, because it felt so common, and she had been common her entire life, until Sammy had changed that. That day he had begged her to come to dinner with his family.

They'll love you. They'll only be irritated I didn't bring you sooner, but she was not ready to take a chance on it, to risk saying the wrong thing or acting the wrong way and him changing toward her. *They aren't like that*, he told her, and now she knew he was right. Sammy's sister had found her, his sister loved her because she loved Sammy.

Irene had thought of keeping the baby, worried on it. When the baby was hot on her at night, she thought of Sammy, how he felt pressed against her, and the last time she saw him, before he cut across the river. If she had been with him, he would not have tested the ice. They would have taken the long way across the bridge. That night, her father had come home early from his shift, and Sammy had hurried, crawling out her bedroom window with his pants only half on, and telling her not to worry.

"It's so cold outside," she had said, and he said he would only walk to the school for Kathleen's basketball game and then get a ride home from there.

She remembered his face as he was trying to buckle his belt while leaning across the windowsill to kiss her.

"Tomorrow," he had said. "I'll find you tomorrow at school."

"I love you," she had whispered, and for that she got his slow, ragged smile. Like her, none of the Henderson kids had worn braces.

"I love you too, Ireney," he had said, and turned his head with a full breath, to take off running in the night, headed for his family, the family who held her now, and she wanting to go with him, but the last glint off his shoes had already disappeared.

By then she had already felt the tension at her belly, and the heart of their child, and she had told him, even though she thought he would be angry, or worse, that he would be as scared as she was.

At first he didn't say much, other than to ask her if she was sure, and she had said that she was very late, and very sure.

He considered this, looked at her. He had looked at her in a way that made everything inside of her well from the bottom of her pelvis to the top of her throat. She would get an abortion if she had to, even if they had to go as far as St. Louis, if it meant keeping him.

He had said that they would figure it out. He had said she should finish school, and then they should get married.

She had wanted to know if he was asking her, and he gave her his craggly smile and said she had to wait until he had a better job.

"I don't care about your job," she had said.

Then he put his hand on her, above her hips, and she could feel the warmth of his fingers there with the warmth of their blooming child. She thought maybe she should ask him to promise—a ring did not matter, only he mattered—but she did not, because she was sure he meant it. He would marry her, and they would raise the baby together.

* * *

When Kathleen asked her about taking the child, it was not that she wanted to give up the baby. She had never wanted to give up the baby. She had wanted a part of Sammy, but the baby would be better off. She did not think she could do it on her own, and she did not think she could have a regular adoption, never seeing her first born again.

"I promise," Irene said.

"I promise," Kathleen said.

Irene remembered how Kath had squeezed her hand, their fingers laced together.

Even before she was late, she had been sure in the pregnancy. Her breakfast would never settle, and her chest was so sore. The smell of her own cigarettes came up hot in her nose, and she had quit even though her father still smoked inside the house. She was not sure if it was better for her to smoke so she could smell his ashtray less or better for her to stay quit, because it was just a little less nauseating. She supposed it did not matter, because she had not lasted long. When she found out about Sammy, the first thing she did was raid her father's pack, like she had done as a child, like she had been doing for years, and sit on the creaky steps of the back porch and burn each one down to the last shred of filter, choking on her own breath, the taste of salt and char at her lips.

She was only a freshman in school. Sammy was not the only person she had been with, but she wished he were. It was his first time, and she wanted to share that with him, this boy who was almost a man—she could see it in the way his shoulders were broadening, hear it on the rough edge of his voice, smell it when he met her after his job at the stockyard where he carted sawdust and straw and kept the floor of the pens clean, while his hands blistered and the muscles on his arm formed a knot; he was so light, like her, but the night he ran from her father, he was heavy enough to shatter the plane of ice. Still, she dreamed of them as a family. Their child, young but strong. Their home, modest but clean. She did not know his sister then, but she knew Kathleen worked in the hospital kitchen and still went to school, and maybe she could put in a word for Irene. In their life, money would always be a little tight, and the edges would never be perfectly smooth, but they would reach to each other in the hard times, and they would feel the other reaching back. They would grow old and stubborn, and the child would help them. On their front porch, with boards missing and beaten by weather and dirt, they would clasp their hands together, remembering what it was like to be young.

* * *

They would have to tell Kathleen's parents, but Kath said they could trust them, plus they needed some help. The guidance counselor, the one who had tried to make Irene leave school, had scared them. Funny, how a simple thing like policy had made it real.

Kathleen's mother suggested her old cousin who lived in Denver. Widowed—*better off,* her mother said, *her husband was never right for her*—and her son was away, in the service.

Kathleen's mother said they would need to help the aunt around the house, because she was old and alone, and that they would need to insist.

Irene saw Kathleen nod because she was used to getting directions from her mother, and Irene nodded because she was not sure what else to do. Kathleen said she did not remember ever meeting Aunt Mae, even after her mother found an old photo.

Aunt Mae had moved to Denver because she hated it in the small towns. She had grown up in the mountains with an outhouse, but it was in the city that she had found her life.

"What else?" Kathleen asked.

Her mother shrugged. "She can tell you, if she wants to. I know she had her baby young, too, though," she said, looking at Irene. Kathleen's mother said Mae had been a teenager, and she only a child when it happened.

The other siblings, they decided they could not tell. They would let them believe what they hoped everyone else would believe—the baby was Kathleen's, and she was mum on the father. It felt like a treacherous secret to keep, keeping part of Sammy away from them, but they agreed it was the best way to keep the child close, and the best for Irene, not yet fifteen.

Irene hoped her friend, her lover's sister, would not feel shame in this, and she wondered about the counselor at school, who had already noticed her, who had already tried to kick her out, and she decided that he would probably forget all about her and just think Kathleen was another wayward girl, if he even heard about her, since she would be graduated by then.

Irene's father, they would not tell. They were not sure how to handle this, but Kathleen's mother said she would think on it. She had known the man since she was in school herself, and she had never liked him. She apologized to Irene for speaking of her family like that but she spoke with such vigor it made both girls wonder if there was history with them. She said it was his meanness that made Irene's mother leave, and Irene blanched, realizing people around her knew more about that time than she did.

"I heard she went back home," Irene said.

Kathleen's mother suggested one of the women Kath worked with at the hospital kitchen—Francine Parker—might know. She and Irene's mother had been friends, a long time ago.

"If you get her drunk, she might tell you," Kathleen's mother said.

Irene was silent. She did not want to ask anyone about her mother. She did not want to get Franny drunk. Her mother knew where she was, so she could have come. Her father had never moved, probably never changed the locks. She wondered if he had ever tried to look for her or if he had pined. What Kathleen's mother said, she knew, was right—he could be mean, mean as a deep cold, mean as a slap, but he was not always that way. She was surprised, sometimes, that he had not found an aunt or a cousin to drop her off with, but maybe there was a limit to one person. Maybe he could not go quite that far. Maybe he kept her, his penance, in the shape of a girl. There were good memories with him, and she wondered if it would make him even meaner, if she kept this from him now.

"I think we have to tell him," she said. "It will be easier for me when I come back."

Kathleen's mother sighed, and she wiped at the table. She nodded and said that it was Irene's choice, that they would support her either way. Irene startled some, realizing that this was what family meant.

* * *

Though most of her morning sickness was gone, when Irene took the steps up her own porch with Kathleen's mother, she thought she would double over. When she turned the knob, the door opened easily. They never locked it. Nothing to lose, less to steal.

Her father was not home yet, so they tidied up and checked the fridge. Kathleen's mother found potatoes in the pantry and said she could make a quick soup with what was there.

"Sometimes a meal makes news easier," she said, and Irene said she thought her father would like that.

"Do you know how to do a biscuit?"

"Not really," Irene said.

Kathleen's mother rolled her eyes, just barely, and asked her to get flour, soda, and salt. First she sniffed at the flour, and then she spooned some out with a teaspoon and checked it. The flour was old, but okay. She chopped up the few wilting vegetables from the fridge and put them in the pot to boil down while she walked Irene though the biscuits. Irene followed her instructions like a prayer, with hope for abundance and good things. When her father got home, she was just sliding the pan out of the oven—perfectly golden, and on her first try—while Kathleen's mother was putting the browned cubes of a cheap cut of beef into her broth and telling Irene that sometime she would show her how to do gravy from pan drippings.

"You're a natural in the kitchen," she said.

When Irene heard her father's voice, there was a clatter, for a second, of the biscuit pan onto the stovetop, and the hiss of steam from the soup.

Her father and Kathleen's mother greeted one another, her father looking like he meant to reach his hand to shake in greeting, but then did not.

Irene felt nervous then, her fingers clammy inside of an oven mitt, her belly turning in a way that made her sure it was the child sending her a message, but she could not decipher if it was *yes* or *no*, or somewhere in between. Her father would be wondering why they were there, why they were cooking. It was Saturday afternoon, but his Friday, and Irene removed the oven mitt and brought him a beer. She asked him if he would wait, just a few more minutes, and his dinner would be ready.

Irene set the small table with their mismatched silverware and chipped bowls, and they all sat with the food steaming in front of them, the quick stew and the fresh biscuits, thick and buttered.

"Do we say Grace in this house?" Kathleen's mother asked.

"We never have, but we could," Irene's father said.

No one said a word, but they all tipped their heads in thanks for a meal and in hope for the old wounds washed clean, and the new ones, so raw they were not even showing yet, to heal without a scar.

Their dinner went slowly—compliments first, followed by silence. It was hard for Irene to say anything. The room felt pressurized, and she could not stop thinking of her bedroom window, the last place where she had seen Sammy alive.

Her father looked like she felt, tired and anxious.

"I'm pregnant, Daddy," she said, even though she had not called him that in years, and he closed his eyes.

He finished swallowing and she could tell he was not sure what to say, and he looked at his bowl, filled with remnants of stew and a shred of biscuit. She could tell he had held at least a small hope that it was going to be a different conversation.

She was glad then that Kathleen's mother was there, glad for whatever history they might have had, and when Kathleen's mother told her to go to her room, she went, as obedient as a girl half her age, her stew only half finished and the biscuit crumbled at the side of her plate. She wondered if this was what it was like to have a mother—someone who knew what to do—and she heard them talking about her in a hushed tone, just out of reach.

It was already planned. At Aunt Mae's, Kathleen would finish the few classes she needed to get her early graduation, and Irene would study at the unwed mother's home. The baby wasn't due until summer, but they would try to stay away from town for a few months after, to let Irene recover and Kathleen adjust.

The voices started to raise. Her father grumbled, and there was the sound of a beer bottle being launched into the bin, glass breaking, and the refrigerator door yanked open and slammed shut as he grabbed another. Kathleen's mother, trying to stay calm, but sounding urgent. *It's better—we're not—goddammit, Don.*

She listened to them argue for a long time. She was not sure what her father wanted, but she could tell he was getting angrier. He kept the low tone that she knew meant he was very upset, and the smoke from cigarette after cigarette wafted into her room. Finally, she opened her bedroom door and went into the living room, deciding that if she was old enough to give birth, she was old enough to talk to her own father.

As she came around the corner, she looked down, avoiding the soft spot underneath the hallway carpet, going toward him where he sat in his chair next to the sofa, where Kathleen's mother perched, leaning toward him.

He opened his arms to her, and she fell to his feet.

* * *

The Florence Crittenton Home said they would help with the paperwork and that Irene could deliver there and see their doctor. They said it was not so irregular to have girls staying at a family residence. They were short on beds, anyway.

When they had talked the whole thing through, before telling her father, Kathleen's mother had shaken her head, and looked down. "You're both so young to have to be working so hard already. I wanted it to be different for you, Kath."

"It's different," she had said. "I'm choosing this."

"I chose it too," her mother had said, her tone getting sharp. "I know what it's like to be young."

Kathleen had stared at the cloth that covered the table. "It's for Sammy."

Kathleen's mother had sighed, and she pulled Kathleen close to her, and Irene saw the hope. The youngest daughter, her tomboy. Kathleen had been the one who might get out. Maybe it would be good for them to be with Aunt Mae. Aunt Mae sounded brave.

For Sammy's child, Kathleen would work, and she would save. Irene would study, and she would keep herself healthy. After the baby came, Kathleen's parents would sign responsibility for the adoption, but Kathleen would raise the baby, as hers. This also was not too irregular, the home assured them, but the woman who they spoke with wondered aloud if it was a good idea to go from one unwed mother to another, even while agreeing that it made a difference since Kathleen had her family and would be a high school graduate. Irene was only fourteen, so young. Too young.

Irene packed her things very carefully in a suitcase loaned to her by her father. In the days since their dinner, she felt closer to him. She wanted to tell him that the baby had been an accident, but not a forever kind of accident, just a timing one. Sammy wanted her as his bride, and they might have even given the child a sibling, if they had not rushed everything

If the ice had held.

She wished that night that she had not made Sammy so scared of her father, so that when her father had come home, instead of running off he might have been calm as he slipped back into his pants and come around to knock at the front door, winking as he asked if Irene might be at home.

Every day, in a way she never had before, she wanted to ask her father if he had ever heard from her mother, if there was something she should know, but she was not sure how to start the questions. She wanted to ask him what he thought—should she write her? She would tell her that she understood now, she understood the fear of having another person inside of her, she understood how it changed everything.

Before her mother left, even though there had not been much family around, she had an aunt and uncle who came around often when she was little, and they would bring her teenage cousin, Lucy Estelle. In elementary school, if Irene was sick, she had stayed home by herself, occasionally looked in on by a neighbor.

Her aunt and uncle had died in a highway accident when a semi-truck full of chickens had run over a passenger sedan, and after that, her mother left, and she didn't see her cousin.

From what Irene knew, they had been just behind the car that was hit, and her uncle swerved to miss the wreck of shattered glass and feathers, overcorrecting, sending their truck off the deep side of the road, jumping the ditch and tumbling down an embankment. They might have been okay, but no one found them for a while, no one saw what had happened or the wheels of their truck, wrong way up just out of the line of sight. There was a girl in the sedan who lived, but Irene did not know who she was. She was ten when this happened, when her father had buried his brother. Their own parents were already gone.

Still, even when Irene's mother did not come back from spending some time with Lucy Estelle—to get her settled, she had said—he held on to Irene. He had done more than she could do. She figured her father must be like a lot of people, struggling to keep his life going, trying to go forward.

Maybe what had made him mean was that somehow he had seen it all coming, and he had to live knowing he would have so much sadness.

He was supposed to drop her off at Kathleen's, and Kathleen's parents would drive them both to Denver to the home, but in front of the house, he asked if Irene minded if he took her himself.

"I'll just follow behind them," he said.

"Of course," she said.

"I want you to come back home after this," he said.

"I will," she said. "You can come visit," she said, and he nodded.

He tried, she thought, and she loved him for that.

The highway felt very slow as they went to the city, the sides of the road flanked by rangeland with just the outline of the foothills visible in the low fog. She was not sure what to say, so she scooted into the middle of the truck's bench seat and leaned on her father's shoulder. She could not remember ever sitting with him like that.

What had he thought about, the night his wife did not come home? What had he thought about, as the dark grew deeper and she, their child, their tiny, dark-haired girl, keened and howled? She could almost remember, if she clamped her eyes shut and leaned deeper into him, with the hum of the road, the tobacco smell of his jacket, the way he would have picked her up, and pulled her to him. Maybe he decided then how they would be—that they would stay together.

He must have waited a few days, even weeks, for his wife to return tearful, broke, or missing the mountain skyline. Irene wanted to tell him how much she forgave everything now, now that she knew what it was like to be sure the person who had helped make a child was never coming back.

The highway was very straight, with wide-open lanes, and the bumper of Kathleen's parents' car easily visible. They followed at a safe distance, and Irene felt her father roll back his arm some, to make more room for her, like she suspected he always had.

Chapter Thirty-Four
Melanie

Summer, 2007

Melanie was thinking of Irene's voice as she drove to the hospital. Wrapped in the clean upholstery and polished plastic of her car, she tried to balance safety and urgency. When she imagined her mother, at first there was a curtain of blood, but then she blanked this from her mind, and focused on what was in front of her—the city streets with light afternoon traffic, the summer sun lighting the dirty curbs and reflecting off the filmy building windows, and the brake lights of the truck in front of her with one bulb smashed and hanging like a broken tooth, the other missing its lens.

When she was anxious at work, she tried very hard not to speculate about what would or would not happen, and she used this approach now. She thought of being at her desk, with the glow of the Repti Glo terrarium lights and the yellow walls she had painted herself; she thought of being irritated at her email or her instant message or at Alex or another of her co-workers. In her car, she rolled her shoulders to loosen the tension, the hum of the road was calming to her, just like the buzz of the servers and the whirring fan of her computer, the drone of her reports spooling off the printer.

The drive was progressing just fine, she thought, until she came down the crest of a small hill, and her tires collided with an already partly smashed corrugated box. The sound of rubber against the cardboard jolted her, and her eyes opened very wide for a second and her breath caught. *It's nothing, just garbage*, she thought, and she reached for the radio dial to make sure it was switched all the way off. When she blinked, the imprint of unattached limbs and digits, not gory, just images like illustrations from a textbook or models made out of clay, flitted under her lids, and blinking harder only made her tear. At a stoplight, she closed her eyes fully, clamping them shut. She concentrated hard, but eventually a scrap of fingernail slid away, a knuckle found its mate with a joint and a finger, a wrist that flicked and turned on an arm that bent at the elbow to wave floated to the side of an intact torso. She was trying to will the body whole, and she heard Irene's words of caution again, while the car behind her honked. Opening her eyes, she saw the light had turned green, and she hurried through the intersection, going a little more quickly than she meant to, and because the car felt wobbly rounding the next turn, she braked harder than she needed, slowing almost to a stop. Touching the accelerator very gingerly, she slowly gained momentum while the driver behind her honked again.

At the hospital, the parking garage was still dusty with ash blown in from the fires, the covered concrete having missed the rains, and the winds having been still for some days. Parking carefully, perfectly straight between the white lines, she was relieved when she turned back the ignition and heard the engine disengage.

Inside the hospital, the time it took to check in felt like forever. There was the front desk of the emergency room with its sign to notify the attendant *immediately* if one was experiencing chest pain—a good shortcut, she noted, if she were to ever need it, but her mother had not come in this entrance, and she probably would have not walked. Melanie waited her turn at the desk, identified herself, asked if she was in the right place, and identified her mother. *Kathleen Henderson*, she said, saying her mother's name as if pushing the syllables from her mouth was about more than simply vocalizing them, as if her tongue between her teeth, tapping the roof of her mouth, was a ritual, as if the sound could make her mother appear and hold them both.

The front desk attendant checked the records, marked some paper, pressed a button at her desk, and told Melanie to go through the double doors.

"134-B," the attendant said. "It's kind of a walk—if you come back again, come in through the other side of the building."

Melanie did not know if that configuration of numbers and the letter meant good or bad, but she thanked the attendant. *Good*, she thought. *They are letting you go in.* Or, *Bad. They are letting you go in to say good-bye.*

After a long corridor, she followed the signs for B ward, passing through set after set of double doors, all opening wide enough for gurneys and tandem wheelchairs and closing with the gentle whoosh of hydraulics. Behind the last doors, there was another set of waiting rooms, these ones slightly more equipped for the long haul and out-fitted with square furniture and coffeepots with coffee that she could smell had been brewing for too long. There were cups for the water that came from a rattling stainless steel box mounted to the wall and a vending machine with most of the slots empty and dark behind the smeared glass.

Still walking, she was nodding at each of the nurses, nodding at the other hallway pedestrians whose shoes squeaked on the polished tiles like hers did, and nervous because she did not know exactly what to do. The order of the rooms was confusing, 136 followed 128, and she looped several times before she saw the turn she had missed.

The bed in 134-B was unmade and empty, and she was not sure if it was okay to sit on one of the chairs in the room. She wondered if she was remembering the room number correctly, so she went to find the closest waiting area. There were signs instructing that mobile phones should be turned off, but she reached for her BlackBerry anyway to text Irene. *Where are you? I'm here*, she typed.

They must be gone for X-rays, or scans, or whatever it was that the doctors needed to look inside of her mother's body, she thought, so she poured herself a cup of the bad coffee and settled into half of a threadbare sofa, and opened her laptop.

There were no windows in the room, and the overhead lights were cranked to a level of artificial brightness that made it feel like night had fallen, and fallen deeply, even though she had only been there for a few minutes. The coffee was bitter and very hot, but she welcomed the warmth of it. As she swallowed, she felt the liquid travel down through her throat and land in her belly, and she closed her eyes to the feeling of heat and of being aware of her body, intact and alert.

There was no wireless connection, but she did not tether her phone. She had a spare power cord in her laptop bag, so she plugged in just in case there was no outlet later. On her screen, the organization of her inbox was comforting, and as a distraction, she pulled up her industrial report to make edits to a difficult passage. The paragraphs of text were very dense, and she had been working on bulleting out some sections and adding more charts to others. The corporate reader, she knew, could not focus on page after page of sentences. They liked their information bite-sized and already concluded.

"Melanie?"

She looked up over the top of her screen at the woman across from her, slumped back into the cushion of the worn furniture, and recognized her, almost.

"Hi," Melanie said, trying to keep the upswing of inflection out of her voice so her greeting would not sound like a question. "How are you?"

"Here," the woman said. "We are here," and she motioned to the man next to her. The man, Melanie placed immediately: Brian from Chicago, whom she had gotten drunk and spent the night with. Now his hand was limply clasped with the hand of the woman who had spoken her name. She had not noticed them when she had come into the room, preoccupied, she had not seen anything familiar about either one of them. Where was Irene, she wondered, and she checked her phone.

Brian would not look at her.

"We met when I did an audit, when your company got acquired, right? I'm Jenny," the woman said, and Melanie did remember her, remembered that she had liked her. Jenny had talked about her kids and about trying to get back to work now that they were older.

Melanie closed her eyes, cradled the paper cup with the coffee, took a deep breath.

"Yes," she said. "It's good to see you."

Brian would still not look up, and Jenny did not introduce him. They all sat in the quiet. Her laptop made a pinging sound, so she closed the lid.

It was Jenny who spoke again, finally. "My mother," she said. "Car accident."

"Mine too," Melanie said. "I don't know how serious it is."

"Unfortunately, it's not the first time," Jenny said, and went on to tell how her mother, Lucy Estelle, was a hopeless drunk, and yet she insisted on driving. Today, in broad daylight, she had taken the car Brian, her husband—she motioned to him, and he nodded almost imperceptibly and then kept scrolling through his phone—had bought when their first baby was born, and then rammed it into another car.

"She's not a baby anymore, though," Jenny said. "Our daughter. She's in second grade."

"Was she in the car?"

"No, no. Just my mother in law. Thanks for asking. Thank goodness it wasn't Stella. Or Connor."

Melanie wanted to say, *Right, they go to private school*. Or, *I think I might have seen their picture*, but then she remembered Brian had not shown her any pictures, he had shown her travel receipts and rupees, spread them out on the rim of the bar counter like a reef, and the reef made a harbor, and inside of the harbor Melanie and Brian could have been anyone, but they had been themselves, telling one another their real names and talking about their real lives.

Melanie felt her stomach turn. "I hope the other driver was okay," she said.

"We don't know yet," Brian said. He still would not look at her, but she kept her eyes fixed on Jenny anyway.

It had to be both of them. This woman, Lucy Estelle, must have rammed her mother, and how strange, she thought, to watch Brian hold his wife's hand. How strange the way they three spoke, politely, even if one mother might have killed the other, and to discover this link now. They might have been friends, if things were different. Only a few days ago, his voice was on her line at work. Maybe it was her penance, Melanie thought, for indulging this woman's husband, for the note she had left in his trousers.

"Oh," Melanie said, the coffee poking at her. "You know, if you are interested, they ended up taking most of your recommendations, it just took some time."

"That's nice to hear," Jenny said. "I wasn't sure about that place. And it had that bad air-conditioning."

"Well, that's still not fixed," Melanie said. She let herself smile. It was okay. She was making small talk with Brian's wife, and she was not sure if he had shock or resignation on his face.

"We listed the building as a liability in the report," Jenny said.

"Interesting," Melanie said. The coffee cup was crumpled in her hands.

"It's funny, how all those things turn out," Jenny said, and she got up from her chair to refill her water. The machine clanked when it expelled ice and hissed when it ran liquid.

"Yes, very funny," Melanie said.

Brian's eyes stayed locked to the floor.

Jenny went back to her seat with her husband, and Melanie got a new cup of coffee and drank it, even though each sip tasted progressively worse. She opened her laptop again, but this time the order of her folders failed to produce the same calming effect.

They waited. At intervals, Jenny or Melanie would chat with one another, absently, as Brian stayed silent. Melanie wanted to ask Jenny, *Do you think your mother killed my mother?* but she did not, and she checked her phone compulsively for a message from Irene.

When a nurse came, the two women jumped from their chairs.

"Henderson?" the nurse asked. Her scrubs were purple and crumpled.

"Me," Melanie said, gathering her laptop bag.

"She's back in her room, you can go to her." Melanie nodded and turned down the corridor, not waiting for any news of Jenny's mother.

In the room, Kathleen was near sleep, and swollen looking. Irene rose to hug Melanie and then immediately sat again.

"They're keeping her overnight, to be sure," Irene said.

Melanie nodded. "The other woman?" she asked. The monitor beeped in the background, and a tube—oxygen, she assumed—whooshed.

"We don't really know," Irene said. "She was worse, though, maybe some broken ribs. A concussion. Both cars are totaled."

Melanie could not think anything other than that ribs did not sound so bad. Ribs would heal.

She asked her mother how she felt, and her mother said she felt bad, but okay. She asked if she had seen the other driver, and her mother said she had seen nothing and that she only knew it was a woman because she had heard someone say so.

The monitors beeped, and the oxygen line wheezed. "I know her daughter," Melanie said, "From work."

"Small world," said Irene. "What'd she have to say?"

Melanie thought for a moment. Her mother, draped in the hospital gown, Irene's face, ashen and tired around her eyes. She wondered for a moment, how Irene had gotten there first, but it didn't matter; Irene had always been there. She remembered a long time ago, when Irene's father had died, her mother had pulled her out of school to go to the funeral. She was in sixth grade and they were supposed to dissect a starfish that day, and she had been looking forward to it—she had done her homework, and she was excited to peer into its arms, or its central body. Her textbook said the fossil record for sea stars dated back to 450 million years, and this was amazing and unfathomable to her. She was very angry that her mother was making her miss it for the service of an old man whom she hardly knew. Instead, she could have been with her scalpel and rubber gloves, uncovering the mysteries of the universe. The man was just a man who the few times she had met reeked of smoke and was covered in liver spots and hugged her too close.

"Mel?" Irene said.

"Sorry," she said. "She said she was sorry."

"Me too," said Kathleen, her voice muffled some from painkillers.

Melanie stayed with Irene in the room until the hospital staff came to move her mother to an overnight bed, and they walked with her through the hallways as the gurney was being wheeled, holding her shoulder and hand. When they passed the waiting room, she looked for Brian and Jenny, but neither were there. She hoped Jenny's mother was as okay as she could be, and she hoped she was not going to have to go to court; she knew her own mother would never press charges. Her mother had always been good at accepting when bad things happened—she shrugged, she licked her wounds, and she kept it to herself.

Chapter Thirty-Five
Jenny
Fall, 1988

Jenny was young when her father left. There was one picture in a scrapbook her mother kept (the stranger-man cradling a baby to him, his hand covering her head, his eyes looking straight to the camera, not to her). Now all she had of him were the features in her own face that she could find no anchor for on her mother's.

* * *

Once, when Jenny was in the fourth grade, there was a blue pickup truck parked among the school buses with a man at the wheel. The man was watching out, it seemed, for every girl who passed, and Jenny felt the bottom part of her stomach drop. *Jenny*, she heard him call, *I know you know me*, and she did know him, in the same way that he, who had not seen her in nine years, knew who to call out to. Her bus was just behind his truck, so she had to walk fully past him. *Jenny*, he called, *come say hello to your dad.* He reached across the cab and swung the passenger-side door open. She was old enough to understand he was good looking, in his way. She was old enough to understand why a different girl might hitch up her skirt and hop into his truck for a ride along the river, but she kept walking to her bus. *Jenny!*, he called, and crawled across the bench seat and scrambled onto the sidewalk. *Get in the truck*, he said, just as her foot touched the first step of the school bus stairs, the door open wide for her.

"I'm your dad," he said. "Get in the truck."

"Can't," Jenny said. "Mom's waiting for me." The first word she had ever spoken to her father: *Can't*.

"I'll take you home directly," he said, squinting against the low afternoon light.

The school bus driver had her eye on Jenny, and she unbuckled her seat belt, got up, and extended her hand. "Come on," she said.

"Mom's waiting," Jenny said again, over her shoulder, because it was true. *I don't know you*, she thought, but she did. She saw her face in his, and they had the same streaky hair.

"I promise I'll just take you straight home," he said, but the bus driver was coming down the steps and pulling Jenny inside and hustling her into one of the rear seats and sitting her down next to a high school boy. *Watch her*, she said, and went back out to the man on the sidewalk, the man was climbing back into his blue pickup, peeling out of the dirt-paved school lot, screeching through the intersection in front of the school, and barreling onto the highway, just like her mother had always said, not in a hurry for much, except to get out of there.

* * *

In seventh grade, she went to Denver for the state science fair. She had placed third in her school's contest, for a project called "Fire & Burning." It was about chemical reactions. She had lit matches, flicked lighters, even torched a pail of garbage (with her mother's permission) and then labeled and arranged her findings on a three-fold poster board. She had not worked that hard on the project, really—the other two winners had done much more than she had. "Air Pressure/Water Pressure: Pressure

Under Pressure" and "Gears: Compare the Effectiveness of Different Lubricants" had won first and second, respectively. Jenny was a very distant third.

Still, she set up her poster board on her table in the auditorium. Her mother had sewn her a tablecloth cut down from an old sheet that she sent through the wash with bright red powdered dye, and then trimmed it in yellow rickrack. Jenny agreed the cloth gave her station flair, but she did not believe it would actually help her rankings. This did not matter to her mother, who was there straightening the display and beaming. And for just a moment, she thought she saw her father slinking through the crowd, his heavy boots streaking the floor. The names of all the kids at the fair had been in the paper. She did not think he was the type to read the paper, but she realized it was not impossible that he would know.

She did not need to win the competition, she only wanted to make a good showing—her mother was already proud. When the results were posted, Jenny's schoolmates ranked tenth and eleventh, she far back at thirty-four out of forty entries.

"I'm still happy for you," her mother said.

What did her father know, of sulfur, of phosphorus? Her mother's name was Lucy Estelle because Lucy meant *born at daylight* and Estelle meant star. Her mother was plasma held together with gravity. Her mother was thermonuclear fusion of hydrogen and supernova. Her mother knew fire.

"Thanks, Mom," Jenny said. She looked again for her father as they packed the display up. She would keep the tablecloth to drape over her dresser, and she would take it to college, where she used it on an altar when she was experimenting with paganism, and she would have it with her years later when she married—the red long faded, and the yellow border turned more to gray, and the cloth so holey it had to be cut down and re-hemmed to handkerchief size. When she married Brian, she wore the scrap in her garter, something old.

"Did you see him?" her mother said when they drove home.

"No," Jenny said.

"He was there," her mother said.

"He wasn't," Jenny said, not sure why she was lying. The car hummed.

Fire is the oxidation of material in the process of combustion.

Ash is the residue after a sample is burned, and mostly salty.

Jenny knew that biology was strong, but it was not everything. If flame was the visible part of fire, she closed her eyes to him. If heat was energy transferred from one place to another, she was nonconductive, a shield to him. In the wild, fire burns clean through the understory, leaving the canopy of trees and clearing the ground for the newest green shoots. The grasslands look leveled, at first. The forests look destroyed, at first. The dirt, scarred with charred seeds and blackened branches, seem barren until the smoke clears and the budding begins, pushing past the charcoal, into a clear expanse of sky. Whenever Jenny reached, it was with her mother's fingers laced through hers. Above them, damp, dew-heavy clouds. Above them, rain.

* * *

When Jenny had her eighteenth birthday, her mother made a cake in their small oven and put one candle on it, the wick hungry at the cheap colored wax drizzling onto the buttercream. The cake had risen high and light, and her mother had sung "Happy Birthday" in her low, trembling voice. They each had a corner piece, which was what they liked best, and the rest of the cake remained like a partly toothless smile.

When she was Jenny's age, Lucy Estelle was grieving her parents and preparing for a baby. At her age, Jenny was unsure about what was next and happy to still have her mother's friendship, after everything. The house had hardly changed; there were some different curtains and cookware, but the structure was the same as the day her grandparents had walked out of the front door and locked the latch against their own not coming home. Jenny knew this story, the story of Lucy Estelle—without a key, because she had never needed one since someone had always been there—who waited for her parents on the steps until the sun went down, the air so dry her heart pumped dust.

* * *

Jenny had not gone far for college, the point was that she had gone, even if just to the north, in Fort Collins, on a scholarship that barely covered costs, but barely was better than nothing. She lived in the dorms at first, and while she did not argue with the other girls, she did not get on with them either. She kept to herself. She had already decided on a practical major, accounting. Her roommate, from Nebraska, was studying the classics, and she invited Jenny to nights of performance art with her troupe, but Jenny never went. She liked being alone in the dorm room or by herself at a table in the library. Her first year, she went home for the summer and camped in her old bedroom. She looked for a job but found nothing, so she cooked for her mother, cleaned, and gardened. Her tomatoes grew high on their stakes; her herbs, bushy; her corn, long and tall. She shucked the ears at the kitchen table, where she had done her homework for most of her life. She slept with a full belly in her childhood bed, wrapped in the same itchy sheets. Her mother was happy to have her home, proud again.

In the fall, she did not return to the dorms—too expensive, too tight. She rented a studio apartment close to campus in the renovated VA hospital. Her room had tile halfway up the walls, and she thought it must have been a ladies' room once, powder pink with gray grout. She liked sleeping in the apartment without the breath of her roommate. She liked having her own bathroom and a kettle that no one else touched. In the mornings, she woke up and made herself coffee and sometimes smoked a joint over her tiny range, blowing the smoke through the rattley exhaust fan.

Once, she heard a knock, and she looked through the peephole, and she swore she saw her father. She swallowed hard and undid the dead bolt, but when she opened the door, there was nothing but air whooshing into an open hallway.

The second summer, she did not go home because she wanted to keep her apartment. She had a part-time job at a deli, and they told her they could have her on full time through the summer, since the other students were leaving. There was a man who washed dishes and had tattoos on his forearms who also worked there. He smelled like sweat and looked at Jenny in a way she could not name. He was close to her age, but he seemed older. He was a version of herself, if her mother had been more reckless, if her mother had not had the house and they had floated between sympathetic relatives and friends, with no place to call their own—or if her father had been around, bringing trouble.

First, Jenny and this man went only for coffee after their shifts ended, but the coffee turned to a night of beer back at her place. He did not have a place, really. She could not work out if he was staying at the shelter near the deli or on the kitchen floor, but either way, he complimented her on her apartment, how clean it was, how cozy. The second time they started with beer and finished with whiskey, finished with Jenny saying she was so, so tired and crawling into her bed in the studio; in her studio, the bed was always there, as a warning or invitation, and the man, Rich, unlacing his shoes and peeling off his socks, crawled in next to her.

It was the first time she had had a man in her bed, but she did not tell him and she did not cry.

In the morning, he was up before her, cooking coffee on the small stove—like she did, the way she had learned from her mother—and digging through her cabinets, making biscuits, whistling in delight that she had real butter.

He brought her a cup of coffee, and she propped up on a pile of pillows to drink it.

He made breakfast, and she was still not out of bed, her thighs sticky and her breasts hurting. He sat with her while they ate, forks clinking against her secondhand stoneware.

He asked if he could use her shower before he left for his shift, and she loaned him a clean T-shirt. On his way out, he kissed her between the eyes on the forehead, and after he had latched the door, she got up and saw that he had tidied up the kitchen. The bathroom was still steamy and warm, and she washed slowly under the hot water. Drying herself with her only towel, she saw that he had left his dirty shirt folded on the back of the toilet tank. It smelled like the deli and the detergent they used, and of him.

For the rest of the summer, Rich was in her apartment. She saw the lines around his eyes get a little softer, especially when he mentioned how nice it was to have a regular place to stay. Jenny got softer too, in the belly, from his cooking. At the deli, they were nice to each other in the same way all of the employees were nice—they depended on one another to keep the place going, and everyone needed the job. In early July, she gave him a key, and she came home from the late shift one evening to find him making sandwiches in the kitchen, which he wrapped in wax paper and tucked into his knapsack.

"Let's go to the park and watch the fireworks," he said. "America's birthday."

"I'm tired, Rich," she said.

"Everyone's tired," he said. "Gunpowder will help."

They walked to the park and spread out on a blanket, and Rich held her hand. He had tattoos on his fingers and up his forearms, one on his back, one on his stomach, deep-blue ink just like the summer light that never seemed to let the sky turn all the way to black.

She thought when school started again in the fall she would not see him anymore. She would not have time for lazy mornings or late nights. They had not started to talk about a future. The closest he got was to stop asking her if it was okay that he stayed the night, and that had happened only after she offered the key. She liked seeing him sleeping in her bed. She liked that when the cashiers at the deli split up their tips to the backroom staff, he dropped his share of quarters into her laundry jar. She washed his apron and his jeans with hers, and folded his shirts into perfect, neat squares. He had his knapsack and duffel bag parked under her bed. Everything he owned fit inside. She told him about growing up, the house, her mother. He did not tell her his story—when she asked about his parents, he always said, *Another time*, so she stopped asking. She told him he should study if he was going to work in kitchens, because there were better jobs out there.

"Not just a line cook," she said. "Be a chef."

He laughed at her then and told her he had not finished high school, and she told him she thought it didn't matter, he could still go on, but she still stopped by the university library the next day, telling the graduate student at the reference desk that she was not sure where to start.

"My friend needs his GED," she said, and she was pointed to an entire section, and the graduate assistant took Jenny through the stacks helping her find the curriculum guidelines, and then sat with her while she used the computers to find a test location, taking their time because it was so quiet during summer session.

She went back to her apartment with a bag of books and a few printed pages from the Internet and waited for him.

"You could finish by the end of summer," she told him. "I made you an appointment for the exam."

He said he was not sure, but he agreed to at least try.

There was enough room in the apartment for a small table, where Jenny did her homework. She started reading ahead for the fall term, while Rich worked through grammar and math and social studies. She liked this life with him, quiet and marked by the sounds of pages turning, the scratch of a pencil against paper, the swoosh of an underline.

On the day of the exam, they had both requested to be scheduled off from work, and their boss raised an eyebrow.

She rode the bus with Rich to the testing center at the public library and held his hand. He had his knapsack on his back and a notebook under his arm, just like any other student. It was August. He passed easily. They celebrated with cheap champagne and a stir-fry.

She was grateful to him when September came. He did not make her ask for her key back or make her pick a fight. She came home from the late shift, and his duffel bag was gone from where it had peeked out from under her bare bed frame, and the key to the apartment gleamed on the table, resting in the center of a piece of torn notebook paper. *Thank you, Jenny*, he had written, and signed his name with a heart around it.

He had not said anything in the few hours their shifts crossed that day, and he had not said anything to her the night before, only held her so close there was nothing but heat between them. She took some quarters from the laundry jar and went to the corner to call her mother. The phone rang until the answering machine picked up, and Jenny could picture the house perfectly, her mother's voice on the answering machine tape sounding through the empty rooms.

Chapter Thirty-Six

Melanie

Summer, 2007

At work the day after the car accident, Alex stopped in her office doorway, but he must have thought better of it, because he didn't say anything before he turned to continue down the hallway. Later, he hardly acknowledged her when she said hello to him in the kitchen.

"Do you have plans for the Fourth?" she asked him.

"Nope," he said, quickly putting cream in his coffee and then exiting.

I deserved that, she thought.

She had spent the night in the hospital with her mother, she and Irene each angling for a little space on the bench in the room, or sitting in the hard-backed chair next to the bed, both being jolted from their tenuous sleep by the tiniest beep from the monitors and from even the suggestion of a labored breath from Melanie's mother.

At 2:15 in the morning, Irene was perched over Kathleen, smoothing her hair. Melanie got up to stretch, and put her hand on her mother's hand.

"She's really fine," Melanie whispered. "We're the ones freaking out."

Irene smiled at her. "You'll never know what she did for me Mel."

"You've been friends forever," Melanie said. "I get it."

"We've been friends since you," Irene said.

"Is that why my dad hates you?"

"He doesn't hate me," Irene said. "He just doesn't understand me. He can't. It's okay. I made my peace with him a long time ago, and then when he and Kath split it didn't really matter anymore."

Melanie nodded. "I just want her to go home."

"Me too, girl. Me too."

* * *

It didn't take very long to find him—a web search and several phone calls, then the administrative assistant was putting her through to Brian's cell.

"How's your mother-in-law?" she asked when he answered.

He said he meant to call, and he said Lucy Estelle was fine. Bruises, a cracked rib, a lightly fractured wrist, but okay. He asked after her mother, and Melanie said she was fine, too, and coming home today.

"Good," Brian said. "I'm glad it wasn't more serious. Lucy is going to hate rehab."

She listened to the static between their mobile phones. He said it was a funny coincidence, and she said that she did not think it was funny at all, and maybe not a coincidence.

"I didn't know you were superstitious," he said.

"I'm not," she said. She remembered as a girl how she'd clung to her horoscopes, but it had been ages since she had read one. The idea of some external order no longer appealed to her.

It sounded like Brian was typing, or maybe it was just the towers clicking as the connection relayed. She was not sure what to say next, and he was silent, but they stayed on the line for another minute, listening, until she said to him that she hoped he could work everything out with Jenny, and he said that Jenny had no idea, and Melanie said she thought he was wrong about that.

Maybe Jenny did not know about them, Melanie said to him, but she knew something—she had not introduced him to her, because maybe she knew better than to introduce her husband to a woman who looked vulnerable, or she maybe did not think he would empathize.

"So, she definitely knows something," Melanie said.

Brian sighed a little. "Maybe."

"Give her some credit," Melanie said.

"Okay, listen, I shouldn't, but I want to ask your advice"

She pressed the phone to her ear. "Of course."

He said Chicago had been the last time, and, what if he kept it that way? What if he promised himself, and if he kept the promise, would it be okay to never tell Jenny about all of the other women, to keep it all a secret?

Melanie considered this. "If you mean it," she said. "Then, yes, it's okay. It would only hurt her to tell. If you don't mean it, you're just a bigger ass."

"I mean it," he said, and she thought she heard something drop in the background, maybe his voice breaking.

They said good-bye and hung up. Melanie put her phone back into her purse and looked at her work. She wondered what her father would say about the accident, but no one had told him, and so she wrote him a quick email with a summary, *She's fine, she goes home today, you don't need to do anything.* She checked the clock. It was lunchtime.

What she wanted more than anything was to wipe her hard drive and delete her user identities and unscrew her Repti Glo terrarium bulbs and walk out of her office, cash out her savings and take her mother and Irene off to a new place where they could all start over, where life was gentler.

She poked her head into Alex's office and told him if anyone was looking for her that she was going home early.

"I put my out-of-office reply on my email," she said.

He tipped his head to indicate that he had heard her, but he did not say anything.

Melanie knew her mother would be home by the time she got to the apartment, and she would be convalescing nicely. Irene would be there, because Irene would have driven her, and Irene's heels would be kicked off by the door. She would be making a soup or a smoothie, something liquid and vegetable and healthy to keep Melanie's mother's strength up and to keep her hydrated, and Melanie would be grateful for Irene, who was usually there anyway, but always there when it mattered.

When Melanie went into the apartment, she was still thinking about quitting her job and taking her mother and Irene away, where it would be just the three of them, and they would keep a clean and spare and solitary home. Maybe sometimes they would have visitors, or other people would orbit in and out, but they three would stay close, and they would not do dangerous things like drive or talk to married men. They would keep an abundant garden and have fresh hydrangeas and spinach year round.

The screen door banged behind her, and she heard Irene shout a greeting from the kitchen. Melanie's mother was propped up on the sofa watching the news with the sound off, the way she preferred.

Melanie took a chair at the same scratched and pitted kitchen table where she had done countless hours of homework. She felt the static of the place, but it was not sad like it was sometimes. Irene brought her a glass of water, and they both moved to the living room with her mother, Irene at the foot of the sofa, and Melanie in the side chair.

In the afternoon sun that bent around the open space in the blinds, the room looked almost pretty. Irene's pedicured toes sparkled iridescent coral, and Melanie's mother's hair shone a bright auburn. The apartment was quiet, with just a low glow from the silent television screen.

She was happy to be there, with them.

Chapter Thirty-Seven
Kathleen
Summer, 1975

There was a man sitting next to a girl on a park bench. The girl, Kathleen, had the infant, Melanie, with her, a small and wrinkly baby, who had her face scrunched to the sun and her legs swaddled. The war had ended a few months ago, but the man was in his uniform, so either he was still a soldier or he was on his way to learning how to not be a soldier. Kathleen did not know which, but she was lonely, out on a walk with the baby, and she sat down next to him. She said hello, even though he did not look like he wanted to talk.

She'd rather be with Irene, but Irene was supposed to be letting go and Kathleen was supposed to be bonding.

"I'm Kath," she said. She was sweaty all over, from the heat and from carrying the baby. She wondered why she thought it was a good idea to take the child to the park, but the ladies at the home had told her she must do things with the child without Irene, and so she had taken the bundle, out into the summer heat, when she would have rather been with her friend who was recovering from a difficult labor. Irene's milk was coming in, but the home had told her to bind her breasts.

Aunt Mae said to give the baby a few days at least to breastfeed.

She didn't trust formula, but by the third day she helped wrap the bandages around Irene anyway.

They had all been instructed to forget, to move on, but Kathleen would not forget, and Irene would not forget.

* * *

Irene was supposed to be healing and adjusting, and it was hard, with all of them at Mae's. In the night, when the child would cry, Irene would cry too, but it was Kathleen who went to the baby, who tried to comfort her, who heated a bottle, while Irene's breasts swelled and Mae paced the kitchen when some kind of knowing that neither of the girls could place, even though they were grateful for her.

Kathleen was not sure how her friend was supposed to follow the home's instructions, when the child was calling for her and Irene's body was calling for the child. She thought it might be easier for Irene to go back to her father's, but she would not say this to Irene.

Irene had offered the child, Sammy's child, and still it was Irene who had it the hardest, puffed up everywhere but empty inside, her shirt soaking through the worn elastic bandages Mae had dug from the cabinets.

When Kathleen confided to her aunt, Mae said to let it run its course. Kathleen was relieved. She didn't want her friend to go, really, but she also did not want her to be in so much pain.

"It will be worse for her if she feels like she's not welcome," Mae had said. "Wait on it."

* * *

On the park bench, the man in uniform was quiet. Probably he was deciding if he should talk to this girl and her baby, but then the light changed a little. Kathleen hoped he was realizing he was home and the war was over. That the sun was hard but not unlovely. That he could converse with people, he could make friends.

"Andrew," he said, awkwardly after the pause between Kathleen offering her name and him responding, and he turned a little, and put his hand out, stiffly. She extended her own hand, even though her palm was probably the sweatiest place of all.

"How old?" he asked.

"She's two weeks," Kathleen said.

"You don't look like you had a baby two weeks ago," he said.

He was the first stranger she'd talked to, and she was not sure what to say. *How does he know?* She panicked, but she concentrated on keeping her face calm.

"I'm not sure what you mean," she said.

"I mean, you look very fit," he said. "And I'm sorry. That's not my place to say."

"She was easy on me," Kathleen said, not sure if this was the right thing or not. "Her daddy's passed," she offered, so the man would not think she was being improper.

"The war?" asked the soldier.

"Yes," she said, and she held Melanie tighter. She did not like this, it felt wrong to her brother Sammy, but there was blood between the child and her, and she had only just realized they needed a story. She couldn't believe she hadn't thought it through already, or that Mae hadn't, and the man, Andrew, has just made it easy. Sammy would have looked as handsome and as strong in a uniform, he would have talked nicely to a sweaty young mother on a park bench, if he had the chance. They visit some more, exchanging pleasantries, and between silent patches they watch the other people in the park.

"I would like to see you again," he said.

"You have to meet my aunt first. I'm staying with her. Phone and we can make an appointment," she said, being formal on purpose.

Andrew did phone, and when he came over the next day, Kathleen could see Mae asking every question she could think of while the former soldier sat in the little parlor.

"It's unlikely that you know my son," Mae said, "But I have to ask. I've not heard from him since the child was born." She said his name.

"I don't recognize him," Andy said. "You can't take it as a sign, though, about the baby."

He was taking a risk, talking to Mae like this, Kathleen thought, but war might have changed his thinking, making him superstitious about everything, just like an old woman.

"The mail, ma'am, the mail is very unreliable," he continued. "You might get nothing and then get five letters at once the next time you check."

"That has never happened," Mae said.

"It happens," he said.

Mae said that in April when she heard the United States was pulling out, she was sure she would see her son soon, and that these last months have been the hardest.

"Of course," Andrew said.

"Your folks must be happy you're home," Mae said.

"They're gone, and I'm an only child," he said. "I wouldn't have joined up otherwise."

Mae nodded.

The following day, when Mae checked the mail, there was nothing, nothing still, but there were also no army people who come to her door to bring her the worst news.

Whenever Andrew came to see Kathleen, they visited at the house, or they went only a few blocks away with the baby. She could tell he thought she should leave the child with her cousin, Irene, but she would not.

Only weeks passed before he offered her a ring.

He said to Kathleen that it was not completely logical for him to have come to love her after such a short time, but he did. He said he knew she and Irene were going to be leaving Denver soon, and he admitted that Mae had said as much, and that Mae had pushed him.

When he dropped to his knee, Irene and Mae were there in the parlor with its sagging furniture and dusty side tables, and Melanie was yowling. The ring was a slim gold band, set with one amber stone.

That night, in the spare room where Mae had crammed two twin mattresses, Irene reached across the patch of open floor, touched Kathleen's hand. She begged her to remember their promise.

"I will," Kathleen said.

"You should stay here with Andy, but I'm still going home," Irene said. "School's going to start. I can hardly imagine."

"I know," Kathleen said. She did not want Irene to leave.

"What's he going to do when he finds out you're a virgin?"

"I have no idea," Kathleen said.

Irene's leaving was nothing much. Her father came to pick her up and Kathleen embraced them both. Melanie was fussing in a way that alarmed Kathleen, but she tried to ignore it, and she saw Irene was trying to ignore it too.

Before her wedding night, Kathleen, on Irene's advice, pushed her finger inside of herself as far as it would go, until she felt a catch and her knuckle was wet with a tiny bit of blood. She washed her hands and telephoned Irene long distance, a little breathless, telling her that it worked.

* * *

Andy and Kath decided to go to the courthouse, where Irene stood for them, and after, Kathleen's parents and Aunt Mae and Irene's father and the baby went to the park bench where they had met and broke a bottle of sparkling wine that they were pretending was champagne over it. While everyone was laughing at the crack of glass and the spray of bubbles, Andy took Kathleen's hand and made her swear she would never tell Melanie that her father was gone, and he promised he would raise her as blood.

From the corner of her eye, Kathleen could see Irene, sipping out of a paper cup poured from one of the other bottles Mae had brought. She had turned fifteen, but looked older, in a becoming way. The sun was bright on her, and her father had her elbow, and she had kicked off her dress shoes. A little tipsy and starting to sing a drinking song they both knew while spinning on the grass, they reached for Aunt Mae and Kathleen's parents until they'd made a rowdy circle. While the other people in the park looked at this family, they would never know it was started from circumstance and made by vows.

Melanie was in a stroller in the shade, and the circle moved until she was in the center of it. Mae and Kathleen's mother's shoes were off now, too. Other people in the park were approaching, and Mae hardly stopped her jig to pour them their own cups of wine, inviting them to dance on the crispy grass. Irene waved to Kathleen to join them.

Her new husband held one hand, Irene the other. The circle moved. Melanie screamed with joy at the commotion, slapped her tiny fingers together, surrounded by their promises.

Kathleen couldn't help but think of Sammy, who would never get to hold Mel, Sammy who seemed so close in the light of the park— he would have loved this exact kind of celebration—Sammy who had broken through the ice, and Kathleen who tried to imagine it as a spray of diamond or crystal.

The dancing broke up and Kathleen poured another paper cup of wine, took one drink for herself, one for her brother.

If, if the ice had held, she thought, but in the heat it was hard to think of ice, until she caught Irene's eye again.

Swear, Irene mouthed.

I swear, Kathleen mouthed back.

There were more and more people gathering, a crowd drawn by a crowd.

Melanie, in her stroller, still smiling.

The wine was almost exhausted but someone arrived with beer and the party erupted again.

Even though Melanie was not fussing, Kathleen went to her and lifted her daughter to towards the sky, sun at the child's back.

The group was circling again, a rope of family and strangers around her, whooping and cheering and chanting, and Kathleen could not help but to get onto her tiptoes so she could reach Melanie just a little bit higher, melting away any of the cold or ice that might be left, the heat one more way to seal the secret.

Acknowledgments

Parts of this novel have been published in different form in the journals *10,000 Tons of Black Ink*, *Descant*, *The Tusculum Review*, *Hawai'i Pacific Review*, *The Green Hills Literary Lantern*, and *The Tampa Review*.

About the Author

Wendy J. Fox is the author of *The Seven Stages of Anger and Other Stories*, and the novel *The Pull of It*. She received her MFA from Eastern Washington University, and her work has been published or is forthcoming in many literary reviews, websites, and blogs. Find her at www.wendyjfox.com and on Twitter @WendyJeanFox

Also from Santa Fe Writers Project

By Way of Water *by Charlotte Gullick*

Struggling to feed their children in an unforgiving California forest when there are no logging jobs to be found, Jake and Dale Colby make personal vows that only make matters worse. Jake will not accept help from the government or his neighbors, and Dale won't allow him to hunt, believing her faith will sustain them. But one other member of the family makes a promise to herself. Seven-year-old Justy believes that she alone can hold the family together, even when her father's violence resurfaces.

"By Way of Water *is a work of exquisite beauty.*"
— Jayne Anne Phillips

eightball *by Elizabeth Geoghegan*

Fueled by an abiding sense of loss, the eight stories in this collection take you on a journey across the exploded fault lines of intimacy, unfolding across cities and continents.

"*The quiet power of Geoghegan's voice reaches both heart and bone.*"
— Francesca Marciano, *author,* The Other Language

American Fallout *by Brandon Wicks*

For Avery Cullins—library archivist, former teenage runaway, and gay man from a small Southern town—"family" means a live-in boyfriend and a surly turtle. But when his father, a renowned nuclear physicist, commits suicide, Avery's decade-long estrangement from his mother, now hobbled following a stroke, comes to a skidding halt.

"*Compulsively readable...a really great book.*"
— Matthew Norman, *author,* Domestic Violets

About Santa Fe Writers Project

SFWP is an independent press founded in 1998 that embraces a mission of artistic preservation, recognizing exciting new authors, and bringing out of print work back to the shelves.

Find us on Facebook, Twitter @sfwp, and at www.sfwp.com